GROSS MISCONDUCT

A COMEBACKS NOVEL

A.J. TRUMAN

TRUMAN BOOKS

1

GRIFFIN

I'm in the middle of fixing the engine on a client's Cessna plane when my boss alerts me that I'm being arrested.

As far as I know, I haven't committed any crimes. I haven't run any red lights or robbed a bank. I'm the most average of average joes. I stand up from my workstation and rub the grease off my hands.

"The po-po's waiting for you," he says. His pale, bald forehead creases with concern. Since I'm taller than him at six four, he has trouble meeting my eyes. Today, he won't even try.

"Did they say why?"

He shakes his head no. "You better go in and see what they want. I can have Corrado finish up with the Cessna."

My stomach feels leaden. Annabelle and June flash in my mind, their sweet, angelic faces crumpling to tears when they find out their daddy's going away. But for what? What did I do?

I walk past my boss to the exit. I adjust my eye patch over my left eye. Hopefully, the patch either garners me sympathy or makes me intimidating to the officer. Both could work in my favor.

I venture through the cavernous space of the hangar to the narrow corridor of offices. I'm glad I never got a job that required me to sit in such a soul-killing setting. Although, now that I'm on the verge of getting arrested, perhaps it would've been the smart move. Guys who wear ties and sit in cubicles didn't go to jail, or if they did, it would be to one of those Club Med-style jails with tennis courts.

I exhale a deep breath and shake myself out before I turn the knob to my boss's office. The cop stands next to his desk, all business, all scowl, his uniform navy and crisp. He's more slender than I would imagine a cop to be.

I'm a large guy, although my midsection has the inevitable gut of middle age. Guys subconsciously step aside when I venture down a sidewalk. I've got a few inches vertically and horizontally on this cop, yet that doesn't stop me from gulping back a nervous lump.

"Officer," I say. I wonder if I should try to shake his hand.

"Griffin Harper?" His voice is eerily monotone, as if he's the Terminator or something.

"Yes?"

"Sit down." He points to the chair across the desk, not the special ergonomic chair my boss got last year.

I do as he says, my heart thumping in my ears. My mom taught me to tread lightly when dealing with cops. "What is this about?"

"You're under arrest."

"For what?"

"For not joining the Comebacks. You're a bad boy, Griffin."

Before I can question why an officer of the law called me, a forty-four-year-old man, a bad boy, he throws on a pair of reflective aviator sunglasses and takes out his phone.

"And you need to be punished." His surly stare instantly switches to a sneaky smile as he presses something on his phone.

The opening chords of the *NSYNC song "I Want You Back" fill the office. I can't remember what I ate for breakfast yesterday, but my teenage lizard brain refuses to forget the shitty songs popular in my youth.

My arresting officer begins shaking his hips, thrusting his junk in my direction. He mouths along to the song and does some choreographed moves. His hand accidentally smacks against the office wall, and he lets out an expletive under his breath but soldiers on.

He pushes apart my legs and shimmies between them, sliding to the ground and springing back up. He drags his tongue across his teeth in a failing effort to turn me on.

The officer, if we're still calling him that, spins around and grinds his ass against my junk before I scoot the hell back and out of the chair. I stand as far apart from him as this tiny office will allow. Through the window, I catch my boss and a gaggle of female coworkers ogling from the hall.

"What the fuck is going on?" I think now's a good enough time as any to curse at an officer.

"I'm Officer Jasper here to tell you that the Wolf Pack wants you back," he says, slightly out of breath as he continues to dance.

My eyes travel to the Jasper the Stripping Telegram Artist logo imprinted on his phone case.

"And if you don't show up tonight, then you're under arrest."

At that, he rips off his pants and throws them in my face.

———

I STROLL into Summers Rink that night ready to kick ass and take names.

The massive facility has a dated quality to it with graying walls, a digital scoreboard made of bright red dots, and the same old banners advertising the same small businesses hanging on the walls. State of the art, Summers Rink is not.

But like your childhood home, it's easy to find its flaws charming.

There are two rinks in the facility. On one is a free skate zone ranging from kids trying figure skating loops down to those hugging the wall to keep their balance. On the other rink, I find a familiar group of guys way past their prime trying to play hockey.

I charge up to them. We all played together at South Rock High School decades ago, back when we were unstoppable. That might as well have been a completely different life. The only thing that's unstoppable is the march of time. As soon as they see me, Hank Rush signals to someone above the scoreboard.

"I Want You Back" blares through the sound system. The guys try to harmonize on the chorus, but it's a patchwork of missed cues and garbled lyrics. I put my fingers in my ears toward the end.

"You fuckers," I say.

"Griffdog!" Hank yells.

"We got your attention." Bill Crandell skates up to me with my former teammates close behind. They take off their helmets. Sweat beads on their rugged faces.

"I thought I was actually getting arrested."

"It was Hank's idea," Bill says. Corporate life has forced him to keep his beard and hair neatly trimmed, but no job is straightlaced enough to take the goon out of the man.

"Jasper's good. I hired him to go to Des's last chemotherapy session in a doctor's coat and bedazzled thong." Hank gives me a thumbs up, his goofy smile unchanged from high school. With his thinner but still shaggy blond hair and noticeable gut, he looks like Jesus's deadbeat brother. Hank has always been on the huskier side, perfect for protecting the goal.

"Thank you for that. His rhinestone-covered junk will haunt me forever." Des rolls his piercing eyes, a slight smile on his full lips, as if he's perpetually in the middle of a photo shoot. Even in his forties, Max Desmond is still a pretty boy.

"Hank's idea actually worked," Bill says. "You're here."

"I'm *here* to tell you guys it was a shitty idea."

"A shitty idea that worked," Hank calls out.

"You've been trying to get me to join the Comebacks since January, and it hasn't worked. Take the hint."

"You could've told us this via text." Hank crosses his arms, a sense of vindication coming over him.

"Admit it, man. You're curious. Marcy says you still come for free skate, sometimes even playing around with a stick," Bill says. Marcy Summers took over the rink from her parents in the late 1980s and has been running it ever since. She knows everything that goes on here and apparently will back channel it to my old teammates.

"You love hockey. You're still a goon at heart." Des cocks an eyebrow at me.

I take a sharp inhale of the rink. There's a common misconception that water, and by extension ice, has no smell. Perhaps that's true on a scientific level, but for people who spend their life on the ice, it smells fresh, sharp, a bit bitter. For some of us, as much as we want to ignore the feeling, it can smell like home.

"My hockey days are behind me," I tell them.

"Bullshit," Des scoffs.

"It's fun, Griff. It's a beer league. We practice, we play, we go out to celebrate whether we win or lose," says Tanner Chance, the only hockey player I know who is too sweet to trash talk. There's a permanent weariness behind his kind eyes, but if I were raising four kids on my own, I'd be exhausted all the time, too.

"We can't do it without you, especially now that Mitch is out for the season." Bill sighs at the news.

"Shit. Is he okay?" I ask.

Bill seesaws his head. "He threw out his back. Sneezing."

The guys and I burst into laughter at poor Mitch's expense, the sound bouncing off the rink's walls. We weren't that far away from one big sneeze making us immobile. The magic of burgeoning middle age.

"We *could* do it without you, but we don't want to," Des says. "Honestly, it hasn't felt the same without you on the ice. Like it used to be. When we were on fire."

"That was in the twentieth century," I say, which makes it sound eons ago. It was only the late nineties when we played together. And weren't the seventies only thirty years ago? I wish. My girls will sometimes ask me questions about life at the turn of the century, and I realize they're not referring to the 1900s, like they should.

"We still got it." Bill wraps his knuckles on the boards. Time may've passed, but he still cuts an imposing figure in his hockey gear. I'm sure I would, too, but I push that idea out of my head. "I know you still got it, Griff. You were ferocious out there, a fucking animal. We need our defenseman back."

"You're forgetting one important part." I don't have to gesture. Bill's already glancing up at my left eye. Quiet descends over my former teammates.

"You made an incredible recovery." Bill softens his tone slightly. "If you're able to drive, you're able to play."

"It's not that simple," I say.

He shrugs, as if maybe it could be. Bill only saw what happened on the ice that day. He only heard about the surgeries and the pain and the blinding headaches that came with the injury. He never had to worry if he'd ever get his vision back. He didn't feel the anger or heartache of his future going down the drain thanks to one moment on the ice.

"I'll pass. My hockey days are behind me," I say firmly. "No more stripping telegrams or homing pigeons or shit like that, okay?"

I step back from the rink before the smell of the ice and the familiar warmth of the lights make me change my mind.

Bill nods, knowing not to push. "Yeah, I get it. I'm just saying, we miss you out here, Griff." He looks over his shoulder, and the guys nod in agreement.

"Why don't you come grab a drink with us?" Tanner asks, his eyes shining with their patented kindness. "Just as buddies. No ulterior motive."

"It's been forever since we've all hung out. Stupid life shit getting in the way." The fluorescent light bounces off Hank's pale skin making him look almost translucent.

"One drink," I say, fully aware of their intentions. But Hank is right. It has been a while since we've all hung out. Nobody tells you how lonely the busyness of adulthood can be. The tug of their camaraderie is hard to resist.

The guys cheer. I can't help but feel a spark of warmth at their reaction, but I don't let it show.

"I mean it. One damn drink."

Bill turns back to the guys. "One. Drink," he repeats firmly. "If any of you try to make Griffin Harper drink a second drink, so help me I will beat. Your. Ass. I'm looking at you, Des." Bill swivels back to me. "Are we good?"

I shoot him my best fuck-you sneer. I may not be on the team, but that doesn't stop me from getting shit like any other player.

I love it.

But I'm not suiting up again.

2

GRIFFIN

Some guys decide to join a recreational hockey league to feel the thrill of competition. Others just do it for the drinking.

It's hard to tell where my old teammates fall on this spectrum.

"To the Comebacks!" Bill says, hoisting his pint glass in the air.

Even though I'm not part of the team, I clink glasses with them. After their practice, we went to Stone's Throw Tavern, the local watering hole in downtown Sourwood owned by Mitch, our friend with the back-breaking sneeze. It's just off the main drag, with big windows that overlook the Hudson River. In better weather, I could spend hours in the beer garden communing with nature and my drink.

I take a gulp of my beer.

"Pace yourself, Griffin," Bill says, clapping me on the shoulder. "Once that drink is gone, you're cut off." He turns to the other guys around the table. "Because he's only having—"

"One drink," the guys answer in emphatic unison.

Asshats.

Bill's face splits with laughter. Back in high school, he took hockey and life just as seriously as me. Now he's cracking jokes and smiling for no reason. It's unnerving.

"Des, what the hell are you drinking?" Derek Hogan asks in his laid-back drawl. He joined us at the bar once his shift at the fire station was over. He has less hair on his head than he did in high school, but he makes up for it with a thick beard.

"A mediocre martini." Des cheers him with his glass.

I look around the table at my old teammates. We're all older. Time has been kinder to some of us than others. It's funny how certain parts of a person don't change over time. Hank still has his dopey, wide smile. Des cocks his right eyebrow damn near up to his hairline in that same skeptical way when he's listening to some bull-shit story. Tanner's eyes remain sweet as ever. Bill's still got his bulbous nose.

Some of us take a sip of our beer, and some of us gulp it down. Instead of sneaking beer and drinking in a parking lot, we can buy it at a bar. It's not as fun, though. When you're a teenager, nobody tells you how expensive drinks can be.

And this drink is costing more than cash. It's like those timeshare presentations you have to sit through to get a free vacation. Bill turns to me and begins his pitch, telling me all about the Hudson Valley Adult Hockey League. It's for experienced adult hockey players who want a fast and competitive league. Games are once a week for seventy-five minutes. The spring season starts up in a few weeks. I can see the machinations moving in his head. He may be smiling and laughing, but Bill Crandell is still a competitive son of a bitch who wants to win.

"You guys have a good roster. You don't need me," I say.

"With Mitch out, we're down a man. I want another Husky out there, a guy I know can get the job done." Bill's eyes rest on me for a beat.

"That's where you come in, Griffdog." Des points at me and winks.

"Look, I know it's been a while since any of us played. Some are rustier than others." Bill cocks an eye at Hank.

"Sorry I didn't spend my thirties doing fucking squats," Hank shoots back. "But on the bright side, I got a bigger stomach so I can cover more of the net." He tosses a peanut into his mouth, pleased with his math.

"We're rusty, but we're not out. We're still champions," Bill continues, that competitive zing lighting up his eyes. "I've seen the other teams practicing. They're good, but we're better. We're unstoppable."

"We were," I note.

"Are," Bill emphasizes back. "We'll shake off the malaise of suburban and dad life."

"I don't have dad malaise." Des gleefully sips his martini with the calm of a proud, childfree bachelor who has never known a three a.m. feeding or toddler tantrum.

"What do you do with all your free time?" Tanner asks.

"Sex. And shopping. And now hockey." Des chows down on his martini-soaked olive.

"I could make a more effective pitch if you fuckers didn't keep interrupting me." Bill rolls his eyes, although since the rest of us have kids, we're all a bit envious of Des's freedom.

"I'm gonna stop you, Bill." I put my hand on his shoulder before he gets himself revved up. "I wish I could help you guys out, but I haven't played since…"

My throat gets tight. The urge to touch my left eye burns through my fingers, but I resist calling more attention. The scratch of the patch digs into my skin.

"Admit it: you just wear that eye patch to scare us," Hank says, wiping peanut dust off his shirt.

I shoot him a scowl worthy of the penalty box.

"And it works," he says with a nervous gulp.

In the wake of the incident, I went through multiple surgeries to get it fixed, and for a while, it seemed like my left eye was improving. Not long after, a sports website chased me down and convinced me to do an interview. I thought that if scouts read about my restored vision, a miracle after multiple surgeries, they'd consider giving me another chance. But when I went on the ice to show the reporter that I still had the goods, I got so dizzy from blurriness, I threw up. The miracle was short-lived.

Alas, I got no calls. I was officially washed up before my twenty-first birthday, so I couldn't even legally drown my sorrows.

Technically, I can still see a little out of my left eye, but it's so blurry and disorienting that it's easier to wear the patch.

"If there's a time of day where you have less eye strain, we can accommodate practices," Derek says, looking at Bill for confirmation. Tanner nods along in eager agreement. They're really trying to woo me. I can't help but feel a bit puffed up by it. They really think I've still got it?

"You want a guy with a bum eye on the ice with you? I thought you wanted to win." I snort out a laugh.

"If it was anyone else's eye, I'd say no way. But a one-eyed Griff Harper is still a better hockey player than most guys with 20/20 vision. Bottom line, Griff: I know what happened in high school was fucked up. It was." He lets out a quick sigh. The other guys get serious. They were all bystanders, but the memory haunts them, too.

Bill bangs his fist on the table causing our glasses to rattle. "But dammit, you can still play. I *know* you can still play. We made magic once before. We can do it again. Show these young guns that the Comebacks still have it!"

He always had a knack for motivational speeches. Even our coach admitted that Bill's were better than his.

Fuck, I want to believe. I want to let the hope and passion enveloping his words lift me up, like I'm a lost parishioner in a preacher's tent. I almost get there, too. I let myself dream about playing again, the feel of the stick in my hands, the high that comes with the crack of slapping the puck into the goal. When I was eighteen, my hockey career went down in flames, and unfortunately, it needs to stay there.

"Sorry, guys." I pull on a smile to lighten the mood. "My hockey days are over."

Their faces sink, some more than others.

"But the next round is on me," I quickly add, and that gets a round of cheers. We may not be teammates anymore, but we can be drinking buddies.

———

It's amazing how fast time can speed by when hanging out with good friends. We spend the evening sharing old memories and catching up, laughing until it hurts. It's been months since we've all gotten together, but it feels like no time has passed. That's the power of a strong friendship. We share recent stories about our kids, each time Des chiming in that he's so glad he doesn't have them. I may not be playing hockey with them, but I'd gladly join them for after-game drinks. I thought I'd spend a half hour tops at Stone's Throw, but another ninety minutes fly by.

The only thing that pulls me from the conversation is the feeling of eyes on me throughout the evening.

I scan the bar for the culprit, a bit of a challenge with the dark lighting. Through the noise and hubbub, I spot a guy at the bar. Broad shoulders. Fit body. Short, tousled dirty blond hair. My heart makes an extra-deep thump in my chest, wondering if we'll make eye contact, and wondering what that would be like. The bartender hands him another beer, grabbing his attention and snuffing out whatever moment I thought I felt.

"Did you see someone you recognize?" Bill asks.

"No. I thought I did." I brush it off and return to my friends. Des is so fired up about something, his cheeks redden.

"Hold up, Tanner. Did you actually say you wanted to have another kid?" Des's eyes spring open in shock and horror. "You already have four!"

"Lulu is already four years old. I miss having a little baby." Chance gets moony-eyed about the prospect.

A flash of panic zips through me. I barely have a handle on co-parenting two.

"I don't know how you do it, man. One tired me out," says Derek, whose daughter is in high school.

"It's really not that bad. Lena is thirteen, so she helps with the younger ones," he says. "And I always wanted a big family. I'd hoped I wouldn't be doing it on my own, but such is life." Tanner shrugs his shoulders. He doesn't seem mad or bitter about his late wife. He takes it in stride and with the loving way he's talked about his kids, has an aura of gratitude driving him. I could learn a thing or two.

"I don't know why you've all chosen to do this to yourselves," Des says, sipping his martini.

"Do what?" Bill asks.

"Procreate." Des checks himself out in the window reflection and fixes the lapel of his blazer, which probably cost more than my whole wardrobe combined. "When I turned twenty-one, I got myself a vasectomy and a bottle of Macallan single malt scotch. I don't need little Des crotch goblins roaming this earth. Best investment I ever made."

"Is it? Do you still need a vasectomy if, you know..." Hank waves his hand, hoping Des will fill in the blank.

"You know what?" Des mimics his fluttering hand.

"You know..." Hank raises his eyebrows in addition to his hand, abandoning any attempt at being subtle.

"The only thing I know is that your body seems to be malfunctioning right now."

"Because of the t-e-s-t-c. Wait. t-e-s-t-i-s-t. Fuck." Hank scratches at his thick eyebrow. "Does anyone know how to spell testicular cancer?"

"How the CIA never thought to recruit you is beyond me," says Des.

"Does your missing ball ever tingle, like a phantom limb?" Hank wonders. He's never shy about asking weird questions, and frankly, it's one we've been curious about since the operation.

"It's not missing, Hank. There isn't a picture of my nut on a milk carton somewhere." Des knits his eyebrows together. "My other guy is strong as hell and punching above its weight. It could get a woman pregnant if it wanted to. Ergo, the vasectomy."

Hank throws up his hands in surrender.

"At least I have Griffdog, my brother in removed body parts." Des holds out his fist. My left eye wasn't removed, but I'm not gonna leave him hanging.

We bump fists, and for some reason, I instinctively turn to the bar for the mysterious blond. I feel eyes on me again, sending a current of excitement across my chest.

"Now that we've discussed hockey, there's another important topic we need to cover," Hank says, hunching forward in his seat. "Griffdog's sex life."

I feel my face go white. The guys all voice their enthusiasm to my dismay. I chug the rest of my beer. "Where the fuck is this coming from? Why don't we start with you, Hank?"

"A big, fat zero. There's an app that lets you display your dating profile in Times Square, so I may look into that."

"Buddy, we're just a little concerned." Tanner massages my shoulder. His big, blue eyes have the same calming effect as staring into the ocean. "You came out two years ago, which was a really brave and exciting move. You finally decided to live your truth, as my eldest says. But since then, you've never mentioned a boyfriend or even a date."

"Or a hookup," adds Hank.

"Your hand must be *exhausted*," Des says.

It's not too tired to flip him the bird.

My lack of dating life is something I hadn't thought about until I was put on the spot. Our power to compartmentalize and ignore things about ourselves is unlimited. I realize I look like a gay in name only.

Did Mr. Eyes hear any of this? And why do I care what Mr. Eyes thinks?

"We want to see you get laid," says Des. "Well, not actually see it because that would haunt my dreams. But hear about it. You know that you won't find a group of guys more accepting. You're in good company. Derek's dating a guy. Mitch is married to one. Tanner took an online quiz and discovered he's demisexual. I'll fuck anything that walks. Hank made out with a guy at my New Year's party."

"I'm feeling my post-divorce self. I kissed a boy and I liked it. Well, not a boy. A man. Well over eighteen. I think he was thirty-four. His tongue was like the Tasmanian Devil, in a good way." Hank runs his fingers over his lips, smiling at the memory. "But I don't want to have sex with you, Griff, if that's what you're thinking."

"Shame," I deadpan. I'm glad times have changed where we could all discuss this freely. Feeling oddly emboldened, I glance up to see if Mr. Eyes is looking at me again. He's chatting with the bartender.

Tanner rubs my shoulder for support. "I think one of the great things about getting older is discovering hidden parts of yourself. Once I turned forty, I got a lot more honest with myself. I loved my wife dearly, but then I could also see myself falling in love with a guy."

I wonder how many people came out to themselves thanks to online quizzes. Wasting time on the internet had never been so beneficial.

"I'm happy for you guys. But I'm doing fine. I'm focusing on my job and my girls. I'm not looking for anything."

"I said that, too, and then I met Cary. There's a right person out there for you," Derek says of his over-caffeinated boyfriend, and stupidly, I think of Mr. Eyes. My heart stops when I catch him glancing at me. Is he flirting? Am I flirting back? Is it pathetic that this is the closest I've gotten to dating since I came out?

"We haven't brought it up in a while because we assumed you'd tell us if you had something to share. We love sharing," Bill says.

"Yeah, I forgot to mention that Bill is balling his assistant." Des shoots Bill a wink and gets punched in the shoulder.

"Tate isn't my assistant anymore. And we didn't start anything until after he quit."

"Technically, that's not true." Hank raises his eyebrows as he takes a drink.

Bill turns to me, ignoring Hank-bait for once. "It's been about a month that Tate and I have been together."

"Their first date was on Valentine's Day. Awwww." Des makes a heart with his hands.

"Like you, it took me a while to be honest with myself about my interest in guys. Even then, I thought my chance for something real with anyone had passed me by. Love stories don't star guys in their forties. Every time I saw Tate in the office and felt that fire, a tiny part of me would hope that we could have a happy ending. And then one night...one incredible night changed everything."

Bill Crandell gets goopy with an emoji-like smile, a sight I never thought I'd see. Well, this explains why he's not the grumpy asshole that I used to play hockey with. Love has made him happy, almost... cheerful. It's hard to watch.

"I'm still feeling myself post-divorce." I nudge Hank's arm, hoping he'll back me up.

"The point is to get other people to feel you," he says back.

"Coming out's supposed to be the hard part. And then knocking boots with hot guys is the reward," says Des. "Why aren't you giving yourself the reward?"

"It's because he doesn't like fun," Hank says.

"I do like fun."

This is the first time in my life when I could be free and live openly. I could actually date someone. And yet something inside has been holding me back, a little voice of doubt that comes out muffled but still audible. It's scary diving into something new in your forties, even scarier when that new thing is sex.

"Can we change the fucking subject?" I ask. "Hank, tell me more about the guy with the Tasmanian Devil tongue."

———

ABOUT TWENTY MINUTES LATER, we say our goodbyes. I let myself enjoy my beer and the time to myself. My ex-wife Carmen has the girls this week. That's one of the upsides to divorce, a few childfree nights to myself.

The last droplets of beer hit my throat. I glance over to find Mr. Eyes still at the bar watching a hockey game on TV. Still sexy. When I played, I didn't let any guy scare me. I could handle them all. But at Stone's Throw Tavern, I find myself a nervous mess.

Especially when Mr. Eyes turns and winks at me.

Shit.

I nod back, doing the decent thing of acknowledging him. I raise my glass to take a sip, and it takes me a few seconds to remember it was empty and that I'm sucking back air.

It's time I get the hell out of there.

I calmly yet quickly escape to the bathroom to splash water on my face. I am out and proud. My family is okay with it. So are my friends. I could live my truth. I could do whatever I wanted with a guy without feeling guilt or shame. Yet, here I am hiding in the bathroom.

I'm not hiding. I'm leaving.

I splash another round of water on my face. I go to grab a paper towel and find none. Just the air dryer.

Water drips down my face. I can't go out in the cold with a wet face. I can't let Mr. Eyes see me like that and assume I fell in the toilet. Not that I care what he thinks.

I squat under the blower and push it on. Some air dryers blow a normal amount of air. Others blast so much it's like they're launching a rocket into space. This one was the latter. Hot jets of ferocious air explode at my face nearly sending me falling to my ass. I clench my eyes shut to keep from going blind. My eyebrows and beard hang on for dear life as my skin ripples with the sheer force of the blower.

Finally, the fiery hell stops. I catch my breath and touch my face, making sure it's still in one piece. My skin is on fire, but dry.

When I'm able to open my eye, I see a pair of gray ones staring back at me.

Mr. Eyes.

And those dark, fearless, penetrating orbs of his? Even more beautiful than I imagined.

He leans against the sink. "So, are you going to buy me a drink or what?"

3

JACK

Of the many coaches I've had in my life, a lot of their advice tended to overlap. There're only so many ways to tell young gentlemen to never give up, work hard, and believe in themselves. As I shuttled from one team to the next over my career, it became a soup of inspirational advice. But I do remember one coach who put his advice rather succinctly.

If you want it, go and get it. And if you don't want it, then get the hell off the ice.

Simplicity. I like it.

Little did he know that I'd mostly use his advice for getting some ass.

When I wanted a guy, I went and got him. I saw. I conquered. I came. And then I left, usually in the wee hours of the morning before he could invite me out to breakfast.

Tonight, I saw this burly guy with a beard and a solid body that was either a block of muscle or fat. I didn't care which. I just wanted to feel its weight on top of me.

And if you want something, go and get it.

"A drink?" he asks, still squatting under the air dryer. He probably thinks he looks like an idiot. I can't stop ogling his thighs in this position and wondering what it'd feel like to be crushed between them.

And we haven't even gotten to that eye patch, which makes him instantly ten times hotter. Did he get it in a knife fight? Fixing a car? Building a house? Whatever the reason, he can be my butt pirate any day of the week.

"You've been checking me out all night. I might as well get a free drink out of it." I lean against the bathroom door and watch his eyes—er, eye–flit around for an answer. The man's not as suave as I expected, but I can work with that. I can power bottom my way through this encounter.

I hold out my hand and pull him to standing. He's taller than me, built like one of those sequoia trees in California that you can drive through. His forearms are like cannons made of muscle and fur. His hands are rough, calloused, and damn near enveloping mine.

"Jack," I say.

"Griffin," he says back, finding his footing.

Griffin. I like it. Good name. A name I'd be happy to scream out over and over as I'm getting railed.

"How about that drink? Unless you're still drying off?" I ask.

He lets out a deep, grumbly laugh that seems to relax him.

A few minutes later, we're sitting at the bar half-watching the hockey game on TV. Griffin is being the responsible one nursing his beer, while I'm going at a more accelerated pace. I don't want to stretch this out too much. One drink and then it's party time in the backseat of his car. I have work in the morning.

"How's the beer?" I nod at his glass while I'm almost done with mine.

"Good," he replies with a husky grunt that I feel in between my legs. Why the fuck did I ever waste my time hooking up with my contemporaries? Older men are where it's at, clearly. Gimme those sweet, sweet daddy issues.

"So do you just hang out here picking up guys?" He licks foam off his top lip, sending my mind off in tantalizing scenarios.

"No. I have other bars for that. I came in here because I needed a drink. You were the pleasant surprise."

Red pools at the top of his cheeks. He turns his attention to the game. He shakes his head. The way he intently watches, as if terrified to pull his eyes from the TV, makes me believe he's nervous more than anything.

"Are you married?" I ask. "Because I didn't see a ring."

"What? No."

I study him to make sure he's telling the truth. I may be a slut, but I'm not a homewrecker.

"I'm divorced," he says.

His attention returns to the TV. Is he nervous or just an asshole? Griffin doesn't give much away.

"So here's the thing, Griffin. When you grab a drink with someone, it's typical to actually talk to them."

"Sorry. I'm kinda…Sorry. I have trouble talking to cute guys." He gives me a sheepish smile, his beard creasing to make room. There's something oddly wholesome about it. "And it's a good game. Although Denko is passing for shit tonight."

It's something I noticed, too, while I was drinking alone and watching the game. The center has had multiple passes nearly get scooped up by the other team. He's being sloppy, something a casual viewer wouldn't necessarily pick up on necessarily.

I flag down the bartender for a refill.

"You still play?" Griffin asks me.

"What?"

"Hockey."

I do a double take. Usually I have to fake a recovering sports injury to tip guys off that I played. "How could you tell?"

"You have a look to you." His gaze lingers on me. Must be a look he likes.

I thank the bartender when he returns with my drink. "Has being in the NHL permanently altered my DNA or something?"

Nobody can resist a pro athlete. Not women. Not gay men. Hell, I could probably pull my fair share of straight dudes, too.

"You're in the NHL?" His reaction is adorable, as if he's twelve and just met his hero.

"I was. I retired." I snort a laugh. "Retired," I say with air quotes.

"How old are you?"

"Twenty-four. Not a fan of early bird specials. Yet."

"Fuck. Were you really in the NHL?"

"I really was. Four whole years."

"Why'd you stop?"

I find myself without a witty reply. Guys don't tend to ask me that. They're too bowled over by me playing in the NHL at all. "One too many concussions."

Griffin nods, instantly getting it.

"I'm glad I was able to play professionally."

"Who did you play for?"

"The Beavers."

"You miss the Pacific Northwest?"

I seesaw my head. "Depends on the weather."

"How'd you wind up back here?" Griffin's eye lights up with questions.

"I'm from the area. I love it here. My condo at the Bellmore has a sweet view of the river. And I wanted to be close to family. They're my rock." I'm proud of myself for getting that out without throwing up in my mouth.

"You live at the Bellmore. Fancy." Griffin raises his eyebrows, his left one peeking up from the eye patch.

"It's all right. I like its security. Some fans can be a little too passionate."

"What's your full name?" Griffin takes out his phone. He has to hold it at his right side to see, which I find adorable.

I push the phone down. "It's kinda rude to Wikipedia a guy you're flirting with while he's sitting next to you."

"Sorry. You're right." He puts his phone down as blush reddens his cheeks for a moment. "What position did you play?"

"You want to know my positions, you're gonna have to buy us another round."

He lets out another grumbly laugh, and I can tell it comes from a deep, genuine place inside him. The kind of laugh one doesn't deploy during small talk.

Griffin stares at the wall of bottles, his jaw getting tight for a moment. "Fuck. You played in the NHL."

"It was pretty sweet, I won't lie." My stomach twists in a cruel knot. Some lies are easier than others. I put my hand over it to chill.

"That's...nice. Really nice." There's a melancholy dip in his voice, a gray cloud passing over his excitement. "You lived the dream."

"Yeah, I suppose."

"Don't do that. Don't minimize it. You worked damn hard since you were a kid to make it into the NHL. You should be proud, Jack."

The passion in his voice jars me a little. Griffin isn't one for surface level conversation I'm noticing; his genuine aura is refreshing.

I regale him with a few stories about my time playing in the NHL, only sharing the fun, cool moments, the things that people want to hear about. If one wants to get laid, one does not bring up the downsides of being a pro athlete. I rub my leg against his, touch his thick arm repeatedly during my stories. I need to keep this plane on course.

But I also find myself talking more than I want, something I do when I'm excited. Typically, I engage in some small talk, bump some uglies, and call it a night. There isn't much excitement in a sure thing. Most guys aren't a mystery, or at least not one worth solving. There's something about Griffin, his nervousness mixed with his guardedness, that makes me keep wanting to peel back layers.

"What's your story?" I ask, eager for more clues to this puzzle. "You obviously know the game. Were you in the minors?"

"I played in high school."

"How long ago was that?"

He thinks it over. "Late nineties. I'll let you do the math."

I try to calculate how old that makes him. Math was never my strong suit. I'd take out my phone to use the calculator, but that's even ruder than Wikipedia. He's gotta be in his forties, which only turns me on more.

"Were you the star forward?" I ask, half mockingly.

"Defenseman, but a star." He gives a faint chuckle. "I thought I was going to make it. So did my coach, my teammates, my mom. College and NHL scouts were fighting over the chance to talk to me." He stares into his drink. "But one bad collision changed everything. This other player and I were going for the puck. At the last minute, he jams his stick out to stop me. The end of it busts through my face shield and straight into my eye."

I gasp, which I know isn't the respectful reaction, but shock overtakes me as I imagine the scene. Guilt immediately takes over me.

"I'm sorry."

He waves it off. He's probably used to it. "On the way to the game that day, my face shield had gotten cracked because a box in my car's trunk fell on it. That made it vulnerable enough..."

My dad once said freak accidents are just a lot of little accidents piled on top of each other. The circumstances that led to that collision are one in a million, yet one in a million occurrences happen all the time.

"But that other player, he came at me with his stick. You don't do that." His face gets red thinking about his opponent, and I don't blame him. "I'll spare you the gory details involved with reattaching my eye. But after that, the scouts didn't want to fight over me. Go figure." He sips his beer. "My mom didn't have the money to send me to college, and I didn't have the grades to get a scholarship. All I wanted was to play in the NHL. I loved it. Aside from my kids, I didn't know you could love something that much, like it turns your chest into an overinflated balloon always on the verge of popping. I was going to be a hot draft pick, buy my mom a nice house, and give her the life she deserved, show her that all her sacrifice and hard work so I could play hockey would pay off. Fuck, I'm sorry." He rubs his forehead, letting out an embarrassed chuckle. "I'm killing the mood. You don't want a sob story."

I find that I do. It's genuine and honest, a sharp change among my hookups. It makes it really hard to treat this guy as the one-night stand he's supposed to be. My heart beats in my ears, even though my heart isn't supposed to be anywhere near this interaction.

"It's okay." I put a hand on his shoulder, even though I really want to give him a hug. "It sucks."

"It is what it is. Can't change the past. It was a long time ago." He waves it off, like it's well in the past. Or he wishes it were.

"And I know all about wanting to make your parents proud. My dad was the proverbial sports parent. If I won a game, he loved me. If I didn't, he wanted nothing to do with me. He didn't even try to hide it. He didn't buy into that whole 'I love you no matter what' thing that parents are supposed to do."

What the fuck am I doing? Telling him about my shitty relationship with my dad, something I don't even talk about with my friends. It's not flirting material. Something about Griffin makes me want to open up, like I want to match his vulnerability. He's quickly turning me into an unlocked safe, waiting to be yanked open and robbed.

"That's fucked up. I'm sorry," Griffin says. "He must love that you went pro."

"Didn't work like I thought." I bit my lip, leaving it at that because I should not be sharing this shit with a hot stranger. "Do you still get along with your mom?"

"She passed almost twenty years ago."

"And your dad?"

"Heart attack when I was ten."

"Fuck." My math skills are decent enough to know he was an orphan by thirty. Griffin is quickly turning from a bull I want to ride to a floppy eared dog I want to nurse back to health.

"To hockey?" I hold up my glass.

"Cheers." Griffin snorts as he clinks it.

"Hey. Do you want to go somewhere?" I put my hand on his leg, inching up. "I have a view for you."

4

GRIFFIN

We leave the bar and stroll down the empty, main drag of downtown Sourwood. There's an electricity between us that only comes with the buzz of late night shenanigans. That feeling that something is going to happen, a charge between our bodies, a shucking of our responsible daytime selves. My body hums with nerves that the beers in me can't quell.

Jack is much younger than guys I would go for, but damn if he isn't cute. Now that he's standing, I can fully make out his muscular body, the thick thighs and wide back common with hockey players. His thin lips stretch into a cocky smile filled with the unearned confidence of youth. Though, he made it into the NHL, so the confidence is warranted in this case. I'll bet he loved to trash talk on the ice.

"Where are you taking us?" I ask.

"To murder you, of course." He shoots me a wink. What guy gets away with winking at someone without being creepy? Jack does.

I stay focused on his gorgeous features and try to ignore the other feelings brewing inside me. Just because we connected over hockey... just because I told him stuff that I never talk about...just because my palms are sweaty and my heart is racing, and I'm wondering what those lips will taste like...none of it means anything.

"You guys have such a nice downtown. I grew up a few towns over. All we had was a Walmart." Jack keeps walking, allowing me to check out his ass.

The cute downtown of Sourwood has lots of nooks and crannies. Despite the town attracting affluent citizens, the main streets maintain a quaint charm, especially with their view of the Hudson River. I appreciate that it hasn't changed too much since I was a kid. People describe it as a small town feel that's only a train ride away from Manhattan.

We stop at a two-story building at the edge of the road, right before Maple Street turns into a neighborhood of houses. A "For Rent" sign hangs in the empty storefront window.

"Here we are," Jack says. Not what I was expecting at the end of our stroll.

"We're going inside?" I peer in the window. "Isn't that trespassing?"

"I own this building."

I try to play it cool. Real estate so close to downtown can't come cheap. How much money did he make in the NHL to buy random buildings?

"Yeah, I was looking for new asset classes to invest in. That's something my teammates and I were always discussing. You can't go wrong with real estate."

The only "asset class" I have is the small house I could barely afford after the divorce, a house that'd make Jack run the other way if he ever saw it.

"I'm thinking about getting a private plane, too," Jack says. "It's worth it to avoid flying commercial."

"I may wind up working for you then. I'm a mechanic at Jenson Regional Airport." I laugh at the irony, only to mask the twinge of embarrassment I feel. I've never been ashamed of my job, but I've also never personally known someone who owned one of the private planes I serviced.

"Small world," Jack says. "If I do buy a plane, I'll consider storing it at Jenson. You seem like a guy who's good with his hands." Jack flashes me another smile, and I damn near go googly-eyed.

"I mostly learned on the job. I needed something to do after high school when hockey didn't pan out."

"Learning how to fix a plane or a car is much more valuable than shooting a puck," Jack says. Shooting a puck has gotten him multiple asset classes, so I don't know how true that is.

I walk up to the front door and pull. It's locked.

"We're not going in the front door." Jack signals for me to follow around the building to the fire escape. He puts his hand on my lower back to guide me, sending a jolt of heat up my spine.

"You first," he says. "I'll make sure you don't bust a hip and fall."

"I'm not that old."

"I was thinking of old hockey injuries flaring up. Don't worry. I'm not going to check out your ass as you go up." He seesaws his head. "Well, no more than twice."

This guy has zero flirting shame. It makes my head fuzzy with dirty ideas.

"It's okay. I checked out your ass while walking here," I say back. Jack's smile goes extra wide on that one.

The rusted metal of the fire escape chafes my hands, but a rush of excitement makes me push through. As does the knowledge that Jack is likely checking me out.

"I can't believe I'm climbing a fucking fire escape."

"Life is full of surprises. Embrace it," he says.

I haul myself over the edge of the roof. When I stand up, I go speechless.

Moonlight reflects in the ripples of the Hudson River framed by a row of mountains on the other side. A flush of trees canvases the mountain, and bright stars salt the clear, black sky. It's so peaceful and captivating that I forget I'm in civilization at all. This town I've lived in forever can still find ways to surprise me. It's a reminder that we are but a tiny cog in the great machine of nature.

"Worth the climb?" Jack asks, returning his hand to my lower back.

I give him the barest nod yes, as I continue to drink it all in. The older we get, the fewer moments we give ourselves to stop and enjoy ones like these.

Jack watches me. Gone is the cocky flirt for a second, a softer grin lighting his face.

"It's incredible," I say. "Is this why you bought the building?"

"I wish. Added benefit." He shuffles closer to me, putting a firmer grip on my back. His warmth sends a bolt of joy through me.

"My girls would love this. Though there's no way in hell I'm letting them climb a fire escape." I shouldn't be bringing up my daughters when I'm on the cusp of a sexy moment. It's a parent reflex.

"How old are they?" Jack asks.

"Nine and seven. It's a fun age. They're obsessed with *Frozen*. Please tell me you were too old for that movie."

"I was. I was in high school when it came out."

That makes me feel a tad better, but I'm still reminded of the giant age gap between us.

"I'm picturing you belting out 'Don't Let Go' with your daughters."

"'Let It Go.' And yes, I have been known to join in a singalong with them. It's something I never thought I would do. I thought I was going to be a strict dad. Stern. Here to set boundaries and discipline. But nope. I'm a total girl dad. I host tea parties. I can do a mean French braid."

What the fuck am I doing? Yeah sure, rich hockey player Jack will totally want to have sex with a guy bragging about his French braid skills and epic tea parties. Maybe this is why I haven't been with any guys. I get right up to the net, and I still miss the shot.

"Are you turned on yet?" I ask, trying to play it off.

"Actually...kinda?" I can't tell if Jack is being serious or not. But then he skims his thumb down my arm, tangling our fingers together. My heart is ready to leap out of my chest. I breathe in his scent by the lungful yet still want more.

"They must think you're cool. Dad's a big, bad hockey player."

"I don't talk about it." I shrug.

"At all?"

"It's in the past."

"Do you miss it?" Jack peers straight into my eye. The energy vibing between us is like a truth serum I am powerless against.

"Yeah," I say, my voice hoarse, like that one word was pulled out of a deep hole. "I think I do. But I can't play again."

"Why not? If you love it and you miss it..."

My free hand grazes over my eye patch.

"I don't know you, Griffin, but I also know you. And your eye is not the reason you've avoided the ice."

Jack smooths a hand over my patch, our fingers touching. It's the final spark of electricity that throws me over the edge and makes me pull him into my arms for a kiss. I don't know what comes over me. Nerves. Unrelenting desire. Curiosity. Jack.

He kisses me back, his tongue surprisingly tender, the taste of his drink mixing with his cologne and lingering sweat. Kissing a guy is one million times better than I dreamed, no offense to my ex-wife. I thread my fingers through his hair and pull him even closer until I can feel his erection poke through his jeans.

Jack rubs a hand over my beard, making me growl with want. His hand dips between us, feeling the ridges of my chest. He moans against my lips, giving my bottom lip a bite.

I'm lost in his kiss, in how thick and hot he feels in my arms, when Jack steps back and sinks to his knees.

Whoa.

I may be a total newbie with gay stuff, but this feels fast. Like we leaped over a few steps. Do guys always move this fast? Did I let Jack assume that we were sucking each other off tonight by coming up here? Fuck, am I cocktease? Fuck, is he going to expect me to blow him and am I going to bomb? Is he expecting us to have sex on this rooftop?

Panic overtakes me, leaving me scared shitless. My first guy-on-guy kiss was less than a minute ago. I'm still figuring out how to put on ice skates, and I'm already being drafted into the big leagues.

He begins unbuckling my belt. Then he undoes the top button of my jeans. Alarm bells ring in my ears.

Ever so tenderly, I push Jack's head away from my crotch. He resists for a second, thinking we're playing a game, until I zip up my fly. He looks up at me, still on his knees, lust rapidly vanishing from his face, replaced with something much darker.

"Sorry," I mutter. "I, uh...I appreciate it, but..."

"You appreciate it?" He spits out, his cocky smile from before flipped to a menacing sneer. He hops to his feet in one swift move. "Go fuck yourself."

"Wait," I start. I reach out for him, but he's already storming down the fire escape.

5

——————

JACK

The next morning, I wake up with a really bad hangover. Truly horrendous. Like someone is bashing a sack of potatoes against my skull.

I can handle regular hangovers. I'm used to those. Nothing that two Advil and some Pedialyte can't fix.

This is different. This is copious amounts of alcohol mixed with frustration, confusion, and shame.

What the fuck happened last night?

I can't stop thinking about it. Griffin, ever so tenderly, pushed my head back, *away from his crotch*. It was supposed to be the other way around. Hot dick was supposed to be filling my mouth, but instead, cold air hit my face.

When a guy is on his knees blowing you, it's hot. When a guy is on his knees and there's no dick in his mouth, it's not hot. He looks like a beggar. A beggar is not hot. Does he know how many guys would be begging me for sex? Being a professional hockey player turned my dick into a magnet.

That wasn't even the weirdest part about last night.

Talking to Griffin gave me this uncomfortable flutter in my

stomach like the sinking sensation when I drive over a hill just a little too fast. It was a good sinking, if that's even possible.

It's not like I wanted a connection with him, but it kind of seemed like we had one. And it scared me shitless. The faster we could get to hooking up, the faster all that connection and fluttering and sinking could go away. Until he pushed my head back. The record scratch to end all record scratches.

Is this the first time in recorded history a man has refused a blow job?

Last night felt like a heart-to-heart when it should've been a dick-to-ass.

Oh, and the shameful part of my epic hangover? That was when I got home and cranked it to Griffin to help me fall asleep. Masturbating to a guy who rejected me is a new low.

A knock at the door jolts me from my Griffin postmortem.

I sit up on my pullout couch, and my head is clocked with a fresh sack of potatoes. The big, dense ones from Idaho. I shove my hand in the gap between the bed and the couch searching for my phone.

"Yo!" Fuentes yells from the other side of the door. "I gotta take a leak."

"Shit," I mutter. I reach my arm down farther, fingers crawling the dirty floor until they come upon the sleek frame of my phone. "Shit," I mutter again when I see the time displayed on the home screen.

"You need a ride to work or not?" Fuentes bangs again.

"Coming!" I yell.

I roll myself off the couch, holding onto the window to keep from falling. Standing is a new sensation that activates a new level of hangover pain in my head. I blink a few times to ease the agony. Fortunately, it's only a few steps from the edge of the pullout to the door. One of the few benefits of living in a studio apartment.

"Hey," I say when I open the door, but Fuentes is already speeding past me into the bathroom.

"Gotta take a leak," he says.

I stumble into my kitchen area, a nook too small to be considered a room, which is fine since I don't cook. I rinse out my mouth with water then down two tablets of Advil from the bottle in the side drawer. Just knowing they're in my system helps to calm the pounding in my head. Though the sinking sensation in my stomach has not abated.

What's Griffin's morning routine with his daughters? Probably something cute where they all sing *Frozen* songs as they get dressed. He probably lets the girls push down the toaster button, too.

Fuck. Griffin, get out of my head. This is why I stick to fucking my contemporaries. Nothing a twentysomething guy does could be considered cute.

"Aahhhh." Fuentes leans against the bathroom doorway, the blissful feeling of an empty bladder lighting his face. "That was great."

Jay Fuentes has the big smile and perfectly round brown eyes that makes people think he's the wholesome boy next door, but they've never heard his locker room talk.

"Thanks for the commentary. Now move. I have to get ready."

"Did I wake you up?" he asks as I rush past him to the bathroom. "Don't you have work in fifteen minutes?"

"Yeah. It's fine."

"You're going to stroll in late? Your dad isn't going to like that."

"What choice do I have?" I strip off my clothes and jump in the shower. The shock of bitingly cold water sends new crackles of pain across of skin, but it also wakes me the fuck up.

Fuentes sits on the toilet. We've showered and gotten dressed in front of each other in locker rooms for years, so there's no weirdness.

"I have coffee and croissants in the car."

The bathroom is so tiny he could rest his legs on the sink. A stray elbow in any direction could put a hole in the wall.

"Thanks." My stomach growls at the mention of caffeine and sugar.

"When is your car going to get fixed?"

"It's in the shop." I wait for the water to warm up, but it's taking its sweet time.

"It's in your parking space downstairs."

I curse to myself, grateful he can't see my face through the curtain.

"Once I get my next paycheck, I'll be able to take it to the mechanic. And did you know this water takes fucking forever to warm up? You need to get a plumber in here."

"I put in a new water heater two years ago. It's a cold morning. The other tenants are probably showering, too." Without having to stand up, he flicks on the bathroom exhaust fan. "You need to run this fan whenever you shower so you don't get mold."

He pulls back the shower curtain to examine the ceiling and walls. Each of his apartments is like his child, and as a landlord, he can be a full-on helicopter parent at times. I put up with it since he cut me a very fair deal on rent here.

For as long as I've known him, Fuentes was adamant about not having to wear a tie as an adult. After graduating from high school, while I went pro, he lived at home and ate peanut butter and jelly sandwiches to save up a down payment on a dilapidated house. He fixed it up and rented out the other bedrooms, then used that money to buy another house to rent out, then another, and then this apartment building. He has a mini empire in the Hudson Valley region. And I have yet to ever see him in a tie.

Fuentes holds his hand under the shower. "It's warming up."

The water goes from freezing cold to scorching hot in a second. I hop away from the spray, turning the dial to the center quickly without burning off my skin. Finally, the water finds a middle ground. It's the first moment of peace since I've woken up.

"Did you have a wilder night than usual?" Fuentes rests his feet on the sink. "You never oversleep when you're hungover."

Fuentes is one of my oldest friends. He was one of the first people I came out to. If I can't share this with him, then who can I?

"Have you ever met a guy—or a girl in your case—and you're flirting, and things are going well, and they leave the bar with you, and they go with you to a rooftop, and...then they turn you down?" I scrub shampoo through my hair as I try to make sense of where the night derailed.

"They did all that and then they said no?" Fuentes gives me a double take.

"They pushed my head away from their crotch, which was very visibly tented with a boner."

"Shit. Are you serious?"

"Oh, and then they said, 'I appreciate it.'"

"That's...huh. Never had a girl say that to me."

My hands scrawl through my hair, water mixing with the foamy shampoo as anger rises inside me. "I'm all about consent. He said no, I backed off. But we were having a good night. Everything was going great. I took him to my rooftop."

"Which rooftop?"

"The one for the building at the end of Maple."

"That's *my* rooftop," he interjects. "I better not find any used condoms or else I'm evicting you."

"You won't. He's the only guy I've brought up there."

"Oh." Fuentes's voice has a very curious tone to it. "Jack's in love."

"I'm not in love. Fuck off. It was a nice night out. I wanted to seal the deal."

"You've sealed the deal with plenty of guys. You never brought any of them to the special rooftop."

"It's not special."

"That's what you called it. I'm just using your words. You said it was your favorite place to think, that the view always cheered you up."

I shut off the shower, my jaw tight. I can't believe I took Griffin to my rooftop where he made me feel feelings then rejected me. "Hand me a towel."

Fuentes grabs the one hanging off the back of the door and tosses it my way.

"Sounds like you're into him," he says.

"Well, he wasn't into me."

"And there were no signs that maybe he didn't want to hook up? Maybe you missed them?"

"I wouldn't have missed a red flag like that. He was the one who held my hand. He kissed *me*. On my special rooftop." I rub myself dry. I toss Fuentes my towel. He hangs it back up while I give myself a rushed toothbrushing.

"Damn, that's cold." Fuentes shakes his head. "Fuck him, right?"

"Right. Why do I keep forcing myself to learn this lesson? People can turn on a dime. They care about you until they don't." I wash out my mouth and storm into the main room. I grab clothes from the overstuffed dresser that barely fits along the wall. It's one of the few remaining items from my old, pro-athlete life, and I didn't want to part with it.

Fuck Griffin. He cracked open a door within me that had been nailed shut years ago. I was off my game and nearly let him in. He got me talking about things that I never wanted to talk about, like my dad. Thank goodness I didn't share anything about my mom. Last night was amazing and incredible and never should've happened but it did...and then he pushed me away.

"Fuck. Him." I slam the dresser drawers shut. I turn to Fuentes for a style check. The man wears a T-shirt and jeans every day since he's his own boss. I get to as well, but I also have to wear a purple apron, which kills any kind of power vibe.

Fuentes gives me a thumbs up and tosses me the apron, bunched up at the foot of the pullout couch.

"You seem pissed. You know a good place to take out that aggression? The hockey rink." He takes a flyer from his pocket and hands it over.

The bold letters at the top scream Hudson Valley Adult Hockey League. That was all I needed to read to know I wasn't interested.

"I can see your eyes glazing over," Fuentes says, opening the front door. We shuttle out and hustle down the stairs. "It's a fun, recreational league for guys who used to play hockey. Miller and I formed a team. We want you on it."

"I haven't played hockey since I left the NHL." I scurry down another staircase, Fuentes right behind me.

"That was only two years ago. You're still sharp. Hell, I hear there're guys who haven't played in decades who are suiting up."

I laugh at the idea of playing middle-aged dads.

"It's one game per week on Sunday mornings. Not like you're going to church." Fuentes unlocks his car, a brand-new, gleaming black truck. He claims he needs the space to haul supplies for maintenance. I think he just wanted a big fucking truck. "Don't you miss playing?"

It was the same question Griffin asked me last night. Again, I freeze up in response.

"Those days are behind me."

"It'd be so baller to have a former pro hockey player on our team."

"Having me on there isn't the flex you think it is," I say. I shove the flyer in my pocket before buckling up. "I'll think about it. Now drive like the wind."

6

JACK

Here's what people don't tell you about professional athletes: most of us don't rake in millions of dollars. A few players at the top make a shit ton of money while the rest of us fight for proverbial scraps. Most hockey players are middle class guys earning a living in a sport that has an expiration date.

We all go into the sport wanting to be one of those top players with the huge paychecks and endorsements. But for most of us, we play in their shadow. We keep our heads down, play the game. We collect a salary that most people would salivate over, but when you factor in taxes, agent fees, lawyer fees, and manager fees, and add the fact that the average career only lasts five years...that money doesn't go as far as you think. Especially when you think the good times will last, when everyone around you is telling you you're going to be a breakout star, so you spend like that. You can take a chance and invest in your teammate's restaurant or a friend's startup. You don't need to squirrel away money for your post-hockey career because your post-career is light years away, and it will include lucrative jobs like TV commentator or head coach. For most of us, we don't become stars. We're just the other guys on the team supporting the star player.

When I was drafted into the league out of high school, I thought

I'd made it. Everyone around me told me I'd made it. Yet in that first year, I rode the bench and got little playtime. The star players were supposed to retire, but they decided to stick around for another year. The heat around me dissipated over the season. I tell people I played for the Beavers to keep it simple, when actually I wound up getting traded to four teams in four years. I got the message: I was good enough for pro hockey, but not great.

Good enough to seduce guys into fucking me, but not great enough to make them want to stay. Once people saw the real me, a guy with no money, no career prospects, and no superstar athlete clout, they bolted. My friend with the startup and teammate with the restaurant, both of which went under? Never heard from them again, although judging by social media posts, they're still living rich lives.

Being a hockey player with a big dick and a small bank account can only take a guy so far. Fortunately, I learned that lesson early on, so I didn't waste my time searching for anything more than a good lay.

Although *one guy in particular* has really messed that up for me.

"You're late," Dad says when I get into Ferguson's, a big box home improvement store where my soul goes to die on a daily basis. Even though he's wearing a garishly purple apron, he still manages to look intimidating, his chest hulking out and threatening to break the apron straps. Forty-four and still hitting the weightroom regularly. He claims it's to relieve stress, and yet he seems perpetually at a low-grade rage.

He gets in my face and studies my eyes. "And hungover."

As much as I want them to, my eyes can't lie. They get super bloodshot when I drink. No amount of Visine can clear it up. It was my tell when I snuck out to drink in high school, and Dad yelled at me then. He'd get furious. *You don't go pro by getting drunk!*

Nowadays he doesn't yell. He just looks more disappointed in me than usual.

"It's only twenty minutes. Fuentes was late picking me up," I lie. Fuentes said I could blame him. Wasn't like he could ever be fired from his job. He turned out to be the smartest one of all of us.

"It's not his responsibility to be here on time. It's yours."

"The store doesn't open for another forty minutes."

"Your shift started twenty minutes ago," he says, and that's that. Growing up, Dad was a foreman at a factory that manufactured industrial kitchen equipment. He holds tight to clocking in on time. When the jobs were shipped overseas, he had a hard time finding something new until eventually following former coworkers to the new Ferguson's in town. Because he doesn't have a college degree, it's hindered his ability to move up the ladder. That, and he isn't the best people person. He's gotten better about snapping at customers, but it still happens from time to time.

"Why haven't you gotten your car fixed yet?" he asks as he adjusts a sale tag on a display.

"I'm working on it."

Dad shakes his head, a common reaction to anything I say nowadays. He turns on his heel and walks down the large, imposing lighting aisle where every freaking lamp is on. He shakes his head, talking to himself, then swivels back to me as if we're already in mid-conversation. "And twenty minutes is a big deal. I've already stuck my neck out to get you this job. The least you could do is show an ounce of respect."

"I'm grateful. I appreciate it." Just like Griffin appreciated my almost blow job? Now is not the time to think about that catastrophe.

"Do you? You don't act like it."

I get the feeling Dad wants me to thank him every single day, and even then, it wouldn't be enough.

"Maybe my flowers got lost in the mail."

"Don't get smart with me."

"I..." But there's no valid excuse. I got too drunk, I slept too late, and I can't afford a decent car. I'm still haunted by watching my old Audi convertible get repossessed. "I'm getting it fixed."

"How do you really not have enough money to get your brakes fixed?"

"It's like two grand!"

"What are your expenses? Your friend's cutting you a good deal."

"I still have to pay rent."

"What about an emergency fund?"

I shrug my shoulders, exhausted all over again. "I don't have one, I guess. I spent it all on hookers and blow."

"Jack," he growls.

"Sorry. Sex workers and blow."

"You think this is funny? You think life is one big joke?" He gets right in my face. "Well, I got a great one for you. A real humdinger. Okay, picture it: this hotshot rookie rides the bench most of the season because he can't outshine a center who's pushing forty. When he finally gets called up to play, his first chance to show his coaches and the fans what he's made of...he accidentally passes the puck to his opponent, who then scores the winning goal." Dad lets out a barking laugh tinged with acid. Despite the loud chortle, there's no joy on his face. "What do you call a guy who sinks his career in under a minute and ten seconds? Fifteen years of hard work down the tubes."

I ball my fists and do everything I can to hold in a reaction. I won't give him that satisfaction.

"I don't know about you, but I call him son."

"What do you call a player who thinks he's destined for greatness but can't even make it out of high school hockey?"

"You watch your damned mouth, boy." Dad gets right in my face, jaw just as tight.

Imagine working with someone you can't stand. Now imagine that person is your father. Is it any wonder that I'm regularly hungover? I can't be around Dad without frustration bubbling under both of our surfaces.

"You've never taken a hit like I took back then. It was a sucker hit from a real asshole, some hot shit trying to prove himself. Messed my shoulder up real good." Dad rubs his shoulder for effect. I've known lots of hockey players with shoulder problems, so I know he's not faking it. But it was over twenty fucking years ago.

"I could've been drafted. And if I was, I wouldn't have let myself fade into oblivion," he spits out. Family really knows how to jab you to inflict the most pain with the least number of words.

Toby, the assistant manager, marches up to us. He doesn't have to wear the apron. He gets to dress business casual, his shirt and pants perfectly pressed. He has a smarmy smile and well-coifed hair that lets everyone know he's counting down the days until he gets promoted into a corporate role and can leave this shitty store in this shitty town.

"Gross Senior and Gross Junior. Good morning!" Toby's utter fakeness is so yucky it makes me second-guess if I'm actually attracted to men. "There was a spill in the garden center. One of the trees fell over, knocked into a display of pots. In the future, we need to be more careful about how closely we stock items."

He watches Dad until he utters an apology.

"Yeah, I was just following the display plan sent by corporate," Dad said, never one to admit fault. Ever.

"Can you guys go clean it up?"

"Sure thing," Dad says.

"Excellent." Toby looks me up and down, notes my coat in my hands. "Did you just get here, Jack?"

"He's been here. He was cold. Needed his jacket from the back room," Dad says. I nod along.

"It's a cold one. Hopefully spring gets here soon." Toby gives us a wave and keeps moving, typing away on his phone.

Dad and I head to the garden center not uttering a word. Hundreds of pieces of broken pots litter the floor. He curses to himself and shoves the dustpan into my hands.

I squat down while Dad sweeps. His broom stops right before a pile of broken pieces hits the pan.

"What's that?" He points to my side where Fuentes's flyer has fallen out of my pocket.

"Nothing. Just some hockey thing." I toss it atop the dustpan pile.

"What hockey thing?" He leans down and picks it up. He immediately starts skimming it, his broom hanging slack against his chest.

"It's nothing." I collect the pot pieces with my hands. "Fuentes and Miller are putting together a team for this amateur adult hockey league. They asked me to join, but I don't think I have the time to commit."

Dad snorts, something close to a genuine laugh from him. The sound and reaction is so unexpected I have to do a double take.

"What's so funny?" I ask.

"Nothing. Just you playing hockey again."

The words sear into my skin. "I said I'm not doing it."

I dump the dustpan into the trash.

"It's for the best." He sweeps another round of broken pots into my pan. "Your hockey days are over."

He lets out another snort. It makes me want to gag.

"Says who?"

"Says the league and anyone who watched you play. By your last year on the ice, you were...you were definitely not at your peak. That's for damn sure. I still tuned into your games, and they were all painful to watch."

"I'd been traded to four different teams in four years." It's hard rebuilding trust with a new coach, constantly being the new guy, finding my groove with teammates who never expected me to last. After my fourth cross-country move, the exhaustion hugged me like a weighted vest. My body was tired from playing. My mind was tired from thinking about how I fucked up my career. My heart was tired from caring.

"You lost it, whatever you had." Dad keeps sweeping, as if he's talking about car keys and not the thing I revolved my life around. "No sense making another fool of yourself here. Can you imagine? A professional hockey player getting his ass whipped by a bunch of amateurs."

He lets out another snort. I've barely known Dad to laugh at anything, and now he's acting like he's watching the funniest stand-up in his life.

Anger gushes through me. I am a damn good hockey player. I made one really bad pass in one very important game, but that doesn't get to wipe away the years of effort and energy I put in. He can hate me for being late. He can hate me for not being a wealthy athlete that can rescue him from this life. But he doesn't get to say I'm a shitty player.

Dad crumples up the flyer and tosses it into the trash. I immediately fish it out.

"Actually, I've changed my mind. I feel like getting back on the ice."

I haven't lost anything. It's merely been in hibernation.

"What are you doing?" he asks as I untie the purple apron of doom.

"And another thing: I quit."

"The hell you do."

Dad's snort laugh is the straw that breaks this camel's back. I can't spend another shift under his disapproving eye.

I whip off the apron and throw it on the ground where it lays with the shattered pots. "Next time, don't set up these displays so close together."

I turn and stroll out, like one of those cool guys in movies that doesn't look back at explosions.

"Come back here!" he yells.

I ignore him and keep walking.

7
———

GRIFFIN

My former teammates watch from the front steps of Summers Rink slack-jawed as I walk up the concrete, cracked-filled path, two big lampposts guiding my way. It's still dark out this early in the morning, but even with my eye closed, I could make it to the front door. The building is at the end of a cul-de-sac in an office park, the pot of nondescript gold at the end of a winding path of anonymous buildings and warehouses. Were it not for the skate logo on the front door, nobody would ever know this was a hockey rink, the place where legends were born and built. Also the place with free skate most afternoons.

"Holy crap," Tanner says.

"He lives," Des remarks.

Bill and I exchange a nod of acknowledgment.

Hank starts a slow clap, which the others join in on. It reaches its deafening climax when I reach the front door. Nobody ever saw a bunch of guys this excited before six in the morning.

I want to tell them to shut up, but I find myself the teensiest bit choked up. I don't deserve any of this fanfare, but I'm grateful they think I do. I missed the camaraderie of a team as much as the game itself.

"I told you stripping telegrams work!" Hank says to Bill.

"He's back, gents. He's fucking back." Bill claps me on the shoulder and guides me through the door.

"I showed up at a practice. One practice," I tell him. It doesn't mean I'm going to be a permanent fixture on the team. I have no idea if I can still play.

"We'll take it one practice at a time. We got the lineup back. The original lineup." Bill rubs his hands together. We were unstoppable. Me, Bill, Des, Tanner, Hank, and Derek. I don't know if history can repeat itself, but we'll sure as hell see.

We all walk down the hallway, past bulletin boards and flyers advertising peewee leagues and lessons. I come here regularly to skate, never to play. It's a familiar place, but this morning, it feels different.

Bill checks his watch, then peeks in at the rink. "There's another team just finishing up their practice. Gents, finish up your snacks, and then let's get suited up."

Hank crams another breakfast bar in his mouth. He rips open a fresh box and offers them around.

We go into the locker room, the rank smell a primal sensory memory of playing in high school. No amount of air freshener can rid this place of its signature stank. We get into our gear and skates. I found pads and a jersey at a resale shop since my old stuff is too small. But my skates still fit like a glove. And my stick feels warm in my hand.

I check myself out in the mirror. Fuck. I'm really doing this. I'm actually going to play hockey.

"Looking good, Griffdog." Hank claps me on the shoulder. Like me, his gear is a mix of pieces from different sets. We look like hockey quilts, but damn if we don't look good.

My teammates and I exit the locker room back into the main hallway. The team on the ice is fully engulfed in their practice with no sign of stopping. They're also adorned in matching black uniforms.

Des lets out a yawn. "Where the fuck is he?"

"Who?" I ask.

Just then, Derek bursts through the front door carrying two trays of large coffees.

"Here you go." He doles out the coffees. "Look who the heck it is."

His face lights up when he sees me then pulls me into a bear hug.

"Where've you been?" Hank asks, nearly chugging his coffee.

"I just got off a twenty-hour shift at the firehouse. I'm going to practice for an hour and then go home and collapse." Derek leans against the wall. He's the only one who got iced coffee, even though it's cold out. He looks at me and cocks an eyebrow. "You sure you want to get back into bed with these animals?"

"Don't scare him away. We finally got him to say yes," Tanner says.

"Chance, how the fuck are you so alert at this ungodly hour?" Des asks, sipping his coffee as if it's literally giving him life.

"I've been up since 4:12 this morning. Dean had a nightmare and then wanted to build blocks," Tanner says, as if it's a regular day for him.

"I wouldn't wake up that early unless I was catching a flight." Des shakes his head.

I've been there, as have all of the other dads. Sometimes, you just know it's going to be an extra-long day.

I gulp down the coffee, the refreshing liquid so soothing and rich that I have to remind myself not to chug it or else I'll burn my throat. "This is amazing."

"Caroline's," Derek says.

"This is Caroline's coffee?" Caroline's is the greasy spoon diner in town. They're known for having a varied menu, with all of the entrées being good, not great. I imagined their coffee was whatever was on sale at the store.

"It is. They import it from somewhere. Cary is a coffee fiend, which is odd since he's naturally caffeinated."

I'm still wrapping my head around Derek being bi. And Bill. And Hank making out with a guy with a Tasmanian Devil tongue? It's a new world, and I'm glad I live in it.

"Go change," Des says to Derek, pointing to the locker room.

Bill paces outside the rink, a tight grimace on his face. "They really should be finishing up by now. Some of us need to get to the office."

"You have emails to send, assistants to bang," Des says.

"For the last time, Tate was not my assistant when we got together." He whacks the back of his hand at Des's crotch.

"I'm wearing a cup, baby. But if you want my dick, just ask." Des winks at him.

"Speaking of dicks," Hank begins, and I know this sentence won't end well, especially when he turns to me. "I think something went down with you and the blond at the bar the other night."

"The blond that Griff was blatantly checking out?" Des asks. The other guys gather around.

Shit. And I thought I was being subtle. I really am a newb at this stuff.

"After we left, I had to drive back because I forgot my phone," Hank says. "I like to play this game that's basically a Tetris rip-off when I'm on the can. I left my phone on top of the toilet at Stone's Throw."

"Why are you giving us all of this unnecessary detail?" Des asks.

"I like my stories to have texture. Anyway, when I went back to the bar, Griff's car was still there. I asked the bartender, and he said Griff left with..." Hank does a drumroll on the bulletin board, making me blush even more. "The Blond!"

The guys let out loud ooooohs and whistles like they're audience members in the cheesy sitcom known as my life. I want to deny it, but there's too much evidence. My face feels so red it could be mistaken for Mars.

"Maybe they just left the bar at the same time by coincidence," Tanner says.

Hank lets out a booooo like he's now an audience member at a trashy talk show.

"You can tell us what happened, Griffdog." Des throws an arm around me. "Did you finally pop your gay cherry?"

I flash back to the rooftop, when all the green lights were there. Jack was gorgeous. He was a key unlocking all of my deepest fears and secrets. How was it so easy to talk to him when I barely knew him? How could I pass all these guys in public and feel nothing, and then spend a few hours with Jack and feel everything?

And then how could I walk away from the greatest kiss of my life, a kiss I initiated?

My head was still a mess from that night. My heart was in worse shape. It shouldn't be possible to feel a connection like this with someone so quick.

"Nothing happened," I tell them. It's mostly the truth, which makes it easier to hide what did happen.

"Nothing?" Hank asks, deflated. "I'll bet he was into you. Even for a hot night."

I'm still kicking myself for getting scared and waiting until the last minute to pump the brakes. But I don't know if I'm built for meaning-less flings.

"Maybe it could've been something more serious," says Tanner, perhaps reading my mind. His eyes widen with eternal hope.

I shake my head no. As a divorced, has-been athlete with one fucked-up eye, I don't bring much to the table. And very quickly, Jack would've realized that. I'd rather wonder about what could've been than deal with the cruel rejection reality would've brought.

"Bill, what do you think?" Hank asks our captain, pacing furiously by the rink.

"I think this team needs to get the hell off the ice. Grab your skates and sticks. We're going in."

We march up to the rink. The team is deep into sprints, seeming to have no intention of winding down.

"Hey!" Bill calls out. They ignore him. "Hello! This is our practice time," he yells.

"They're fucking with us," I say under my breath. In hockey, actions matter infinitely more than words. I step onto the ice and stop a puck in the middle of a passing drill.

"Hey!" I yell as loud and forcefully as I can. I pick up the puck and throw it onto the bench. "You're on our time."

I motion for my teammates to join me on the ice. It's quite a contrast, our mishmash of hockey gear versus their sleek, matching black uniforms with a stick logo that could double as a knife, but I don't let it intimidate me.

"We have the rink now for practice," I say to the sea of black. "Who's your captain?"

A guy skates forward from the pack. He takes off his helmet, and my head and my heart and the rest of me plummet through my skates.

Jack might be wearing a hockey uniform and bulky gear, but that spiky blond hair and thin-lipped smile is unmistakable.

"Nice to see you again." An amused grin hits his lips as he silently puts all the pieces together.

My mouth goes dry. Seeing him in person again reminds me of how gorgeous he is, how my body craves his features.

"Jack," I say, my body tingling at the sound of his name on my tongue.

"Of all the ice rinks..." There's a menacing calm to him that makes me believe that any intention he had of wrapping up his team's practice is long gone now that he sees me. He skates to the center of the rink.

"What are you doing here?" I ask.

"We have to practice," he says. "First game of the season is coming up."

"For the rec league?"

He nods, completely unfazed at seeing me. He hasn't flinched once, whereas I feel stark naked despite wearing an ungodly amount of gear.

"You're playing in the league? But it's for amateurs only. Not for professional hockey players." I skate closer and catch a glorious whiff of him, sending me back to that rooftop.

"I'm not currently in the NHL. So according to the league's rule-book...I'm a Blade." He high-fives his teammates.

"This is an extracurricular league. Guys play for fun."

"Really? Because you seem like a guy who isn't capable of fun. You seem like a guy who might seem like he's up for fun, but then actively *pushes* fun away." Jack shrugs his shoulders, a coldness permeating his fake smile.

Fuck. This is a non-checking league, but Jack's going to shove the shit out of me the first chance he gets.

"If any of you dinosaurs have an issue with my playing, you can take it up with the league," Jack hollers over to my teammates.

"Dinosaurs?" Des cries out. "We're not even fifty!"

"Well, good for you," Jack shoots back. "We can't be held responsible for any broken hips on the ice. And nice jerseys. Very homey." He looks back at his teammates, who chuckle at the joke. "Anyway, this is our ice. We have it booked."

"No. We have it booked," I growl. I skate up to his face. I still got about two inches on him.

"Actually, we have it booked." Jack skates to the players' bench where his phone rests. He pulls up an app noting the time blocked off.

"The rink has an app?" I teepee my eyebrows together as I study his phone screen. I turn back to Bill for backup. He skates forward.

"I made the reservation on the website. Maybe their systems aren't synched," Bill says.

"Well, cry into your flip phones. We have this rink, and we gotta practice." One of Jack's teammates fishes out the puck and brings it over to him.

"Look, we were probably double-booked. It happens," Bill says, trying to keep the peace. Jack just keeps glaring at me. "You guys got some practice in. We need to get some practice in. We'll each have an abbreviated practice today, and we'll get it squared away for the future."

I look to Jack and give him a nod. It can't get any more fair than that.

Jack doesn't blink. "Nope. We were here first. You can hang out on the bleachers until we're done."

"You fucking serious?" Bill hisses. I block him from charging into Jack, which is like holding back a bull. It only makes Jack chuckle.

"Bill, I got this. Go back with the guys." I give him a reassuring nod. Bill stares down Jack as he skates away backward.

I get closer to Jack so nobody else can hear us. "Look, I can explain about the other night. You don't have to take it out on my teammates."

Jack throws his head back and lets out a laugh as plastic as my helmet. "Griffin, that's rich. Don't worry. The other night meant absolutely nothing to me."

He doesn't blink when he says it. It's a chainsaw ripping through my heart.

"I had a conversation about hockey with a guy who, it turns out, couldn't get it up. I know that's common with guys your age. Whatever."

"What? Uh, no. No, no, no." I might have no experience with guys, but I definitely wouldn't have trouble in that department. With a mouth as acidic as his, I'm glad my dick got nowhere near it.

Jack skates in a circle around me. "How about we play for it?" He asks loudly enough so guys on both teams can hear.

"For the rink time?" I ask as he nods.

"One-on-one. First one to score, their team can practice today. Loser has to find a new time slot."

"Deal," I say without giving it much thought. Sure, Jack was a pro hockey player, but in an alternate world, I could've been, too. I can take him.

"Hell yeah! Let's go Griffdog!" Bill shouts. My teammates join in, bolstering me with support. Jack thinks he's such hot shit. He's about to get his ass kicked.

He flashes me one more cocky smirk that gets me funny in the tummy. I clench myself. I'm here to win. No, not win. To wipe the floor with this guy.

The Comebacks and the Blades skate to their respective sides and watch from their team benches, whooping and cheering us on. Jack and I skate to the center of the ice.

"First one to score a goal," he says.

We shake on it.

I place the puck between us. We knock sticks three times, then we're off. Or rather, Jack is off. His stick catches the puck so fast it defies physics. Before I can register, he's zooming down the ice. I break away to catch up to him, pushing off so hard my legs build with soreness, which I ignore. I've had no chance to warm up, and my body is still asleep, not to mention this is the first hockey I've played since I was eighteen.

But I can still take him.

He pulls his stick back to shoot, taking a few seconds of sweet time, and I swipe the puck away. I bolt to my end of the rink.

A gust of wind rushes through my beard. I don't get halfway to the goal before Jack is in front of me, slapping my stick away and stealing back the puck. I recover quickly, but he already has the puck in his possession.

I don't let up. The cheers of my teammates infuse me with power. I skate backward blocking his path. His glinting blue eyes catch on me, transfixing me for half a second I can't give away, but damn are they gorgeous. Even if they're narrowed at me.

I keep skating backward trying to wrangle the puck from his stick, but Jack's too fast with his stick handling, shuffling it like a three-card monte. He tries to skate around me, but he senses I won't let up.

"You handle that puck well," I say.

"Not as well as I would've handled your cock."

His blunt admission makes my mind go to a *very* dirty place. The distraction is just long enough for Jack to shoot the puck between my skates and into the goal.

The Blades cheer from the sidelines. The Comebacks not so much.

Jack's teammates surround him in victory. Between the gap of bodies, I can feel Jack's eyes on me. They're staring the sharpest of daggers.

8

JACK

By day, Dominick Miller helps people find serenity as a yoga instructor. Yet on the ice, he is one angry, aggressive mother-fucker. I'm glad I play as his teammate and not his opponent.

"Imagine your lungs filling all the way up with air. Breathe in peace and serenity. And then exhale, letting out all the impurities tainting your mind and spirit." Miller sits cross-legged at the front of the yoga studio, his back perfectly straight. His tight athleisure shorts leave little to the imagination, forcing me to stare at a smudge on the mirror.

"Take this moment to connect with yourself. The balance that you seek on your skates will only come from within."

I turn to Fuentes, who does the jerk off motion in response. The room quiets with peaceful silence which is broken a second later by our teammate Ian ripping ass.

"It's okay," Miller says, not missing a beat. "That is a normal bodily function. It means your body is dispelling negative energy."

"Well, in that case," Ian says before ripping off another one.

We all crack up, laughter bouncing off the mirrored walls. Miller clenches his lips and clings to his Zen, though the protruding vein in his neck tells us we're skating on thin ice.

"And now we get into cat-cow pose," he says. He instructs us to get on all fours, alternating between arching our back and making it go concave.

"Yo, which one is the cat and which one is the cow?" Fuentes asks.

"It doesn't matter," Miller says.

Cat-cow is one of the silliest names for an exercise, but damn if it doesn't stretch out my back and relieve the tension. I can feel my spine extending.

"Hey, I can't give you a ride to work tomorrow. I'm taking my mom out for her birthday." Fuentes loves coming up with secret activities for his family for birthdays and anniversaries. Last year, he took his mom on a hot air balloon ride. They're super close, a foreign concept in my family.

"It's okay. I forgot to tell you, I quit my job."

"What?" Fuentes gasps, his hands almost slipping out from under him.

Miller shushes him. "Calm thoughts. Calm thoughts."

"I couldn't stay there. It was a very toxic work environment." Everything with me and Dad is toxic. "Don't worry. I have rent covered this month, and I'll have a new job to take care of rent next month."

"Awesome." Fuentes gives me a thumbs up, but his heart doesn't seem in it. "What kind of job are you looking for?"

"Yoga is meant to be a silent conversation with your spirit," Miller says.

I shrug my shoulders at Fuentes's question. "Whoever will hire me."

"Come on, man," he says, sounding disappointed. "Is there anything you want to do?"

"I don't know."

"You don't want to hop from job to job, only focused on making rent. Don't you have, like, ambition to do something?"

Sometimes I forget that Fuentes isn't just a good friend and a fun hang. He's a smart businessman. His point stings, but it gets me thinking...and the thinking leads to a dead end. My only ambition growing up was to make it to the NHL. That's what I trained for day and night. That's the only thing Dad said I could be. I don't know if I can be anything else except for a hockey player.

"Fuentes, you're fucking up my Zen," Miller says, his hands curled into fists. He takes an abnormally deep breath and exhales. "And Gross, you should be paying attention. You definitely need calm after that last practice."

Is getting judged by your yogi part of class? Miller has us get into warrior pose on our feet. I find it deeply ironic that yoga is about being Zen, yet one of the most popular poses is called warrior.

"The fuck you talking about?" I ask.

"Yeah, what was that about?" Fuentes asks me. "You looked like you wanted to rip the Comebacks player a new asshole."

Maybe it's because that player didn't want to do anything with mine. When I saw Griffin's face at practice, he had the same patronizing expression that he wore on the roof when he cast me aside after leading me on. I look around and find my other teammates eyeing me.

"Excuse me for sticking up for our practice time, for being competitive, for wanting to win! We can't let ourselves lose to a team called the Comebacks for fuck's sakes." I would never hear the end of it from Dad, his resigned satisfaction that he was right—he raised a loser. "Can we go back to stretching?"

I signal for Miller to get on with it. He instructs us to get on our stomachs and move into the cobra position. Again, another yoga position named after a snake that can either kill you with venom or crush you to death.

THE NEXT MORNING, I take a break from filling out job applications online and run over to Summers Rink. I needed to sign one last form. So many waivers to sign since there're so many ways to mangle your body in this sport.

The administrative wing is through a door next to the snack bar.

The smell of popcorn fills my nose as I head down the hall to Marcy Summers's office.

I stop just before her door. Griffin's grumbly voice echoes in the hall. I shift a touch closer for optimal eavesdropping.

"Jack Gross needs to be disqualified," he says.

What the fuck? I knew Griffin wasn't interested in me, but his words are filled with animosity. I guess he didn't like being shown off on his own turf.

"And why is that?" she asks in her thick New York accent. She has the tough, no-nonsense attitude a woman needs in a male-dominated field. Not to mention all the hyper-competitive parents trying to "do right" by their perfect angel children.

"He's a ringer," Griffin spits out. "He doesn't belong here."

"Goodbye, Griffin. Tell your cutie patootie kids I say hi."

I crack a smile. At least someone in that room has my back.

"Marcy, he was a professional hockey player for several years."

"Was. He's not anymore. So long as a player isn't currently playing in a professional capacity, they're eligible to play in this league."

"He has no business playing in an extracurricular, amateur league."

"You make the rules now?"

"This is a fun, laid-back league, and I don't think it's fair to the other players to be thrown in with a pro."

"No hockey league with you in it is fun and laid back," she says.

Go Marcy! I mime a silent cheer in the hall.

"He's unsportsmanlike and obnoxious. Look, I don't want to be a tattletale, but did you hear how he acted the other day? He refused for his team to leave the ice so we could practice. We don't want that kind of attitude in the league."

"We?" Marcy shoots back. "The rink was accidentally double-booked. I heard he played you for it, and it didn't go so well. For you."

I smile to myself, trying to remember how sharp I was on the ice... and trying to forget how good Griffin looked in his hockey gear.

"He's just some rich asshole who wants to slum it in our league,"

Griffin says with such conviction it shakes me for a moment. Whatever connection I thought we had, I really, *really* misjudged. "It's the other teams that I'm worried about. You're going to have players quit the league if the Blades have such an unfair advantage. Or they'll resort to finding their own ringers, and the integrity of the league will be ruined."

"I'll monitor the situation," she deadpans. "I've known you since you were a teen with bad acne. Watched you on the ice in game after game. You were never one to get intimidated, Griff."

"I'm not intimidated by him."

"Are you worried about losing to this guy?"

"I'm not going to lose to him," he says with absolute conviction.

"Really? Because you did the other morning," I say.

There are few things that bring me genuine joy in this world. But the pure shock on Griffin's face as he realizes I heard every word he said about me is definitely one of them.

"Good morning, Marcy! Here's the signed liability form for you." I stroll past him and hand her my missing form. She's everything I envisioned from her voice: big hair, big glasses, a withering stare that could look through the toughest athlete.

"Thanks, sweetie," she says, likely her nickname for all players under the age of thirty.

I turn to Griffin, still white as a ghost. It's the first time I get to see him in good lighting. His confident nose, the dignified wrinkles just starting at the corners of his face. Even in this ugly fluorescent lighting, he's gorgeous. Damn him. His right eye is a vibrant, transfixing shade of green. A spring meadow I could lay in and watch the clouds float by. That is, if he wasn't being such a prick.

"Griffin, I promise, when I wipe the floor with you in our next game, it won't be because I'm a professional hockey player. Or a rich asshole. It's because I'm just a better player than you." I cock my head and flash him the most fuck-you smile in history.

He turns to Marcy, like she's a ref that won't eject me into the penalty box. An amused smile crawls onto her lips.

"What are we going to do about practicing?" Griffin asks Marcy, then flicks his eyes to me. "Because it's obvious the Blades don't want to share."

Marcy types on her computer, a desktop with a fat back monitor that's almost as old as me. "I can move some things around. How're Thursday mornings at seven?"

"That's too late for us. That's crunch time for getting kids to school," he says.

"The Blades will take it." I nod my confirmation to Marcy but don't look at Griffin.

"Thanks," he utters.

"We respect our elders. Is that sportsmanlike enough for you?" I shoot him a glare.

I leave Marcy's office and pass a group of figure skaters practicing triple axels on the ice. I call an Uber, ignoring how much it's going to cost. The faster I can get away from Griffin, the better. I hate that I still think he's cute even though he has such a low opinion of me.

"Jack."

Fuck. Griffin jogs to catch up to me outside. I try to ignore how good his chest and belly look in flannel.

"Where's your car?" he asks.

"I called an Uber."

His eyebrows jump. "Nice life," he says.

I don't bother correcting him about my financial status.

"Jack," he begins, then trails off.

"You're trying to get me thrown out of the league?"

"You're a ringer!" He clenches his eyes shut then reopens them, calmer. "I'm sorry."

"You're a sore loser."

"And refusing to get off the ice so we could practice? Acting like a total asshole? What do you call that?"

Fire blazes up my neck at the accusation. "I can't believe you tried to get me ejected. And that you thought it would work."

"I didn't expect someone who played professionally would want to join a league like ours. Especially because you didn't seem in love with the sport the other night."

I step closer, my scowl shushing him good. "You don't say another word about the other night, okay?"

I want it wiped from my memory. I want the warm and fuzzy feeling it still gives me to vanish for good. The Uber remains five minutes away. Fuck.

"Look, if we're going to be in the same league, it's best that we clear the air," he says, putting on his best captain voice.

I sit on a bench and cross my arms. "Okay. Clear it."

Griffin stumbles, his face going white again. "I...I had a great time with you the other night. You're funny, smart, warm."

"Whoa, whoa, whoa. Are you giving me a break-up speech?"

"What? No. We were talking and getting along—"

"Getting along?" That is by far the worst euphemism for flirting I've ever heard.

"I didn't know where you were taking me."

"Did you think I was kidnapping you?"

"I thought we were going to grab coffee or something," Griffin says, each word in his excuse another car in this pileup.

"Grab coffee? In the middle of the night?"

"And then suddenly we're on a rooftop."

"You make eyes at a guy—"

"You made eyes at me first," he objects.

"You have a drink with him. You flirt with him. You leave with him. You go to a quiet, secluded place with him. What did you think was going to happen on that rooftop, Griffin? We were going to play Scrabble and make friendship bracelets? There was really no other time during the evening when you could've bailed. You had to wait until I was on my knees like a fool?" I could use some yoga to keep my embarrassment at bay. I hate that I was made a fool, and Griffin won't even own up to it.

"I'm sorry. I..." Just when I think a real answer is going to come out of his mouth, he clears his throat, as if shoving it back down. "I enjoyed spending time with you, and maybe we can be friends."

I'm starting to realize that Griffin isn't the suave, charming guy I thought he was. It's like he's never been with a guy. How did he ever find his ex-wife? A mail-order website? Perhaps getting pushed away from his crotch was the best thing that could've happened to me.

"I think the friend ship has sailed. And now I find out that you tried to have me tossed from the league?" I laugh again, and I realize that it's masking anger. "You know what comes next, Griffin?"

"What?"

A smile slashes across my lips. "Payback."

9

GRIFFIN

My frustration over Jack fades away the second I open the front door to Carmen's house.

"Daddy!" Annabelle's and June's voices echo in the hallway as they barrel toward me. Their small bodies move with such exaggerated movement that it convinces me their bones are made of bouncy balls.

"Angels." I scoop them into a hug, each arm wrapping around a daughter. I know my days of doing this are numbered. Each time I see them, they look more like burgeoning teenagers.

June breaks from the hug first and tugs at my sleeve with utmost urgency, her eyes going so wide they take over her face.

"We built the ice castle!" she says. "It's so cool!"

Annabelle, her quiet second in command, nods along. June grabs my hand—I remember when her fingers could only curl around my thumb—and drags me to the living room.

In the kitchen, Carmen makes quesadillas on the stove. She waves to me.

The girls plunk me down on the floor. They've arranged pillows and blankets into a droopy structure that only they're small enough to crawl into.

"This is the ice castle!" June exclaims. "Annabelle created it with her hands."

Annabelle does a spell, complete with sound effects. She then joins her sister inside. The pillows wobble as she shimmies through the opening.

"Annabelle, careful!" June warns.

"That's a nice ice castle, better than the one in the movie," I say.

"It's really big in here," June says through another opening made from arranging the throw pillows to form a window. "There're almost too many rooms."

"How many bedrooms?" I ask.

"Seven."

"Wow. Lotta bedrooms." I whistle. "Have many people do you have living there?"

"It's just me and June," Annabelle says, getting a word in edgewise with her sister, not always an easy task. "But one of the bedrooms is for our pet reindeer, George."

"His room is at the other end of the castle because he chain smokes," June tells me. "We're trying to get him to quit."

Kids' imaginations are the most creative things in the world. It's like one big game of Mad Libs.

"One of the bedrooms was turned into a pool," Annabelle says. "A pool with a waterfall."

I'm about to ask how a pool and waterfall in an ice castle don't turn to ice themselves, but I don't want to ruin the fun.

"We caught George smoking a cigarette in the pool." Annabelle shakes her head. "We really want him to quit."

"I told George I don't want any smoking in my house." Carmen squats down next to me. "I'm going to have another talk with him."

She kisses me hello on the cheek. From the outside, we look like the perfect family. Too bad Carmen and I are both gay. Now that our secrets are both out, our relationship post-divorce is much better than when we were married.

"Time for dinner," she says.

"But I want to stay in the ice castle," June says, her voice immediately going to a whine. "Can we eat in here? We have three dining rooms!"

"Three? Impressive," Carmen says. "But will the hot cheese melt the ice castle, though?"

The girls trade a look of panic. I suppose some logic is welcome here.

A few minutes later, we're sitting at the kitchen table digging into delicious, mouthwatering quesadillas. Carmen was the cook in our marriage, spoiling me with yummy Mexican cuisine. She says cooking is a way of reconnecting with her mother, who passed when she was a teenager. My meals usually come out dry and oversalted. The girls love staying with me because they know they're getting McDonald's for at least one meal.

"So guess what? Dad joined a hockey team," I say.

The girls are unfazed, but Carmen looks up from her meal. "You did?"

"Yeah. Some of the guys from high school put together a team for an amateur adult league."

"That's great. I forgot you used to play." Carmen and I met in our thirties. Her brother used to work at the airport with me. Deep down, we were both scared of coming out and unknowingly used each other as beards. Eventually, Carmen got tired of playing heterosexual and came out to me when June was three months old. It was an especially exhausting month; both girls weren't sleeping well, and the tiredness acted like a truth serum. She said I was gay, too, but that I wasn't admitting it to myself. The bold statement plus sleep deprivation led me to look in the mirror and have that honest conversation with myself. I was gay.

"Huh," Carmen says, contemplating my new activity. The only thing I told her about my time playing was that I lost my eye. Hockey Griffin is a totally different Griffin from the one she knows.

"Maybe you can come to a game," I say to the girls.

"Is hockey scary?" Annabelle asks.

"What if you get hurt again?" Fear casts a shadow over June's face. "What if you lose your other eye?"

"I didn't lose my eye. It's still here. It just likes to sleep a lot, like a cat."

The girls nod, but they don't seem as convinced. The energy plummets at the table, making my heart tighten.

"This is a non-checking league, which means all the players are nice to each other." I take an exaggerated bite of my quesadilla. It gets laughs from them.

"Nic*er*. But there're still fights, probably some cursing, too," Carmen says.

"I think the girls have heard most of those words."

"Doesn't mean they need to hear it from their dad."

"I'll be on my best behavior. You can bring the swear jar with you."

There are kids that go to hockey games all the time. I went when I was younger than June. The girls could see me in my hockey jersey, slicing through the ice and scoring a goal. Seeing them in the stands, getting to experience that with them, makes my heart fizz with excitement.

"We'll see," Carmen says. She isn't a fan of sports. Never wanted to watch a game with me. I think that drove the wedge in our marriage more than our predilection for the same sex. "More importantly, we have some birthdays coming up."

She was always a master at changing the subject. That was how our marriage survived for as long as it did.

Annabelle and June are two years apart, almost exactly to the day. Carmen went into labor at Annabelle's second birthday party. June may be younger, but she's the leader of their pack.

"Two special girls will be turning nine and seven in style," Carmen says. "At the Hadley Tea House."

"We're having it at the Hadley Tea House?" Annabelle asks in high-pitched delirium. June's jaw openly falls to the table.

The girls scream with glee. I wince to block out the noise. My heart goes out to all dogs on the block.

"What's the Hadley Tea House?" I ask.

"It's this old-fashioned high tea room. A few girls in their classes have had parties there. It's really cute."

"Isabella H. AND Isabella J. had their parties there," Annabelle informs me. "Isabella H.'s was better, but don't tell Isabella J."

I pretend to zip my mouth shut.

A tug of regret pulls at me for only learning about their party plans now. I won't deny that Carmen's been more hands on with their day-to-day lives. She's up on what's going on at school. She keeps track of their doctor's appointments. She probably can tell the difference between Isabella H. and Isabella J. I'm by no means an absentee dad, but I should be doing more.

"What if I built you an ice castle for your birthday?" I blurt out.

"What? Are you serious?" June asks. The pure excitement comes off her body in waves.

"Yep. Not real ice, of course. But I want to build you girls your own ice castle in the backyard. It could be a treehouse." We have a huge oak tree in the yard with thick drooping branches.

"Are you serious?" June yells, clutching her heart. She and Annabelle trade a look and scream some more.

"Anything for my girls."

Carmen raises a concerned eyebrow at me, wondering if I'm serious. I have to be. It's already out there. I've never built a treehouse, but I've put together airplane machinery.

How hard could it be?

THE NEXT DAY, Hank comes with me to start getting supplies for the ice castle treehouse. He helps me devise some rough blueprints and a list of what I'll need. He worked in construction before becoming a plumber, which he prefers because it's mostly indoors.

Hank has us go a little out of the way to a home improvement store that he says has the best selection of wood and better pricing.

"That's a lot of purple," I comment as we pull into the Ferguson's parking lot. I pass this store on the highway all the time. Its big, purple logo is a visual marker that my exit is coming up.

Hank gets out of the car and pulls a folded piece of paper from his pocket. "We'll start in lumber, then we can move onto brackets and whatever tools you're missing."

"Thanks for helping me with this. I don't exactly know what I'm doing." The sun is especially bright to match the extra windiness of this March afternoon. "I've built things before, but never a treehouse."

"Happy to help. I built one for my son when he was little. It had a slide and a zipline, but he only used it as another place to read books," Hank says with a touch of confusion. "And not comic books. Actual books. I found him reading *A Brief History of Time* when he was eleven. *For fun.*" Hanks laughs to himself and smiles warmly at the memory. "I don't know how I wound up with a brainiac son. Genetics are weird."

"It sounds like you got a good one there, Hank."

"Don't I know it." He grabs a shopping cart.

The automatic doors part as we approach. The cavernous, warehouse feel of home improvement stores can be overwhelming. Sometimes, I feel like I walk a mile just to find a screwdriver.

"Land ho!" Hank yells out, pointing to the opposite end of the store. I try to shush him but have quickly learned that Hank Rush can't be shushed.

Hank steers the cart past mowers and power tools and appliances, and it seems like we've barely traversed the store.

"Now, are you thinking plywood, or do you want something more durable like some kind of cedar? Hear me out: western cedar. Shit!" Hank stops his cart short, barely avoiding a collision with a Ferguson's employee. *Ask Me Anything: Ted*, reads his name tag. "Sorry about that."

"It's okay." the man says through gritted teeth. I can tell he wants to say something else but doesn't want to get fired.

He looks up, and time seems to stop. Stop and rewind. Something about his face strikes a familiar chord, and as my brain scurries to put the pieces together, the employee seems to be doing the same.

That scowl. I remember it on the ice. It's wrinkled and weathered, but eyes don't age.

"It's you," the employee says, gritting his teeth even more. "Griffin fucking Harper. Nice eye patch."

"Thanks to you," I mutter back, my hands instinctively curling into fists. "You know, you never apologized for blinding me in one eye."

"You slammed into me. You fucked up my shoulder. Fucked up everything."

"Likewise." Even after all these years, I still want nothing more than to put my fist through his face. It's been years, but nothing's changed at all. This asshole didn't apologize, didn't even acknowledge what he did when he jammed his stick into my eye in a wildly illegal move. The epitome of gross misconduct.

It's because of him that I missed my shot at the pros, that I let down my mom, my friends, my coach, and forfeited my potential. All because he wanted to take down South Rock's top player by any means necessary.

"Fuck you," I spit out, white hot hatred pounding in my ears. "You're still a piece of shit."

He turns a shade of deep red I didn't think possible on a person. He's fighting every urge not to throw a punch. I dare you. I fucking dare you.

"I don't think Ferguson's has what you're looking for. I recommend Home Depot."

"Fine." I walk away, Hank following behind me. He's white as a ghost, as if he just witnessed a bad car accident.

"Home Depot has a great selection, too," Hank says. He pushes the shopping cart into the row of unused ones. The automatic doors part for us. "Was that the guy..."

"Yeah." I feel my eye patch, my rage subsiding with each step away from the store. How is it fair that one random stranger can have so much control over the direction of my life?

I unlock my truck. Hank slides into the passenger seat.

"Fucking Ted," Hank says with visible disgust. "I'm going to send in a complaint to Ferguson's corporate. I wish I'd gotten his last name."

And then the realization slams into me like his hockey stick all those years ago.

"Gross." The name sends a shiver as it leaves my lips. "His last name is Gross."

10

GRIFFIN

Bill squared away the rink space issue with Marcy during the week. She's not the type to apologize, but rather blamed it on the digital upgrade that she's been forced to adopt. She was able to schedule our practices on Thursday evenings. Bill wondered if he should say something to Marcy about getting back our old time. We lost it fair and square to the Blades though, something that makes my blood boil all over again now that I know the truth. We couldn't tattle to the teacher.

I get to the rink after work and feel like I've stepped into a daycare. Tanner's kids are running up and down the bleachers playing tag, screaming and laughing. Hank's son Brody sits on the top bleacher with a textbook open on his lap. The inane chatter of a YouTube personality echoes from the tablet of Rowan, Bill's daughter. It'd be nice if Annabelle and June were able to come to a practice once. Something to work on with Carmen. Hearing about my eye injury turned her completely off hockey.

"I bet Wayne Gretzky never had to put up with this," Des mutters as we get onto the ice.

"You won't even notice they're here!" Tanner says, ever the optimist.

"Dad! Davy won't share his tennis ball!" yells his six-year-old son, Dean.

"Davy, share your tennis ball!" Tanner responds from the ice in his best calm-dad voice.

"No. I found it on the ground. It's mine. I already licked it!" Nine-year-old Davy says.

"Well, you can't argue with that logic," Des snarks to me.

Tanner turns to us. "One second. I'll be right back. Start without me."

He darts off the ice. Des claps me on the shoulder. "Thanks for losing us our morning slot, champ."

"It's all right. This is a challenge, but we've dealt with worse." Bill skates to the center of the rink.

"We have?" Des asks.

Bill thinks for a moment. "Figure of speech."

"Leave the guy alone." Hank skates up to us from the goal. He's wearing his old South Rock High jersey, which rides up on his pads as if he's wearing a belly shirt. Unlike '90s-era Britney Spears, he doesn't have the flat stomach to pull it off.

"What's going on with your jersey?" Bill asks. He tugs it down. The jersey pops back up like a window shade.

"I shrunk it in the wash."

"Are you sure it shrunk?" Des winks at him.

"It did! I used to be able to fit into it no problem," Hank says.

"Was that before or after you were legally allowed to vote?"

"Excuse me for wanting to boost morale. Sorry I don't wear bougie gear from wherever you get your shit. My jersey isn't from Brooks Brothers."

"I don't think Brooks Brothers manufactures jerseys for the modern businessman, Hank," Des says. He is truly a master of sarcasm.

"One-balled Dickheads 'r Us then," Hank shoots back.

Des bristles at the reference to his nuts but keeps his sardonic attitude. "You mean the toy store that's been out of business for like a decade? A-plus on your timely insults. Let me know when I should expect your Myspace jokes."

Hank has no retort, so he does what any goon would. He shoves Des. Des shoves him back. Hank might be larger surface area-wise, but Des is the stronger one, his arms like cannons.

"Guys! Break it up!" I push them off each other. "Save it for the other team."

"Once we get back on the ice practicing together, all this noise will fade away." Bill always knew how to regain control and get us back into the zone. "I'm getting Comebacks jerseys made that will fit everyone. We've dealt with loud, obnoxious fans at games. A few kids running around is an upgrade from that. And as for evening practices, it's the only time that was available. It is what it is."

His eyes flick to me for a second, and I know what he's thinking: I fucked this up because I couldn't get one on Jack.

Well, apparently Jack has been playing me this whole fucking time, a long con of revenge for his dear old dad. I'm wise to his game, though, and I won't be a sucker again.

"I won't let it happen again," I say to the team. I picture wiping the ice with Jack, wiping that cocky grin off his face.

"Good," says Bill. "Let's get practicing."

We begin skating around and stickhandling to warm up. Bill has us come to center ice for drills. He splits us into two teams and introduces a puck onto the ice. Derek and I have to keep it away from Tanner and Des while staying in the neutral zone. Bill practices taking shots on Hank at goal to keep him warm.

Tanner stifles a yawn into his arm as he effortlessly passes to Des. We used to joke that those two shared a brain because they rarely had to signal to each other for passes.

"Don't yawn. That'll make me yawn," Derek says, powerless to stop his yawn.

"Keep it up," Bill yells back to us. "Our first game this weekend is against the Rangers. Don't be too worried. They're park rangers. I think we got this."

"Beating the Rangers will be good practice when we eventually play the Blades," I say, finally intercepting a pass between my two foes. My hand grips my stick tighter.

"You're so focused on the Blades," Des says.

"They have a ringer on their team. Of course I am."

Des studies my face, as if looking for other evidence. I won't give it to him.

"You keep mentioning their ringer," Tanner says. "I think he's getting in your head."

Buddy, he's already there, try as I might to get him out.

"Of course he's in Griff's head. The guy beat him one-on-one," Derek says.

"Was this the same guy flirting with him at the bar?" Des asks.

"You don't know the half of it. He's Ted Gross's son," Hank says, yelling from goal while stopping one of Bill's shots. Impressive. "We figured it out the other day. The guy is still a raging prick."

I do a quick lap around the empty half of the rink to avoid my teammates' stares.

"Ted had his son join the league to mess with Griff." Hank shakes his head.

"That's fucked up," says Des.

"Des!" Tanner nudges his chin to the kids in the stands.

"Hank can say prick, but I can't say the f-word?" Des rolls his eyes.

"Can you guys stop talking about me and Jack? Not like there is a 'me and Jack.' I don't want anything to do with Ted Gross's demon spawn."

I do another lap to clear my head. When I return to center ice, I scoop the puck away from Des, charge down the ice, and nail a goal on Hank. No matter what happened in my one-on-one showdown with Jack the other day, I still got it.

"F' the Blades. Long live the Comebacks!" I yell.

———

Practice is rigorous and thorough. Bill believes in pushing us hard in order to make us stronger. He compared it to snakes shedding their skin. This might've worked when we were teenagers, but now in our forties, I'm finding that my body doesn't bounce back nearly as well as I'd like. That's the problem with getting older. In my mind, I still feel eighteen. It's the rest of my body that's determined to age.

After getting showered and dressed, the guys and I roll out of the locker room, kids in toe, feeling like a million bucks. We strut down the corridor to the exit, chests big and puffed, imaginary crowds fawning over us. We completed a challenging practice, doing things most guys our age wouldn't dream of doing. When Jack gets into his forties, I doubt he'll still be playing hockey.

Why does my mind keep going back to him?

"He's just one guy," Bill says as we head for the exit. Can he read my mind? "Jack might be good, but he's just one guy on a team."

"He's not that good," I say.

"He SUCKS," Tanner's son Davy yells.

"Davy. Language," Tanner shoots back.

"The rest of his teammates are good," says Hank, walking behind us. "I caught some of their practice. They've got the moves."

"Well, so do we," Bill shoots back. "We can't let the Blades get in our heads." He turns to his daughter Rowan, and they share a nod of agreement. Then Bill turns back to me, his hand on the door. "Any of them."

I give him a salute. Message received.

Bill pushes open the door. "Fuck me."

"Bill," Tanner hisses, nodding at his kids at his side.

But Tanner follows Bill's eyeline. We all do, and we all have the same reaction.

"Fork me," Tanner mutters.

His minivan is mummified in toilet paper. As is Hank's two-seater. As is Des's Lexus and Bill's SUV. They are big white puffs in an otherwise empty parking lot.

The guys run to their cars to assess the damage.

"It's two ply!" Hank and his son Brody rub toilet paper between their fingers.

"What a waste of perfectly good toilet paper, Dad," says Brody.

"What the..." Bill says, his usually stoic face filled with shock and a bit of horror. But he's not looking at his car.

He's looking at mine.

When my eye lands on my truck, it's as if a pilot light clicks on inside me, releasing a flame of anger.

My pickup truck isn't merely mummified in dry bath tissue like my teammates' cars. It's encased in a thick layer of wet toilet paper stuck to every inch. The wet, half-dried toilet paper has the bumpy look of a vintage popcorn ceiling. It covers my windshield, doors, truck bed, even the side mirrors.

I run my hand across the driver's side window, the mushy sloop sliding off the car and plopping to the ground. I'd had to wade through dirty diapers and sick kids, and yet the feel of the wet paper on my hand ranks as one of the grossest things I've experienced in my adult life.

"Who the hell did this to my beautiful Lexi?" Des says, ready to go full Liam Neeson in *Taken* to protect his car.

"The ringer," I mutter.

Bill comes over with an ice scraper. I don't take it from him. Instead, I start laughing. A low, maniacal, crazy person chuckle ripples from deep inside my chest out of my mouth, causing my teammates to take a half-step back.

"Gentlemen," I say. "Looks like the Blades want a prank war."

11

JACK

I'm jolted awake by Fuentes pounding at my door.

"Dude, we got practice!" he yells.

Shit. I look at my phone and realize I forgot to set my alarm. I roll out of bed and throw on sweatpants and a sweatshirt. I gargle with a cup of mouthwash and meet Fuentes in the hall.

I was never a morning person. Early practices and early flights while I was in the NHL made me perpetually tired. I subsisted on coffee and the adrenaline of play time, when I did get play time.

"Did you forget to set your alarm again?" Fuentes asks as we descend the stairs. I nod yes while swishing mouthwash.

Outside, it's cold and dark. No surprise for early March. A light dusting of snow covers the cars in the parking lot. Maybe if it was Christmastime, it would be a pretty scene, but by this time of year, I'm so over snow.

I spit my mouthwash into the bushes.

"Hey!" Fuentes says.

"It's not going to kill the bushes," I say. The man is very touchy about his property.

We hop into his car where Miller waits in the backseat, eyes closed and exhaling a loud breath.

"What the hell are you doing?" I ask.

"I'm getting focused for practice. I'm finding my center so I can play with intention."

Somehow, the more Zen Miller gets, the more of an animal he is on the ice. We had our first game on Sunday. Miller got thrown into the sin bin twice for checking an opposing player. He let out a stream of F-bombs as the ref pulled him away that would make Samuel L. Jackson blush.

We drive down roads coated with gray slush, the gross comingling of snow and grease. The ugliest part of winter. It kind of reminds me of the goopy shit I covered Griffin's car with the other day.

"What's so funny?" Fuentes asks.

I giggle like a damn middle schooler. "Guys, remember when we TPed the Comebacks' cars?"

They burst into laughter at the memory. It's like we're sixteen again, hanging out in our car during lunch period wondering if we should cut the rest of the day. Having a good laugh with your friends is good for the soul. It's chicken soup for shitheads.

"I'm impressed we got it done so quickly. Teamwork makes the dream work," Miller says. He pulls out his phone and plays the video we secretly took. The guy dropping to his knees over his Lexus was priceless. I know I want nothing to do with Griffin Harper, but the look of utter shock on his face is somehow adorable. There's an innocence to it, like a peek at the boy inside the man.

Not that I should be finding anything about Griffin adorable.

"You really went to town on the pickup truck," Fuentes says. "Wet toilet paper is a pain in the ass to get off."

"He deserved it for trying to get me booted from the league." Among his other sins. "His car is fine. His teammates helped him get it off. What's a season of hockey without some pranks?"

"You think they'll retaliate?" Miller asks.

"Nah. They're too scared. They know they can't top that." I put my feet up on the glove compartment. Fuentes knocks them off at the stop light.

"How goes the job hunt?" Fuentes asks.

"It's going."

"Didn't you have an interview yesterday?"

"It was more like an interrogation. Bernice, the grandmotherly manager, started asking me all these questions about plants and cacti." I interviewed at My Flower of Need, a plant shop in Sourwood. I figured since I sometimes worked the garden center at Ferguson's, I'd have it in the bag. I didn't know I needed a fucking PhD in botany to work there.

"Plants need water to grow. Isn't that the most important thing to know?" Miller asked.

"You'd think!" I shake my head. "She said it's a specialty plant store, so they need someone with specialized knowledge. I'm a fast learner! I learned how to play *Halo* in like a day."

"Bummer. Onto the next!" Fuentes makes a right, passing the local library, which has a fancy fountain installed in front.

Fuentes has been supportive of my job search, helping me format a resume. But under the best friend guise, I can sense the landlord wondering if he'll be getting a rent check next month. I had enough in savings to cover March rent. April may be questionable, but he doesn't need to know that yet.

"I'm thinking that retail isn't for me. I want to work in an office," I say, imagining a cushy desk chair, business cards, and free snacks.

"Um, okay. But I think most office jobs require a college degree. Maybe? I don't know." His face pinches as if bracing for impact. Fuentes never wants to be the bad guy.

"Not all of them. Some of them ask for equivalent experience," Miller says, saving my ass. He's done more research on these jobs than I have, apparently.

"Have you been thinking about what exactly you want to do in an office?" Fuentes looks over at me, and for the first time, I see concern in his joyous eyes.

"I don't know. Something...with accounts?"

"You're asking a lot of questions," I tell Fuentes. "I'll find something. I've been at it a week. Chill." I pat him on the back to calm him down.

"Have you made a vision board? You should make a vision board," Miller says.

I point my thumb back at him while looking at Fuentes. "That's a solid idea. I'm going to make a vision board."

Whenever I sit down to think about what I want to do with my life, I get intimidated by the question. Other kids got to dabble in different interests. They got to sign up for clubs, activities, and camps. They got to take various classes in college. All I've ever known is playing hockey. Dad set my life up for that purpose. Thinking about the future only makes me feel more like a failure. I can't shake the idea that this is not how my life should be going.

Fuentes exhales through his nostrils, preferring to stare ahead at the road.

"What?" I ask, anger mounting at his reaction.

"I wish you took things more seriously. Jobs, hockey..." Fuentes trails off, biting his lip to stop from saying more.

"Whoa. What's wrong with my hockey playing? We won our first game." I turn to Miller for backup, but to my shock, Mr. Chakra averts his eyes.

My lovely ride with my buds has turned into an ambush.

"What the fuck is going on?" I ask, seconds from jumping out a moving vehicle.

"You were...rusty on the ice," Fuentes says, and I can tell it's twisting him up being the bearer of this bad news. "I mean, you played *fine*. Good, even. You were extremely competent."

"Funny. None of those sound like positives," I shoot back.

"I didn't see your soul out there." Miller claps me on the shoulder.

I dig my fist into my thigh. I wanted to give him a knuckle sandwich chock full of soul.

"What Miller is saying is that something was missing," Fuentes says quickly to keep the peace. "We've played with you for years. We've watched your games. You're an awesome player, Jack. When you're locked in, you are on fire. But it kind of felt like you were going through the motions on Sunday. There wasn't any fire."

I stare out the window at the rolling hills of houses as I replay Sunday's game in my head. I landed good passes, scored a goal. But as I reflect, I can't think of any WOW moments I had, the kinds of moves where I felt in tune with the game, every part of me harmonizing.

"You were on fire when you went one-on-one against that Comebacks player with the eye patch," Miller says. "It was like you hadn't missed a step since the NHL. I was mesmerized. No wonder he tried to get you eliminated from the league."

My heart does a quick flip as I remember the challenge. Was I flipping over the excitement of the game or the opponent? It had better not be the latter.

When Fuentes turns off his car, the cold seeps in fast. I don't like waking up early and practicing in the cold, but at least I can do it alongside my best friends.

Fuentes pops the trunk and hands me my gear. "You're a great player, Jack. I'm guessing you're just a little rusty and you'll get back into the groove for the next game."

———

I REALLY TRY to focus during practice. I even do some calming breaths when the guys aren't looking. Perhaps Miller is right, and I need to center myself in order to find the fire. I had it for all those years. Fires don't just disappear.

Practice goes well for the most part, but I can't shake the lingering rustiness. I can't get out of my head. I keep flashing back to the passing debacle from my NHL days, to my coaches' expressions as they watched me. When I was getting drafted, everyone pretended they loved me. But as soon as I wasn't useful, I was kicked to the curb.

After practice, we hit the showers. I turn my shower to extra hot, and finally, I find some semblance of calm.

"I'm still laughing at that video," Fuentes says beside me. "When that guy wiped the TP off his truck? Classic."

I laugh, too. Griffin had the best reaction. He is a perfect straight man for pranks. Well, not that straight. And that cute smile of his when he probably realized it was me.

Sigh.

No. I will not think about Griffin anymore. Especially while I'm soaping myself down.

"Did he ever say why he cockblocked you?" Fuentes asks.

"I don't care." Griffin did a poor job trying to explain, acting like it was no big deal. He was just another person who pretended to like me and then bolted. I shudder with embarrassment as I remember his hand pushing me away. "I can't wait to kick their ass."

"It won't be that hard," says Fuentes. "They all look exhausted."

"I almost feel bad about playing them. I don't want them to throw their backs on the ice," Miller says.

"They'll all win gold at the Dad-Bod Olympics." I laugh to myself, even though Griffin sure gave me a good run on the ice.

I'm the first to leave the shower. I wrap a towel around my waist.

When I strut into the locker room, something feels off in a way I can't explain. The hairs stand up on the back of my neck without explanation.

I zero in on my cubby, where the white paint of the wall behind it is visible. I push aside my coat to where my clothes are hanging. Or should be hanging.

"What's up?" Miller walks past me.

"Check your cubby." I frantically search my cubby, pushing the coat aside again, looking on the shelf above, checking in the space where my shoes sit. My clothes are gone.

"What the fuck!" Miller's reaction catches up to mine. He throws his coat on the floor, revealing a cubby just as empty as mine.

A piece of paper flutters to the floor. I find the same one on my bench. It's blank except for a logo at the top.

The Comebacks logo.

Other guys pull similar pieces of paper from their half-empty cubbies.

"Looking for these?" Griffin asks from the locker room entrance, holding up my clothes.

Hank, their goalie, steps out from behind him. His arms are full of jeans and shirts and sweaters. "Guess we're not that old, huh?"

"What the—" I instinctively cover my junk.

Griffin flashes a wicked smile that makes him look seventeen. "You may be younger, but we're smarter. Have fun air drying."

My teammates are shocked in place, searching for some article of clothing to cover themselves with. But I'm ready to fight. A smirk jumps on my face. I love the competition.

"Guys...get 'em!" I yell.

We charge for the Comebacks.

"You'll have to catch us first!" Griffin says.

The guys race out the locker room door, our clothes bundled in their arms. We surge after them like runners angling for the finish line. My heart is pumping, and I find myself laughing like a little kid. The cold air hits my half-naked body, my junk sloshing from side to side under my towel. I won't let a little chill stop me from saving my team's clothes. My teammates follow behind me, my band of toweled brethren.

Griffin tosses someone's boxer shorts onto the ice as he runs around the rink. We weave through the benches and concession stand. Someone's shirt goes across the cash register. A pair of pants are tossed over the popcorn machine.

I hurdle over the benches and around the rink, gaining on them. As close as I get, Griffin manages to elude my grasp. These Comebacks fuckers are faster than I expected for a bunch of old guys.

Griffin turns around and runs backward. He throws a pair of boxer shorts that aren't mine in my face, making me stumble.

Fuentes yanks them from my nose and puts them on. "Thanks, man."

My body repulses.

"Give us our clothes back!" Miller yells. "It was Jack's idea with the toilet paper!"

"Traitors!" I yell back to him.

The Comebacks bolt through the rink's double doors into the lobby. One of them with a mane of blond hair and supposedly sweet smile chucks a bundle of sweaters into the skate rental station.

"I know I shouldn't apologize, but I'm sorry about this! Please don't catch a cold!" he yells as kindly as possible as he follows his teammates out the door.

I zoom to catch up with him, finding that the lack of clothes makes me go faster.

"They're heading for the front door," Fuentes yells, desperate. He snaps the waistband of his boxers. "Shit, I don't think these are mine!"

A fresh round of cold air hits my body as I burst through the double doors. The cold can't stop me. Nothing can knock me down. Just as I'm about to grab Hank's shirt to hold him, my damn towel gets caught on the door hinge, pulling me back. I try to rip the towel to break free, but it's surprisingly strong.

"Fuck."

"Ha! Maybe next time, loser! This is what you get for fucking with mature adults," Hank yells back at me as he runs outside.

I pull my towel loose and zoom out the front door. This time, the cold air of outside hits my bones and sinks into the strands of my wet hair. I run through the parking lot and find them hopping into the bed of Griffin's pickup, driven by a teammate with a dark, growly beard, who looks worried like he's committing a crime.

I run right up to the truck, but it pulls away before I can get a good grip. The cold metal slides through my fingers as they drive through the parking lot.

Griffin stands up in the bed and throws the final armful of clothes onto the pavement. He crosses his arms, triumphant. Even though he took all our clothes, I can't help but notice how fucking good he looks. Chest puffed out, impish glint in his eye.

Damn him for still being fuckable.

I shrug my shoulders and give him a nod. Touché.

I flip him the bird to let him know I don't approve of it, but I do respect it.

Griffin nods back. Our eyes lock for a moment, unable to pull away from each other.

"Fuck it," I mutter to myself.

I let my towel drop.

I catch Griffin staring down at my crotch before he meets my eye again and gives me a smirk of approval.

You could have had all of this, Griffin. So enjoy the view because you'll never see it again.

12

GRIFFIN

I haven't heard anything from Jack since the prank. We don't have each other's numbers, and I don't see him around the rink. I know better than to go there during their practice. I'm public enemy number one among the Blades. And rightfully so.

A part of me wishes he'd found my number and texted. Even something about how he's going to kick my ass. I go back to the bar, but I don't see him either.

My team and I lace up for our first game of the season on Sunday afternoon. Nerves jangle through me. My heart races so fast I have to ball my hands into fist to get them to stop shaking. The last time I played hockey, I lost an eye. I lost everything.

"Hey. You okay?" Bill squeezes my shoulder, sensing my nerves. They must be coming off me in waves.

"Yeah. Like riding a bike, right?"

"It is. I wouldn't have stalked you if I didn't think you could do this." Bill stares into me, pulling out my fear. His unwavering confidence helps to put me at ease.

"If we lose, we go out and drink. And if we win, we go out and drink," Hank says.

Bill has us huddle.

"We're not going to let anyone push us around," he says. No matter how fun the game is, Bill takes it seriously. We all do on some level. Nobody wants to lose.

We put our hands in the center and yell "wolf pack" at the count of three. It pumps me full of adrenaline.

"Okay, lace up and let's get out there," Bill says.

We go out into the stadium, and there's a decent number of people in the stands. I gather they're mostly family and friends, with a few hockey superfans scattered in. To me, it feels like the damn Stanley Cup. It's just a fun game, I remind myself. Win or lose, we'll laugh about it over drinks.

"OK guys. This is it!" Bill says just before we go out there.

We corral by the rink entrance.

"Give it up for the Comebacks!" the announcer yells over the loudspeaker.

We yell and whoop and rush out onto the ice to thunderous cheers.

As soon as I step out though, something feels off. I immediately can't find my balance. I lean forward, then back, then resort to windmilling my arms before toppling into Des, who topples into Tanner. Human dominoes.

The crowd stops cheering.

I stand back up to collect myself, yet just as fast, I fall on my ass down again.

"What the fuck," I mutter.

"Uh, Griff..." Tanner squats down. "Did you check your skates?" He points at my blades.

I run my finger over them. They're slick. No cuts.

"You got taped," he says.

I look across the rink, just knowing it. Sensing it.

Jack. Waving. Smiling.

Fucker.

———

I TRACK down Jack's number from Marcy, telling her it was damn near an emergency to talk to him. He left after I spotted him, so I didn't have a chance to beat his ass in person.

"What the fuck is your problem? You covered my blades in tape?" I growl into my phone when I'm back in my truck. After we got the tape off, I was able to skate, but my confidence was rattled, and the bad juju spilled out to the rest of the team. We lost.

"Hey? You like what I did?" Jack asks, cocky as ever.

"No. What the fuck? You fucked with my skates?"

"It was a prank."

"On game day!"

"You stole my clothes," he shoots back.

I grip my steering wheel tight. "That was during practice. I would never prank you on game day and fuck with your juju. Good juju in hockey is sacred."

"I'm surprised you didn't know they were taped before you went out. A win for me." Jack gets quiet when he notices I'm not laughing. "It was a classic hockey prank, a welcome back to the game. I thought you would've taken the tape off before you got out there."

"Well I didn't. This was my first game in a long time, and my first game playing with one functioning eye. I had other things on my mind." Blood pounds at my temples. My first game back, and I fall flat on my face. Multiple times.

"I'll know for next time."

"There is no next time. I know what you're up to. Doing your dad's bidding. Let me tell you something. What happened on the ice was his fault. He charged into me and took out my eye. He messed up his shoulder. It wasn't me."

"What? Griffin, what are you talking about?"

I don't have the patience to listen to his excuses. "Both of you can fuck off."

I miss the days of slamming down a phone to hang up on someone. It's not as cathartic pressing the end call button.

———

A FEW DAYS LATER, I'm still steaming about the prank. The thought of it makes my ears burn. Jack's tried calling me back a few times since then, but I don't want a halfhearted apology. I don't even want a full-hearted apology from him.

"You don't prank a player before an actual game," I mutter to Hank. I slouch in my chair, not for emphasis, but because these auditorium chairs are so damn uncomfortable. They're meant for teenage bodies, not mine.

"I know, I know." Hank is only half paying attention to me. He looks toward the stage waving to his son Brody like he's flagging a taxi. Brody gives his dad a tentative, awkward wave back, immediately embarrassed.

"That's shit you only pull during a practice. Pranking before a game is below the belt stuff."

"It's that whole generation. They don't care about rules, or anybody, so long as it makes for a good meme. They don't have driver's licenses. They don't have sex. All they have are memes." Hank shakes his head. Were we not in public, he'd probably be shaking his fist, too. It's amazing how all of us turn into this person as we get older, whether we like it or not.

Brody sits at a long table with three of his quiz bowl teammates. They all wear matching, baggy South Rock High Quiz Bowl T-shirts. I hate to admit what Hank and I said about these types of kids when we were their age. I'm not proud of it, and since most of those kids are far more successful than me, I've been eating crow my whole adult life. Why do we mock smart kids? They're the ones who become the doctors who keep us healthy, engineers who build our cities, creatives who entertain us, and politicians who pass our laws. Shouldn't they be at the top of the popularity food chain?

"Go Brody! Kick some ass!" Hank shouts out along with a resounding WOOOO that reverberates in the auditorium. Brody blushes and looks down at the table.

Brody's quiz bowl coach, Mr. Bright, hops off the stage and comes up to us. He's young, beanpole thin with a mop of brown curls. He empties some Skittles into his hand and tosses them back like pills.

"Mr. Rush, I appreciate the enthusiasm, but this isn't a sporting event. You may want to take it down a scooch."

"Oh, yeah. Sorry about that, Amos."

"Since we're at my place of work, please call me Mr. Bright."

Amos is good friends with Mitch's husband. We've been around him at social gatherings, where it only takes half a drink for him to let down his professional guard.

"You got it, Mr. Bright." Hank gives him a salute. "Brody has been practicing really hard for this. He's going to kick so much ass the other team will need a rectal exam when it's over."

"You know, I might not phrase it exactly like that." Amos cocks his head. "But I appreciate the enthusiasm."

"You don't want to throw him off his game, like by taping his skates," I say.

"It's not a game. It's a quiz bowl tournament. But sure?" Amos awkwardly places a purple Skittle in his mouth and returns to the stage.

On the way over, Hank was listing out all of his son's academic achievements like the proudest dad in the world. Brody is destined to find the cure for cancer, invent the next supercomputer, or help us colonize Mars. Maybe all three.

"Anyway, cut Jack a little slack," Hank says. "He's not that far removed from being a teenager, and you know how guys are in high school."

"He's twenty-four. He's an adult," I shoot back.

An uneasy feeling churns in my stomach. Jack is nearly twenty years younger than me, and I've still been thinking about him standing naked in the parking lot. He let it all hang out proudly. And well...he had every right to be proud.

"Is there another fucking video of me circulating online?" I ask Hank. Jack's video of the toilet paper incident had over a thousand views online. Hank assured me that was nothing in the world of going viral, but it was still a thousand people seeing us made to be fools.

"I had Brody look, but he didn't find anything."

"Fine. At least he didn't make an even bigger mockery of me." Taping up my skates right before my first game in decades. What the fuck? My cheeks burned with residual embarrassment. "But the point stands: you don't do that to another player. You don't fuck up their actual game."

"He didn't fuck it up, though. We got the tape off before the game started. Watching you go down was kinda funny." Hank stops mid-snort when he notices I'm not laughing. I narrow my eyes at him. "I said it was only *kinda* funny."

"We lost. Because of the bad juju he gave me." It wasn't even close. The other team won by four. The tape incident and resulting embarrassment threw me off my already rusty game, and I wasn't able to recover until the third period. "Every hockey player knows that you don't mess with the juju right before the game. I guarantee nobody in his pro days ever did something like that."

"You're right. He's an asshole," Hank says, but only to placate me. It's the same tone he uses when I critique his goaltending skills.

"He's an asshole. And he's in this league and fucking with me as revenge for his raging dickhead of a father. I'm telling you, Hank, he's going to send this league down in flames."

"I'm impressed. You're new to being gay, but you have the drama queen shit down pat." Hank raises an eyebrow at me. "This is Real Housewives-level. I'm...I'm legitimately impressed."

"I'm not a drama queen," I growl back. I'd rather be compared to an overflowing Porta Potty than a Real Housewife. "I'm pointing out legitimate issues with this new player. You don't think it's fucked up that he's Ted Gross's son? You saw how the guy was at Ferguson's."

Ted hasn't forgotten what happened on the ice. Neither have I.

"It's a little fucked up. But maybe it's just a coincidence that he's in the league?" Hank raises his shoulders to his ears. "He used to play hockey. He misses playing hockey. He found a local competitive league for hockey. I'm going with Gillette razors on this one."

"What?"

"It's a concept in science that says the simplest explanation is usually the correct one."

"Isn't that Occam's razor?"

"Oh. Maybe. I've never used their razors." Hank feels his clean-shaven face. It's a miracle that he graduated from high school. There were times the team would wait outside his classroom to find out if he passed a test and thus had a GPA high enough to play in that week's game. Sometimes, I wonder how Brody could be Hank's offspring, but then I remember Brody is just as sweet and loyal as his old man. Genetics are weird.

"Maybe Jack doesn't like you for a totally different reason. Who knows?" Hank wonders. I haven't told him or the guys about what happened on the rooftop. I'd much rather believe it's a complicated revenge plot led by his dad.

"In all fairness, we stole his clothes." Hank chuckles, remembering the prank. "He wanted payback, and he got it."

"Please. He enjoyed it. He was fucking smiling as we drove away."

Again, my mind flashes to him letting his towel drop, his cocky smirk as he let me soak in what I was missing by leaving that rooftop. I can feel the warm sensation brewing in my core—and heading south. My dick isn't on my side here.

"What I mean to say is that he knew what we did was a fun prank. Taping a guy's blades on game day is a dirty move."

"You're not the first player to get your skates taped, Griff."

"Jack is an overconfident prick."

"Whatever you say, drama queen." Hank shakes his head while staring at the stage, waiting for the event to begin. "You were never the guy to let another player get inside your head. I guess there's a first for everything."

His words shine an unwanted spotlight on me, making me want to hide. "He's not in my head."

Well, which head are we talking about?

"He's totally in your head. He's moved in and already assembled IKEA furniture." Hank chuckles to himself, his cheeks getting extra bulbous.

"No, he's not." I lightly punch Hank's shoulder. "He's pissing me off, that's what he's doing."

"Who's pissing you off?" Derek scoots into our row with his friend Leo. Derek's daughter Jolene sits next to Brody on stage, her radiant red hair unmistakable up there.

"Hey, buddy." Hank leans over me to bump fists with him. "Good to see you again, Mr. Mayor. How's that pothole on Mercer Street coming?"

"It's getting patched up this month."

"You said that last month."

"Well, I mean it this month." Leo has the slicked back hair and polished look of a politician, which makes sense since he's Sourwood's mayor. But today he's here with his dad hat on to cheer on his son Ari, another one of Brody's quiz bowl teammates.

"So who's pissing you off?" Derek leans back in his chair, likely tired from another long shift at the firehouse.

Hank leans over me. "Take a wild friggin' guess."

"Jack Gross?" Derek arches a skeptical eyebrow.

"He violated the sacred rules of hockey," I say, though nobody seems to believe me. "And he's a ringer."

"You got a ringer on your team?" Leo asks.

"Not our team. We play by the rules. It's the Blades. They have a professional hockey player in their ranks." I sit back, crossing my arms. "A professional hockey player who insists on pranking players before an actual game, not during practice."

"His dad is Ted Gross," Hank informs them. "The guy who..." He points to my eye patch. I swat his hand away.

"Shit," Leo says. "And now you're playing his son, who's a pro hockey player?"

"A former pro hockey player," I say. "He wants to take a break from buying buildings and jet-setting to play in our league."

"Yep. He's in your head, he ain't paying rent, and he's never leaving." Hank snorts to himself.

"Hank, I remember what your locker used to be here. I will find a way to shove you back into it."

"The whole Blades team is good," Derek says. "I went to their game. They trounced the Matterhorns."

"Maybe Jack is teaching them his professional secrets," Hank says.

"Which would be another violation of league rules," I point out.

"Were you always this much of a stickler for rules? Just relax." Derek shrugs.

Hank shushes us when the moderator steps onto the stage. She wears a blazer and pencil skirt to go with her serious expression. She kindly explains the game rules. Hank makes the wrap it up hand gesture to us, no doubt because this is not his first quiz bowl rodeo. We go quiet as she jumps into asking the first question:

"Protons and neutrons are made up of this subatomic particle."

Brody buzzes in. "Quarks."

"Yes! Let's go!" Hank cheers.

"Correct," the moderator says, eyeing Hank. "Next question. SB is the symbol for this element on the periodic table."

Brody hits his buzzer again. "Antimony."

"Correct," she says again, betraying no expression.

"Yeah! That's what I'm talking about!" Hank yells.

The moderator stops mid-question. Amos sits off to the side, his face as red as the Skittle in his mouth. Brody motions for him to take it down a notch.

"Sorry," Hank says. He watches with rapt with attention, a gigantic smile on his face. The world of hockey is the furthest thing from his mind.

Jolene and Ari get buzzer time throughout the competition, but Brody is obviously the star of his team. Each time he gets an answer right, Hank lets out a "yes." He keeps looking over at me in amazement, wondering if I'm as floored by his son's intelligence as he is.

At the end of the round, South Rock High is way out in front. Leo leans over, the wheels spinning in his head.

"I can't help thinking about this hockey matchup," Leo says. "We have a professional hockey player and his young guns on one team. And then we have the Wolf Pack on another."

The Wolf Pack was the nickname for our high school hockey team when we were playing. We were a force to be reckoned with, leading the school to back-to-back championships.

"You guys were legends in this town. And now you're back together, the original lineup. It's quite something." Wheels turn behind Leo's eyes, but I don't have time to decipher that look. I have bigger things on my mind.

"I need to prank Jack back. Hard," I say. "Show him that I won't give in."

"Dude, I don't have the time or energy for another prank. Why don't we focus on the games? We're not playing the Blades for a few weeks anyway," Derek says. He knocks at my skull. "Get this guy out of your head."

Easier fucking said than done.

"Yeah, if I didn't know any better, I'd say you have a crush," Leo says.

I feel my entire face turn red. Before I can respond to that accusation, the moderator takes to the podium and Hank shushes us.

"Let's go, Huskies!" Hank cheers. "Let's go Brody!"

"Can you be quiet?" A fellow dad a row in front of us sneers.

Hank gets right in his face. "Hey pal, you wanna take this outside?"

13

JACK

fter sending over fifty resumes to crickets, I finally get a bite to be the office manager for the private airport outside of town. It's located down a windy, wooded road that leads to a big, open airfield. The contrast is startling.

Fuentes pulls into the parking lot. From the passenger seat, I watch single engine planes and small private jets line up to take off. Students at the flight attendant school attached to the airport flutter about outside in their uniforms, the men's pants especially fitted to their buttocks. I could get used to both of those views.

"You're going to do great," Fuentes says, giving me a supportive punch on the thigh. "Don't speak too fast. Don't trail off. Give them some of that big-swinging-dick charm of yours."

I don't know much about the job I'm interviewing for. I think I have to stock office supplies and the company fridge. They didn't require a college degree, though, and they provide full benefits. *Take the interview*, Fuentes and Miller told me in no uncertain terms.

I'll learn as I go. Practice makes perfect, in hockey and in life.

"Are you okay with taking an Uber home?" he asks. "I have to let in the HVAC guy to one of my buildings."

"Yeah." I shake out my hands. I've played hockey in front of tens of thousands of fans, broadcast live on TV. I didn't get nervous like I am now. I feel like an impostor in this suit, in this life.

Fuentes gives me a supportive smile and makes a fist in solidarity.

"Thank you for driving me. For being my fucking chauffeur. And for the apartment. I hit the friend jackpot with you."

Ever since we played hockey as kids, there was never any competition between us, no double-crossing to be coach's favorite. As my hockey career was taking off and getting more attention from scouts, Fuentes didn't act jealous. He was excited for me. I've made a lot of mistakes in life, done a lot of dumb shit. Somehow, I lucked out with Fuentes.

"I was a shit student in high school. Even my teachers didn't think I'd amount to anything. You remember what you always said to me?" Fuentes asks.

A nostalgic smile hits my lips. "You're destined for great things."

Fuentes nods. "You believed in me. Just hearing that made me think my crazy ideas could work. When someone keeps telling you that you're destined for success over and over, it starts to sink in.

"And when you first got drafted, you remember what you did? You rented a limo and threw me an epic eighteenth birthday party. We cruised around New York City with fake IDs like we were the kings of Manhattan. None of us had to take out our wallets once."

We got into this bar that we heard professional athletes frequented and did shots with a bunch of basketball players. We strolled down the High Line at dawn eating hot dogs, beaming with that kind of invincibility and optimism that comes with being on the cusp of adulthood.

"You're a real one, Jack. And real ones look out for each other." Fuentes gives me a fist bump. "I know you're having a hard time, but you're destined for great things."

"Like being the office manager for a private airport?"

"Hey, everybody's gotta start somewhere."

I hold his words close to my heart, forcing them to seep in. They are a shield against the cynicism and depression that has clouded me ever since I left the NHL.

"You got this."

I get out of the car into the cold, refreshing air. I check myself out in the reflection of a puddle. I smooth out my ill-fitting suit. All hockey guys have trouble wearing professional clothing. They're not built for muscles. It looks like I'm encased in a sardine jar, but it'll do. Aside from that, hair is good. Scruff is shaved. Tie isn't crooked.

And yet...I'm fucked.

Because in the reflection, I catch sight of a familiar pickup truck behind me. It was only a week ago that I watched that pickup drive away with my and my team's clothing, a certain surly gentleman flashing me a victorious grin. A grin I should've been mad at, but have kept thinking about. Watching a serious person smile is like unlocking a new level in a video game.

Crap, Griffin works here. I vaguely remember him mentioning he was a mechanic for a private airport when we met. I should've listened harder instead of sneaking glances at his bulge.

Knowing that I'm in the same vicinity as him makes me a new kind of nervous. My stomach regularly does a somersault when I think of him, which is very rude of my stomach considering the guy has no interest in me.

If I can handle getting knocked around on the ice and getting traded every year, then I can handle a regular corporate job. The hardest part will be faking enthusiasm for sitting at a desk. I don't know if office life is right for me. But working at Ferguson's wasn't right for me either. Maybe I need to suck it up rather than trying to find where I belong. I wish that the NHL would've given us some training on job stuff in between all the practice. They likely knew that most of us would need a regular job when our career was done.

I walk into the expansive hangar where people in gray jumpsuits work on fixing airplanes. There are small two-engine planes and a large, private jet in the back.

I've flown on a private jet before. The cool factor wears off quickly. The food is never as good as you want it to be.

As I admire the jet, I spot Griffin working on the bottom of it from a raised platform, deep into his work, sleeves pushed up.

I find myself captivated by his methodical working. The way his brow creases as he tightens a widget. The smear of grease across his thick forearm. The smile he gives his fellow mechanic when she cracks a joke. He's a man in his element, good at his job.

And damn does he look good in his jumpsuit. Fuentes and Miller told me to bring a briefcase so that I'd seem like a more serious person. I now use that briefcase to cover the very serious tenting in my pants.

Griffin turns to get something from his toolbox, giving me a glimpse of his big, round ass jutting out perfectly against the dull gray of the jumpsuit.

Could I stock that cake in the company fridge?

He turns back to the jet, and I dart out of view before he can see me.

———

I MEET with a Black woman named Darlene who's the executive assistant to the airport general manager. As she describes her role at the airport, it sounds like she's the one running this place. We walk past a row of offices until we reach hers. It's cramped, but there're homey touches like plants and pictures of her kids. To our left is the door that leads to her boss's office. Outside her window, a gleaming private jet sits on the tarmac. They look small on the runway and in the sky, but up close, they're huge. It reminds me of people in apartments when massive parade floats pass by their windows.

"That's quite a view!" I say.

"Oh, yeah. There's a musician that lives in the area, and that's her private plane. I can't say whose it is, but if you start working here, you'll probably see her around." The fan side of Darlene makes a quick cameo before she goes back to her business self.

We have some pleasant chitchat about hockey life. Her husband was a fan of one of my prior teams, which led to my resume sticking out in her pile. I breathe a small sigh of relief that she's already on my side.

"So Jack, tell me what attracted you to the role?" she asks. There comes that point in an interview when the pleasant chitchat fades away, and the interviewer inevitably becomes an adversary, judging whether to hire you or not.

In hockey, I'm used to thinking on my feet, pivoting when a teammate is blocked or a shot goes wide. Interviews are a new beast for me.

"Why am I attracted to the role? That's a great question," I say, obviously stalling. The first answer that pops into my head is the truth: because you called me in for an interview and because I need a job. I will do pretty much whatever you tell me to do so long as you give me a paycheck. Too bad honesty is the worst policy in job interviews.

I search my brain for an intelligent sentence, and the best I come up with is, "Well, I've always liked airplanes."

Darlene nods, waiting for more.

"You know, they're cool. Because they're so heavy, but they can fly through the air." I can hear how dumb I sound, and yet I can't stop. It's the same thing that happens when I feel momentum sending me into an opposing player. "And so I'd love to work around airplanes."

And maybe a certain mechanic whose ass looks tasty in his uniform.

She waits a few seconds, as if expecting me to say something better and then realizing that that won't be happening. She gives a polite smile.

"It's pretty fun working here. Airplanes are truly a feat of engineering."

"And it looks like they're serviced well." I clear my throat, trying to clear the image of Griffin. "I mean, your staff...they do a good job. I haven't heard of any planes crashing from here, so that's good!"

Bringing up plane crashes? I'm on a roll.

Darlene gives a cringey laugh, one that politely screams "get him out of here." I need to save this interview. The clock is ticking down, no time-outs.

"But my point is that aviation is an exciting field, and I really like helping people. I love working with my fellow players and helping them get better. Making an improvement in someone's confidence, in their life, is great. And I think that's transferable to making sure our coworkers are happy and comfortable."

Darlene nods along, a grin of appreciation lighting up her face. I breathe out a relieved sigh.

"I believe that a happy employee is a more productive employee," she says. I wish I'd thought of that line. She's good! "As office manager, you will find ways to delight coworkers, whether by making sure they have what they need in the office or planning fun in-office events like the holiday party."

"I love parties!" I refrain from telling her the last party I planned involved a keg.

"Can you talk more about how you work with others? And how you fostered hospitality in your role at Ferguson's?"

"Great question." I would watch one of the star players on an old team say that in press conferences. He said it allowed him to pause and think of a good response. I'm racking my brain for an answer when behind Darlene, through the window, a familiar big ass in a grey jumpsuit slowly comes into view.

Griffin raises himself up on a scissor lift to work on the private plane. His back (and ass) is to us as he works on fixing something on the wing. His back looks impossibly broad against the tight fitting jumpsuit. Pornographic fantasies swirl in my head.

"Um, well, serving customers is all about being hospitable, so I have experience there."

It's hard to stay engaged when Griffin and his delicious, strong body is right there. Did he plan this? Is he messing with me in revenge for the tape trick? Did he put on a jumpsuit that was one size too small, knowing I'd be looking at his ass through the window?

"I always made sure to answer whatever questions customers had. People like when they get answers to their questions."

He turns, so I can see his face. His brow crinkles along the creases of his forehead. He's oddly sexy when he concentrates. I slump down slightly in my seat out of his view. Griffin bends over to rifle through his toolbox, his ass sticking in the air like the air traffic control tower of my dreams. Or maybe that's his dick.

I copped a quick feel when I was on my knees during the rooftop debacle, and the man is packing heat.

"I just want our coworkers to have a happy ending." I clear my throat. "With their holiday party."

"Okay. Great. Making sure people are heard is an underutilized skill in the workplace," Darlene says. "What would you say is your strongest attribute?"

Right now, my cock feels like my strongest attribute because it's on the verge of getting so hard it could put a hole in Darlene's desk. Griffin's ass is still in the air. How many tools is he rifling through? And is he...wiggling it?

I notice he has on headphones when he stands up, the white buds stand out against his dark beard and hair. He gives his ass another shake to whatever he's listening to. Griffin dancing like nobody's looking? Too. Fucking. Cute.

"My strongest attribute is that I work hard." Rock fucking hard. "I don't give up, no matter how difficult a request." I have the stamina to go all fucking night. "I think hard work is a very important asset, especially as I'm learning a new skill." Please plunk your asset directly on my face.

Griffin takes out a massive wrench and begins loosening some widget in the wing. His arms flex their muscles, two thick pieces of rope attached to a brick wall of a body.

"Anything in particular about how you exemplify hard work?" Darlene asks, reminding me we're still in an interview.

"I was learning some stick handling maneuvers from an old coach, and I went over it for hours on my own until I mastered it." I smile at the memory, one of my proudest moments in the NHL. "And at Ferguson's, I always volunteered to organize inventory in the back, which was one of the least favorite things for employees to do." I did it to get away from Dad, but she doesn't have to know that.

"Why did you leave Ferguson's?"

I practiced this answer with my friends. "I'm looking for more of a challenge, a place where I can expand my skillset and grow my career."

She seems to buy it. Meanwhile, in Griffin land, he's working with tools and screws and nails and it's making me hornier and hornier.

He wipes a smear of black grease onto his jumpsuit. He keeps wiping to get it off his hands. And then, I forget to breathe for a moment because he unbuttons his jumpsuit.

Each button unclasping over his broad chest sends another current of heat up my leg. His white undershirt hugs his chest and belly. I know bellies don't have six-packs, but Griffin's might be the exception. It just looks strong and imposing and makes me feel bad for my flat stomach. I want to hug it as I bounce up and down on his cock.

"The office manager role can be a great stepping stone careerwise. It's where I started my career. I never imagined I'd be an EA, but as office manager, you get a lay of the land across all departments."

"That's great! I'm really excited about this role," I say, my eyes darting back outside.

Just as I regain my breath, I lose it all over again when Griffin pulls up his undershirt, using it to wipe his brow.

Holy mother of gay Jesus. I get a full, glorious, there-is-a-God view of his hairy torso, a torso I'm silently begging to rub my face all over. His pecs are rugged and cut, mostly muscle with a little heft of fat. He is all man. He has ensured that I could never be attracted to a man under thirty again.

I would not be opposed to him bending me over that airplane wing.

I shift my gaze down to under his belly where the band of his boxers is visible. Boxer waistbands are sexier than boxers themselves. They are the ultimate tease.

I realize that my dream job isn't to be office manager; it's to be Griffin's full-time cocksucker.

And just as quickly, the fantasy ends. Griffin drops his shirt and buttons up his jumpsuit.

"Jack." Darlene spins around in her chair to look out the window, but all she sees is a mechanic diligently working on aircraft.

"Sorry. Planes are just so cool!" I laugh it off as the lower half of my body cools off.

Her mood shifts to a cooler temperature, or maybe it had already shifted and it's the first I'm noticing. She stands up and signals for me to join her. "Well, it was so great of you to come in, Jack. We're seeing a few more candidates, but we'll let you know when we make a decision." Her hand is essentially guiding me out the door before I can protest.

She leads me to the lobby and gives me a quick wave before whooshing back to her office.

14

GRIFFIN

Working on airplanes is a much more peaceful existence than working on cars. The high ceilings and open air of the hangar makes things quieter. I can listen to music and zone out. I don't have to talk to people, sit in meetings with people, basically do anything that involves interfacing with another human being.

It's a good life.

That is, until someone decides to disturb my peace.

"What the hell was that?"

I look up from the landing gear that I'm tightening up to find Jack glaring down at me. Jack in a suit that is one size too small for his thick arms and legs.

I give the gear one final twist of the bolt before standing up. The owner of this Cessna 150 claimed he wanted to keep flying his plane until the wheels came off, and he pretty much got his wish.

"Excuse me?" I ask. Jack's blue eyes are so filled with fire that they're nearly aqua.

"That little show you were putting on outside."

"I don't follow..." Oh shit. Did I fuck up his plane? I remember him saying he owned one. Rich people loved nothing more than toying with people who worked for them, like we were mice in a cat's mouth. "Was that your plane on the tarmac? The wingtip was already damaged, probably from flying through one too many storms. I noted in my report that you need to order a new part."

"What? No. I...you...out there...with your jumpsuit...and you whipping your shirt off..." Jack paces in the space between the Cessna and my tools. "You were messing with me."

"Now I really don't follow." Was this what it looked like for someone to be having a panic attack?

"I prepared so hard for this interview. I did a mock interview with my friends for Chrissakes. It's the only one I've gotten and now it's fucked because of your hot body."

I'm not sure whether to feel offended, guilty, or turned on by the compliment. Jack seems equally confused, rubbing at his head and mussing up his neatly combed hair. Damn him for looking even cuter with shaggy hair.

"I'm sorry?" I've never had to apologize for being good looking, but I suppose there's a first for everything. Wait, why the hell am I apologizing to him for anything? "Actually, I'm not sorry. If you have a problem with the way your plane was serviced, you can speak to my manager. Otherwise, get the hell out of my hangar."

"Dammit." He plunks down on my stool and lets out a grandiose exhale. He wipes at his eyes, a nuclear mushroom cloud of stress wafting off him.

Fuck. What is it about Jack that makes it impossible to tell him to truly fuck off. I let out a groan and pull up another stool. "We will get your plane fixed. Don't worry. I can see if I have a replacement part here."

"I don't have a plane! I don't even have a job!" He yells, his voice echoing through the hangar. Valentina, the other mechanic on duty, glances up from the helicopter propeller she's working on. I give her the signal that everything's okay.

It's then that I notice Jack's suit isn't that nice. His shoes are scuffed and don't have a designer label. And peeking out his briefcase is a resume with his name plastered on top. Rich people don't use resumes. They use country clubs and connections.

"You don't have a private plane?" I ask, the truth slowly revealing itself. "And you don't own that building you took me to when we met?"

Jack's eyes are like a mood ring changing hues before he has a chance to make up an excuse. The fiery aqua of before deepens to a dark blue-green ocean of regret, informing me that I'm correct.

"I'm pretty much broke," he utters, his voice barely above a whisper. "My friend owns that building. He lets me rent one of his apartments for super cheap. Otherwise I'd be living in my car."

I try to wrap my head around this information, but it's a shock to the system. "But you played in the NHL. I looked you up. You were a professional athlete."

"We're not all multi-millionaires lounging in swimming pools filled with Lamborghinis. I was traded to four teams in four years. I wasn't exactly a star player, and I definitely wasn't paid like one." He loosens his tie, a sense of relief coming over him as he unspools the truth. "I made decent money, but when you give a twenty-year-old all that cash, he's bound to make a lot of stupid decisions with it."

Jack laughs to himself, probably the only way to get over being rich and having it all go away.

"I owned a Lambo. They're a pain in the ass to keep up. They get horrible mileage, and they require the more expensive premium gas." Jack yanks his tie off and shoves it in his briefcase.

"Smart that you got rid of it," I say.

"It got repo'd."

"Shit." My heart sinks thinking about everything Jack went through by the time he was twenty-four. He gained and lost a fortune. Gained and lost a career. "I'm sorry."

"Don't do that. I don't want your pity. I don't deserve it. I did this to myself. I thought the good times were going to last forever, and I made some shitty decisions. Trusted the wrong people." He shakes his head to himself, his eyes darkening.

"Was anything you said on the night we met the truth?" I ask, half-joking.

"Yeah. My dad is an asshole who used me to live out his failed dreams. He thought I would be his ticket out of his shitty life. He did a one-eighty when it was clear I was never going to be the star player. It's quite breathtaking how quickly people close to you can turn." Jack's bottom lip quivers, and for a moment, I wonder if a tear will fall down his face. Instead, he stands up from his stool, gets right in my face, anger seething from him. "He didn't put me up to *anything* with you. I'm not his fucking puppet, got that?"

I nod in understanding, and it gives me a sense of relief. I don't have to hate myself as much for thinking Jack is attractive. It also makes me hate Ted Gross even more, if that was possible.

"Well, good luck with the job hunt," I say. I squat down again to work on the wheel that's loose under this Cessna. Jack walks around my workstation, opening drawers and admiring tools. A wrench falls out of his hand and clangs back into the drawer. He reminds me of a stray puppy that wants attention.

"Can you, uh, pass me that wrench actually?" Since he's just standing around, he could be of use. Technically, it's not allowed, but there are airplane owners who prefer to service their own aircraft. A quick smile flits on his face at the request, which makes the freckles on his nose squish together. Not that I should know a damn thing about his freckles.

I tighten the screw for the front wheel, but it's still loose. I take out the screw and notice the sides have been worn down.

"Hey, can you see if there's a screw in there that matches this one?" I hand it to Jack.

"Sure." He rifles through the drawers in the toolchest. He takes out a screw, compares it to the broken one, studies the grooves, then throws it back because it's not the right one. He does this two more times before handing over a match. The kid wants to work, I'll give him that.

"Thanks." I squat back down. The screw fits in perfectly.

"So like, what's the deal with you and my dad? What happened?" Jack sits on the floor, no cares about messing up his suit. He takes off the jacket, which was squeezing his arms. His shirt allows me to see the curve of his chest better.

"What does your dad say happened?"

"He was going for a puck, and you skated at him full speed and just barreled into him like a bus."

"He barreled into me! I was the one going for that puck, and he came at me stick first." A flash of white hot anger burns in me. I could bend this wrench in half I was so pissed. Ted Gross is crying victim? He still has two functioning eyes.

Jack throws his hands up in defense. "Just repeating what he said many times over the years." He sidles up to the plane, smoothing his hand over the fuselage. "Maybe you guys are both right?"

Everything happened in less than two seconds. Unlike with the JFK assassination, there's no footage to parse and obsess over. But I remember what happened. I remember the last time I saw anything out of my left eye, the image of Ted Gross coming at me like a cannon ball.

"He messed up his shoulder really bad. He was never able to play the same way again. Still hurts him to this day," Jack says.

"You're defending him?"

"Trust me, I'm not. The last thing I want to do is stick up for him." He puts his hand on my shoulder, its warmth calming me down.

"He's not the only one with scars." I don't have to point to my eye patch. Jack's stare gets there on his own. "He never visited me in the hospital. He never apologized. Even if it was a freak accident, fucking apologize."

"What can I say? My dad's an asshole. He was born angry, he's angry every day, and he'll die an angry old man."

"Is that how you want to live?" I hand him the wrench. He puts it away in the correct drawer.

Jack shakes his head no.

"Can you pass me the mirror in the third drawer down?" Jack hands it over. I use it to check around the wheels in hard to reach angles. I want to make sure there are no other loose screws or wires around the landing gear.

"I'm sorry about what happened to you, Jack. That sucks. But at least you got to play. You made it to the NHL. Things might not have gone how you wanted them to, but you still accomplished something great."

Jack nods politely, the way we do with unearned compliments. He takes back the mirror, places it back in the toolchest. "So did you."

I snort a laugh, thinking this is him being sarcastic again.

"I never made it pro. Your dad made sure of that."

"Stop being so down on yourself, Griffin." Jack throws a clean rag in my face. "I'll admit the sad, wounded puppy thing is cute, but it's not accurate."

"I'm not the one who lied about my life, Jack," I shoot back.

"But you're not being totally honest with yourself, either." Jack gets right in my face. I can practically feel his stubble on my cheek. "Yeah, you didn't go pro, but you have a pretty good life. You have a great job, good friends, a roof over your head, two daughters who sound adorable and love you no matter what your hockey stats are. You're doing pretty good for yourself. And trust me, there are lots of guys playing in the NHL who have everything you dream of and are miserable because they don't have what you have today."

Jack's eyes vibrate with an intensity that catch me off guard. His words cut through walls that had been there so long, slicing through the story I'd told myself for decades.

"I should count my blessings more," I admit. "So should you."

"Deal." He holds out his hand for a shake. I squeeze extra hard, but he doesn't wince.

Heat builds between us, spinning around like electricity in a lightning storm.

With a sincerity and urgency I didn't know I had in me, I cup his cheeks in my hands. He doesn't mind the bits of grease streaked on his skin. "You're going to be okay, Jack. I promise you that."

Jack's eyes don't move from me. I stare into him, seeing the fear hiding behind the cockiness. It only makes me want to hold him closer. The moment, whatever the fuck this moment is, swirls around us. I feel my body inch closer, a deep desire to taste his lips overcoming me. Jack shuffles toward me, heat radiating between our bodies.

And then, in a quick jolt, I see Ted Gross's angry face from Ferguson's. I see his hockey stick coming at me. I freeze up, and in those critical seconds, Jack clenches under my hands. He steps back, whatever truths he revealed behind his eyes gone.

"I really need to learn my lesson with you." Jack grabs his jacket and storms out before I have a chance to explain. Well, first I'd have to come up with a fucking explanation.

I glare at the Cessna. The landing gear is gleaming and fixed. At least one thing in this fucking hangar knows how to take off.

15

JACK

I always dread going home. For most people in the world, home is a cozy place, a sanctuary, four walls filled with love and safety.

Most people didn't grow up under the roof of Ted Gross.

Home was where I went to get nonstop feedback on my hockey game, where pressure was put on to win the next game, where a homey touch was forever lacking after Mom left. When I got drafted out of high school, I might've been happier to live in a different city than I was to become a professional hockey player.

"What the hell are you doing here?" Dad asks when I stumble into the kitchen from the garage. He hunches over the small table with a microwave dinner, the purple Ferguson's apron slung over the opposite chair. Lucky for me, he never changes his garage door code. Otherwise, I don't know if he'd let me in.

"I need something from my room," I say.

I look around and recoil at the memories that seep out of the old furniture. Even though Dad keeps the house clean, there's still a dingy, sad quality to it, like being in a club that's no longer cool. He never bothered to replace the family pictures on the wall. Dad's always preferred living in the past. Mom's smile from a Disney trip beams back at me, empty and cruel. I'll never understand how someone could look that joyful and then bail on her son less than a year later. When she left, Dad's idea of fatherly warmth was telling me to channel my anger on the ice.

"I'll just be a minute." I trudge upstairs, past a photo wall of family pictures, pictures from my peewee hockey days, and Dad's high school hockey days. It is the staircase of broken dreams.

My old bedroom is the first one in the hall. The bed is gone, as are the posters I had tacked up. Boxes line the wall under the window. The bookcase that used to be a shrine to my medals and trophies and news clippings sits empty. When I was playing in the NHL, I'd come home to my room in pristine condition, exactly how I left it at eighteen. Now I'm a ghost.

I kneel down and begin searching the boxes, scrambling through years of hockey memorabilia, digging through the good times. It takes epic concentration to avoid reading old articles about "Promising Hockey Star" Jack Gross.

"Shit," I mutter, getting to the bottom of one box with no luck. I pop open the next one. Old trophies clang together. I hate all of them. They're gravestones for success.

After opening all four boxes and coming up short, I search behind furniture and in the nooks and crannies of my old closet. But there's no way it would be there. The lanyard bracelet always sat on the bookcase. It needed to commune with those fucking trophies, according to my dumbass teenage logic.

"Where did my bracelet go?" I ask Dad after stomping down the stairs.

"What bracelet?"

"You know which one. The blue and green one that I wore for every game. It was my good luck bracelet." My junior high girlfriend made it for me at church camp. (We only kissed, and I thought of her brother the whole time.) I knew she'd get pissed if I didn't wear it, so I put it on for one of my games. I wound up scoring a hat trick. From then on, I wore it for every game. Hockey players are very superstitious when it comes to good luck.

Of course I've been rusty and not my best self on the ice lately. I haven't been wearing my lucky bracelet.

"I last had it on the bookcase in my room," I tell Dad, who shovels a sad, shriveled piece of meatloaf into his mouth. "I put it there after my final game when I moved back."

"All your stuff is in those boxes."

"When were you going to tell me you boxed up my old room?"

"You never come home. I figured you didn't want it." Dad's callous expression screams "you snooze, you lose." I'm surprised he didn't burn all that shit in a bonfire.

"So you were just going to throw all that stuff away without telling me?"

"If you want it, it's there. I'm planning to turn that room into a home gym."

"Wonderful," I deadpan. "Do you remember seeing the bracelet?"

He shrugs, and I catch a flash of something dark in his eye. He goes back to watching the news on a small flatscreen sitting on the kitchen counter.

"You threw it out." I clench my jaw. "Of all my shit, that's the thing you throw out."

"I might have. I did a purge in your room, getting rid of random junk."

He knew it wasn't random junk. He saw me put that bracelet on before every game.

"Why do you need it? For that beer league you're in?"

"Yeah," I say confidently.

"How's it going?"

"It'd be going a lot better if I had my bracelet."

"If you need a fucking bracelet to win against a bunch of amateurs, then you're in deep shit." He gets up and takes his dinner to the trash. He washes his cutlery in the sink, dries it, and puts it back in the drawer.

"Griffin Harper is in the league."

Dad's back tenses up. The muscles flex in instant fury.

"When you told me the story of what happened, you left out the part about gouging the other player's eye out."

"He charged at me!" Even now, as a full-grown adult, hearing Dad yell makes me want to cower in fear as if I'm still a little kid. "I had no time to move!"

"You never apologized to him."

"Because I didn't do anything wrong!" Dad wipes his hands and throws the dishtowel on the counter. He squirms from the movement. We rarely had father-son catches because of his shoulder. Maybe that was for the best since he would've been critiquing my pitching the whole time. "At least he can still play."

"It's amazing. He's not bad for only having one functioning eye."

"You're a fan?" Dad asks, disgusted.

"No." A flush of heat creeps up my neck. "I haven't played against his team yet."

"You can't let him beat you, Jack," he says with the seriousness of a father sending his boy off to war. "A professional hockey player getting beat by a middle-aged, one-eyed has-been? It's pathetic."

"Thanks for the vote of confidence."

He puts his hand on my shoulder, a sign of paternal affection that sends a chill through my body. "He is not your friend, Jack. He's not your league mate or drinking buddy. That man took everything away from us."

His voice is fragile and laced with pain. I let his hand stay on me a moment more before shrugging it off. I have a low tolerance for father-son bonding. "Noted."

———

I PLAYED that Sunday without my lucky bracelet and was as rusty as ever. Is it any surprise we lost?

Fortunately, the beauty of a recreational beer league is we can drown our sorrows at Easter Egg, a new arcade bar that opened up in downtown Sourwood. I sit around a big table with my teammates while the bright colors and symphony of arcade noises surround us.

Nobody in the Blades is that sad about our loss. We only talk about the game for a little bit, then the conversation moves to jobs, family, movies.

I can't help but feel an uncomfortable spotlight on me, though. Griffin said it himself: I am a ringer. When you put a former pro on your team, you expect results.

I excuse myself from the table, get some quarters from the bartender, and shuffle to the open Addams Family pinball machine straight out of the early '90s.

"Hey." Miller knocks my elbow, sensing my frustration and current party-pooper status. "It's all good."

"Yeah, I know." I stay locked into the game, fighting to keep the pinball from the gutter for a few more seconds. The last thing I want is a pep talk.

"It's just a game."

"Says the guy who unleashed a string of F-bombs at the player who was hooking you." Summers Rink bills the league games as "family-friendly events." Marcy had a word with Miller about his language.

"I'm a very passionate player," Miller says, inhaling a deep breath and chasing it with more beer.

"I didn't have my lucky bracelet. I've always played with the bracelet." The pinball careens into the gutter, right between my flippers, shutting me up. I can't blame my performance on a piece of lanyard, as much as I believe in good luck charms. "I sucked out there."

"You didn't suck," he says with little confidence. I arch my eyebrow at him, calling bullshit. "Fine, you're still a little rusty."

"When can I stop being rusty?" Is there WD-40 for this problem? Isn't rust irreversible anyway? Rusty machines don't become brand new no matter how much scrubbing you do.

"You need to get out of your head," Miller notes. "You're thinking too much."

"There's a first for everything," I joke. Though Miller might be onto something. I play best when I can focus on the game, but my head's been filled with so much shit lately. Finding a job. Figuring out what the hell I'm going to do with my life. Dealing with Dad's perpetual disappointment. And now Griffin has wedged his way inside my brain. Our conversation in the hangar and the night we met keeps playing in my head. Something about him instantly makes my thoughts untangle and allows me to admit things I've been too scared to say.

Oh, and his bare chest and belly play in a running loop in my head, too. As if I didn't have enough noise already.

"Fuck." I watch another ball fall into the gutter. Game over.

Miller rubs a spot on my back that he's sure holds all my tension.

"These things take time. You haven't played in a few years," he says.

"Neither have you guys."

"Trust the universe. It knows what it's doing."

"Miller, I love you, man, but I also want to punch you in the face when you say shit like that."

"That's fair." He sips his drink. "Can I play?"

Miller and I switch positions. He instantly locks into the game, his eyes narrowing at the pinball swirling through the game, a tiger ready to pounce on his prey.

I check my phone and find an email from Darlene at the airport asking me in for a second interview.

"Yo, I got a second interview." My heart fills with glee. Email is like a slot machine, and I landed on a jackpot. "I got a second interview!"

"No way! That's awesome! For the office manager job?" he asks, not taking his eyes off the game.

"Yeah. I thought I bombed that interview." I remember Darlene ushering me out of there so fast. It didn't help that a half-naked man was distracting me.

"Way to go, Jack." He tries to give me a high five while his eyes stay glued to the game. Miller winds up smacking me in the face, but it's a smack of pure love.

The more I think back on the interview, the more cringe moments pop up in my recollection. Did she really see potential in me after I sputtered through most of my answers?

"Shit!" Miller yells, his face turning cartoonishly red.

Shit is right. Because I keep reading her email.

While I know our first interview got off to a bumpy start, Griffin Harper in the mechanics department raved about you. He said you have a great work ethic. I'd love to bring you in to meet with some other people on the team as well as the GM.

"Oh, I got you motherfucker," Miller growls at the pinball.

I find myself in a growling mood, too.

"Griffin Harper said something to her. He told her how great I am and that she should give me a second look."

"That's awesome." Miller turns and checks out my reaction. "Or it's not awesome?"

Objectively, it is awesome. But the cognitive dissonance of Griffin is astounding. The man opens up to me and gets me to spill my guts for a second time. He acts like he wants nothing more than to kiss me, batting his dark eyes and shooting me the cutest grin known to man. Then he rejects me *for a second time.*

And then he goes to bat for me with Darlene?

What? Ex-fucking-cuse me? Do you like me, do you not like me? You want me thrown out of the league, yet you lobby for me to be your coworker?

Fuentes joins our gathering with shots. "What's going on?"

"This game is a FUCKING PIECE OF SHIT," Miller yells as the warbled game-over noise plays from the pinball machine. "Gomez Addams, I will FUCK YOU UP."

I can practically see the steam coming out of his ears, and I'm right there with them. The source of my anger isn't a pinball machine, but a guy who keeps slipping through my flippers like a dastardly shiny, silver pinball.

Miller shuts his eyes and takes deep breaths en route to his happy place. I prefer to marinate in my righteous anger.

"Well, I know why *he's* angry, but what's up with you?" Fuentes asks me.

"Griffin inserted himself into my job search," I say with disdain. I take my shot and Miller's shot in quick succession. "I have a second interview."

"That's great!" Fuentes takes his shot then begins playing the pinball machine. "You should send him a thank you."

"I shouldn't thank Griffin Harper for anything. The guy gives more mixed signals than a broken traffic light."

"Are we still talking about the interview?"

"After the interview, we almost kissed. Until Griffin very pointedly said 'no thanks.'"

"So he's not interested. His loss." Fuentes's tongue peeks out from his lips as he gets into the game.

"Is he really not interested? I can't tell."

"Uh oh. Jack Gross found a guy who doesn't immediately give it up. No wonder your head looks like it's going to explode." Fuentes finds way too much joy from my personal life.

"Griffin isn't playing hard to get. He's playing some other game with no clear-cut rules. I am tired of him meddling in my life."

Miller returns, face a normal shade of color. "Okay, I'm back. What did I miss?"

"Jack's desire to jump Griffin's bones is eating him from the inside."

"Fuck you, Fuentes." I storm back to the table and say good night to the rest of the team. I take two shots someone left and bolt out of there.

The cold air and alcohol work to clear my head, or try to. But goddamn Griffin is still in there, playing his games with no rules. Why does he have to be so fucking attractive and sweet and thoughtful? It only makes the rejection sting more. Does he think I'm not good enough for him?

I wander down the main drag of Sourwood. Most stores are closed. Lampposts and neon signs of bars light up the night.

Miller says to trust the universe. Well, the universe is quickly proving herself to be a bitch who can't be trusted. Because when I glance down an alley, I spot a familiar pickup truck.

What the fuck is the universe trying to say with this?

I burp and then narrow my eyes at the car as I laugh to myself. I don't know what the universe has up *her* sleeve, but I have a plan of my own.

16

GRIFFIN

It's a good thing our friend owns Stone's Throw Tavern, or else we'd probably get thrown out by this point. The Comebacks are still on a high from our squeaker of a victory at today's game against the God Squad, a team made up of ministers and rabbis from the area.

"It was beautiful. A thing of beauty. It should be in a museum." Bill hoists his beer in the air, and we cheer, glasses clinking against each other in a joyous mishmash.

He's talking about the epic game-winning shot courtesy of Des and Tanner. They had a remarkable opening where they sped down the ice, passing the puck back and forth like a slingshot between their sticks, where Tanner took a shot. The puck sailed into the upper corner of the net. If the goalie had been a tenth of a second quicker, he could've blocked it.

Des and Tanner take in the acclaim. Tanner is more modest. Des, not so much. He motions for Bill to keep talking.

"So what you're saying is that it was the Mona Lisa of passing," Des says, not one to shy away from hyperbole.

"Something like that. I just watched that puck go back and forth.

The God Squad couldn't keep up. It was...it was just like old times," Bill says, a twinkle in his eye. "You still have that old magic."

"Nobody's old here," Des says, throwing back a martini.

Back in high school, Des and Tanner were dynamic twosome on the ice, their passing coordination getting past the heaviest defense. They were so in sync, it was as if they could read each other's minds about where to go on the ice.

"It's a good thing Des is so predictable. That way I always know where the puck will end up," Tanner says, shooting him a playful sneer.

"And it's a good thing that I'm always one step ahead of Chance." Des clinks his drink against Tanner's pint glass, matching sneer for sneer. "It keeps Dear Old Dad on his toes."

"Thanks for making me such a great player, buddy," Tanner says, his eyes staying on Des. He was never one for trash talking.

"Likewise," Des shoots him a wink. Tanner turns back to his drink, but I clock Des's eyes staying on him for an extra second. After decades of friendship and teamwork, they have a strong bond that's heartening to see.

"Aww. Kiss!" Hank says before breaking into a laugh. "Kidding!"

Mitch shuffles up to us, replenishing our peanut bowl. "Congrats on the win."

"How's the back?" Bill asks.

"It's getting there. Definitely by next season."

"Mitch, what are you doing?" Charlie, his much-younger husband, races up to him, panicked. "The doctor said you shouldn't be carrying anything heavy."

"It's a peanut dish," Mitch says.

"Those peanuts are unshelled. They're much denser in weight." Charlie takes the dish from him and massages his back. "Physical therapy is going great. Mitch is making progress. We're taking walks. He's going to be back on his feet in no time, so long as he follows the doctor's orders. No lifting heavy objects." Charlie points his accusatory eyebrows his husband's way.

"I didn't know I married a drill sergeant."

"You love it." Charlie gets on his tiptoes to give his husband a kiss.

Mitch and Charlie have a sizable age gap between them. Charlie used to date Mitch's daughter in college. But they work. They are totally in love. When I see them, I can't help but think of Jack. And kissing him.

Or not kissing him.

He is testing all of my willpower. Finding out that he's Ted Gross's son has made my attraction to him even more fraught.

"Okay, I have to go." Tanner stands up and finishes his drink. "My mom needs to get home in time to watch *60 Minutes*."

Tanner better thank his lucky stars that his mom is still alive and able to babysit his kids. Carmen and I never had that opportunity, and babysitters in Sourwood aren't cheap.

Eventually, the guys start to go home. I should join them. While I loved celebrating the victory with my team, it felt unearned. I barely contributed. I still haven't gotten my groove back.

I say my goodbyes. Bill walks me to the door.

"Good game," he says.

"Bill, don't bullshit me. I was the weak link on the ice today."

He seesaws his head, being careful with his following words. "You're still finding your mojo."

"Hopefully it shows up soon."

"It will." Bill gives me a no-nonsense stare. "It will. You have all the tools. You just gotta remember to use them."

The advice is a bit confusing, but so is playing with lost mojo. Too bad I can't travel back to the 1960s to get it back from Dr. Evil.

I stroll through downtown Sourwood, breathing in the night air. It's nice to be outside in the quiet after being crammed into a loud bar. Moonlight makes everything prettier.

I always park in the same spot in the alley between the bookstore and kids' shoe store. It's quiet, close, and nobody thinks to park here.

Yet when I turn the corner into the alley, I find that I'm not alone. A man stands next to my truck, his back to me.

"Can I help you?" I ask.

"Shit," he whispers, but he doesn't move. Between his legs, I see a line of piss trickle down my driver's side car door.

"What the hell are you doing? There's a public restroom down the street," I tell the man, even though we both know it's too late for that.

You don't take a whiz on someone's car. Save that shit for the sides of buildings.

He says nothing, probably too embarrassed, his frame shrouded in moonlight.

"Stop!" I yell.

He ignores me. The trickle speaks for itself.

I get closer, ready to hurl him onto the main sidewalk. A streak of light from the nearby lamppost provides some illumination. His features come into focus as I approach.

Blond hair, broad shoulders, bubbly ass.

"Jack?" I ask, horrified. "What the fuck are you doing?"

17

JACK

"This is payback." I feel my smile get so big it hits my ear lobes. "For what?"

My brain stops, trying to figure out the right answer. The brilliant idea and my chain of logic don't make it to my mouth. I begin to realize that not getting nookie on a rooftop is no justification for pissing on a guy's car.

But I can't give him the satisfaction of my contrition. I go defiant instead.

"You know what."

"I actually don't." Griffin gets closer but also knows that no man can stop another man mid-stream.

I shake out the last drops and tuck my dick back in my pants. I wipe my hands on my shirt and turn around. "What's up?"

"You fucking asshole. You pissed on my car."

"You did this to yourself!" I yell. The alcohol has fully taken over my brain. I step around him, but Griffin hooks his thick fingers onto my arm and pulls me back. His hot touch burns up my skin, sending shivers of lust raging through my system.

"What did I do? Tell me what I did, Jack."

"You talked to Darlene about me."

"Yeah," he says, confused. "I put in a good word."

"I don't fucking get you!" I push him back, my hands on his broad chest. "You're in my head, and I hate it!"

He pulls me close, his hand staying firmly fixed on my arm. "You're in my head, too! You think I want that?"

"I don't know what you want. I took you to a beautiful rooftop and you pushed me away! I never take guys there because it's special! I took you there because I wanted to experience it with you, even though I just met you, and you...you said thanks but no thanks. You're an asshole! When my bladder refills, I'm coming back here and pissing on the other side of your truck."

Griffin doesn't say anything, leaving me unnerved. His hand digs into my arm, sending more lust shivers through my traitorous body. His eyes are on fire, blazing with intensity as the flames lick at the pit of my core.

Thunder rumbles through the sky. Lightning crackles across the darkness, but it can't match the electricity between us.

"Fucking kiss me already," I spit out, seething with fury.

Griffin tugs me against him, leans his head down, and delivers the most epic kiss of my life as the sky cracks open, unleashing a downpour.

He smashes his lips on mine, making me remember all over again what a great fucking kisser he is. But it's different this time. There's no hesitance, no sweetness. It's heat. It's need.

His lips are fucking magic. Warm and salty with the bitter taste of beer on his tongue. I breathe in his scent, wanting him in all the worst ways. His beard scratches my smooth cheek as his tongue explores my mouth.

Rain soaks through my clothes and my hair. My hands canvass across his broad shoulders, the muscles popping through on his arms, wet clothes hugging even tighter to his thick body.

He shoves me against the brick wall of the alley as his hands dig through my hair, pulling me against him.

"You okay?" he asks, his hand caressing the back of my head.

"Of course I'm fucking okay." I resume kissing, our tongues

tangled in lust. I unleash a moan as he gives my pointed nipple a quick pinch through my soaked shirt.

I finger the strap of his eye patch behind his head as his coarse hair bristles under my pads. His eye patch rubs against my cheek slightly, a new sensation that makes me want to hold him tighter.

I rut against his leg like a hopeless, horny, stray dog. I don't want to give him the satisfaction of knowing he gets me hard in two seconds flat, but I'm way past thinking rationally.

"Is this what you fucking want?" he growls under his breath.

"You wanted it first. Staring at me across the bar."

His hot breath dances on my lips. I scrawl my fingers through his beard.

"You and your fucking beard," I mutter against his lips. "You should shave this fucking thing."

"Not until the end of the season, Ringer."

"Call me Ringer again, you fuck."

He smiles at me but says nothing. What did I tell you? Asshole.

Griffin pushes up one of my legs, letting our bodies get closer as rain streams down our faces and clothes. His woodsy cologne and manly scent, a bit of permasweat mixed in, gets me dizzy with desire. His hands press into my back as I'm pulled flush against his chest. His cock digs into my hip, taunting me.

I grip his cock over his jeans. He lets out a raspy moan and hisses into my mouth. I can get drunk all over again on these noises.

"This is the part where you usually run off," I say.

He stares at me, his eye blown wide and heavy lidded, the lust raging through him just as strong as it is with me. Good, it should be. I should always elicit raging lust within this man.

I stroke my hand over his cock, back and forth, giddy with the thickness I can detect. He puts his hands on my chest, a little unsure, maybe a little scared, which catches me off guard. There's a hesitant exploration. It's a moment of tenderness in this tornado.

I unbutton my shirt and let him put his hands on my bare chest, heat and want sizzling inside me as his fingers slip over the light hairs around my pert nipples, which are as hard as my cock. He gives them a firmer pinch than before, forcing me to throw my head back and moan.

My breath pounds in my ears. My lungs can't keep up. I want him to split me open. I need his touch. We are on a road with nothing but green lights.

"I'm going to give you the best fucking blow job of your life," I say, the statement coming out as a threat.

"You better."

Fucker.

I shove him backward until he's up against his truck. I get on my knees, landing in a puddle, but I'm already soaked. The rain makes his shirt stick to his chest and belly, emphasizing each muscle, each lump. I grip his cock through his jeans.

"You're not running this time," I warn him as I unbutton his jeans. He doesn't stop me, nor does he stop me from unzipping his fly. A lamppost above illuminates us, providing just enough light to navigate pulling his cock from his boxers. He tries to help, but I shove his hand back. I can't trust he's not going to end this. If he really wanted to end this, he could.

His hard cock juts out. Fuck, it's bigger and better than I dreamed about. Yes, I did dream about it and might've been late to practice one morning from cranking it in bed. He's unabashedly hairy down there, almost like he wants someone to dare ask him to clean up.

"We should probably go somewhere—" Griffin starts.

I shove his cock in my mouth, refusing to let him finish that sentence. If we move from this spot, the moment could be over. He could bolt. We have to get this over with and out of our systems.

That's what this is. Getting out of each other's heads by giving head.

He throws his head back against his truck, letting out a groan silenced by the pouring rain. For my ears only.

I take his cock down my throat, letting its salty heat shudder through me. I reach up his shirt and land on his hairy gut. I push down to the base, letting him completely fill my mouth.

"Suck me, Jack."

I swirl my tongue over his crown. "You better be liking this."

He unleashes a groan that rivals the thunder in volume.

I suck him hard and fast, knowing that some lovely couple could walk past the alley any second and stumble upon us. That fact makes me even hornier.

He pulls his cock out of my mouth. Rude. He smacks it on my tongue.

"How badly have you wanted this, Ringer?"

"Not as bad as you," I shoot back.

"You want this cock?" He holds my chin back, fucking wagging his dick in my face. Which sadly, only makes me want it more.

He lifts up his heavy shaft. "Lick these nuts."

I take a ball in my mouth, then go to the other. I can feel their heaviness, full of come. They're musky, manly, a mix of sweat and rain coating them. He jerks himself while I lap up each ball.

"I'm going to make you come so hard." Another threat escapes my lips.

"You're going to swallow every last drop," he growls at me, sending a bolt of heat exploding between my legs.

"You can't fucking tell me what to do," I say before taking his cock again. He juts his hips out to give me a better angle.

"Hands off," he says. I drop my hands to the side, and Griffin grabs a fistful of hair in each hand and fucks my face.

"Take it," he commands.

The feel of his cock filling my mouth, precome bitter on my tongue mixed with the hard taste of rainwater that drenches us. I lose myself in the rhythm, in the waves of lust rolling off both of us. His burly hands tighten around my hair as he pulls me closer, rutting into my mouth.

"Fuck. I'm coming." He lets go at the last minute, as if giving me a last minute choice to back away if I wanted. I'm not going anywhere.

He unleashes a guttural moan that rips from the deepest part of his chest as he empties himself down my throat. I swallow every last bitter drop of come, leaving no stone unturned in my quest to right the wrongs of the rooftop.

He falls back against his truck, holding his cock at the same time. The rain glistens on his meaty thighs. I wipe all residual glimmer of blowjob off my lips.

"Glad we could finally get that out of our fucking systems." I stand up and walk away, leaving Griffin slumped against his car.

18

GRIFFIN

It's kid chaos at my house a few days later. The girls are running around the backyard with Tanner's kids, playing some game that's a mix of tag plus make-believe divided by red rover. In their world, the game has a rigid set of rules impenetrable to us adults.

I think I prefer kid chaos to the chaos swirling inside my head after that drive-by blow job I got from Jack. My body is still on fire from the hookup, flashes of sizzling heat sliding over my skin as I think back to Jack's mouth on mine, his lips stretched around my cock.

Well, my first time doing anything with a guy was memorable, at least.

Tanner and Des have come over to help me with building the ice castle treehouse for the girls. We're putting up the walls today, then I'll paint. I found a soft blue color and glitter additive that'll give the structure a shimmy, icy look. Luckily, today is one of those late winter days that's been more like spring, sunny and warm enough to be outside.

"Did you see the email from Bill?" Tanner asks as he lines up another board, which Des screws in with the power drill. They have a system down. "We have to go to the rink tomorrow morning."

"Our old practice time?" I ask. The time we wanted before Jack beat me for it. "Will the Blades be there?"

"I assume so." He shrugs, out of information.

"I wonder if they tattled about all the pranks." Des, whose phone has been in his hand the entire time we've been working, clicks to the email and reads it aloud. "All Comebacks are asked to attend a quick meetup tomorrow morning at the tail end of the Blades' practice. Yadda yadda, yadda. Blah, blah, blah." Des screws in the nail with the power drill. "That's weird. I play hockey to avoid pointless meetings."

"Do you think Jack is mad about the pranks?" Tanner passes me a plank of wood to nail into the structure. "You two are oil and water whenever you're around each other."

Or maybe we're oil and a match, engineered to explode on impact. My stomach does a roller coaster loop at how combustible we were.

"I don't think it's that," I say.

"You think he's still getting back at you because of his dad?" Tanner asks, aiding me in lining up the plank, a minor difficulty with having one functioning eye.

"No. Jack and I are just opposing teammates."

Des studies my face like one of those quirky detectives on TV who can walk into a crime scene and tell the police exactly what happened.

"Heads!" yells Tanner's son Dean as a kickball whizzes by. Tanner catches it an inch from my face.

"Dean, watch where you're playing." Tanner throws it back to him.

"Sorry." He grabs the ball and races back to the kids.

Des swings the power drill around his finger, a confident smile on his lips. "You know, in my job, I'm involved in high-stakes negotiations. Millions of dollars on the line. It's made me really good at reading the people across from me and deciphering when they're holding back information."

"What's your point?" I grumble.

"You and Jack fucked."

"Des!" Tanner shushes him, nods at the kids not too far away.

"My bad. You and Jack forked."

"We didn't...do that." I think about denying, but my friends would never believe me. And when it comes to sex, Des is fucking clairvoyant. "We did things adjacent to that."

"You finally kissed a boy, and you liked it?" Des asks.

I nod yes.

Des and Tanner hi-five each other, then surround me in a victory hug not unlike what happens when we win a game. They better not think about hoisting me up. I give them a minute to revel then push them back.

"What happened, Daddy?" Annabelle asks me.

"Your Daddy hit a very important, long overdue, milestone," Des says. "He made a new friend."

She gives me a thumbs up.

"Annabelle, why don't you go back to playing? Have you shown the kids your new bracelet?"

She perks up with a fresh wave of excitement and skitters off. I sigh in relief when she's out of earshot. I don't need my dad life and sex life to ever intersect.

"How was it?" Tanner asks. "Everything you thought it would be?"

"Better," I say without hesitation. Better can't even describe how thoroughly reality outstripped expectations. I'd been so scared about hooking up with a guy because I didn't think I'd know what to do. Nobody likes being a forty-four-year-old newbie with anything, much less sexual prowess. Jack pulled me out of my head, though. In that alley, I didn't think. I just did. I let myself get taken over by the moment, let myself take what I wanted from Jack without a thought to the future. A flash to grabbing Jack by the hair and bobbing him on my dick comes to mind, sending a shiver of lust tearing through my chest.

"I'm really happy for you, man." Des claps me on the back.

"How could you tell?" I ask.

"You seem different. A man with the answers to all the secrets in the universe."

I know Des is kidding. He's not that perceptive. But despite my nonstop thinking about Jack, I do feel a kind of invincibility that I can't explain. Maybe this is why teens and twentysomethings can be cocky shits. They think having sex unlocks a new plane of being.

"So when are you seeing him again?" Tanner holds another piece of wood that Des drills in. Des blows the top of the drill when he's done.

"Well, I'll see him at the meeting tomorrow. And aside from that, probably never."

Their shoulders slump at the news.

"It was one-time thing. We had to get it out of our systems."

"No, you don't. It's not gonorrhea. He's young, dumb, and obviously full of come. Carpe that diem. You need to make up for lost time," Des says as his phone buzzes with another notification.

The thought of getting to hold Jack in my arms, to taste his lips, makes me dizzy with want all over again. But the way Jack left as soon as I blew my load down his throat clearly means it was a one-and-done thing for him.

"Just keep this between us. The last thing I need is this getting out, for multiple reasons."

Tanner gives me a salute. Des revs the power drill, which I'm assuming is a yes from him.

June walks around the treehouse, inspecting our work with a shrewd gaze.

"How's it looking?" I ask.

"I'm liking what I see," she says with a hedge, though her beaming eyes tell me she's absolutely in love. She points to an opening above Tanner. "That window needs to be bigger."

"Bigger?" he asks.

"Like a balcony, where I can greet my royal subjects," she explains with utmost seriousness.

He looks at me, and I give the nod of approval. We'll make sure the window sill is tall enough that she or Annabelle won't fall out.

"Done," Tanner tells her with a little salute.

She marches over to Des who is absorbed in typing something on his phone. She clears her throat. It takes him a moment to look up.

"Yes?" he asks.

"Mom and Dad say excessive screen time is bad for you," she tells him. "You've been on your phone a lot today, Mr. Des."

"Screens are only bad for kids. Adults have superpowers that allow them to be on phones however long they'd like." When he doesn't have a hockey stick in his hand, I've noticed that Des is usually glued to his phone. He claims he's constantly having to email people for his job, but when I glance over, more often than not, I find him on social media or Milkman, a gay dating app.

"Humans don't have superpowers," she says back.

"Pretend superpowers."

"If it's pretend then it isn't real." June is nothing if not coldly logical. "Isn't it dangerous to be on your phone while working with sharp tools? Isn't that a bad example you're setting?"

I glance at Tanner, who's seconds away from bursting out with laughter. June could have a very successful career as a prosecutor.

She crosses her arms. Des's eyes widen slightly as he realizes my little girl is serious. That's the thing with kids: they have a knack for being blunt without warning.

"F-fine." Des slides his phone back in his pocket. He waves his empty hand at June for proof.

"Good. Now everyone back to work!" June yells.

"June," I say sternly.

"Please," she adds.

Tanner gives her a stealth thumbs up. June waves goodbye to us. She points to her eyes then to Des before running back to the other kids.

"Did I just get my ass handed to me by a kid?" Des wonders.

———

THE NEXT MORNING, I get to Summers Rink and find my teammates waiting in the front lobby. The Blades are practicing on the ice. I spot

Jack pull his stick back and slam a shot into the empty goal. My stomach takes another spin on an upside-down roller coaster.

I need to hook up with more men. A lot more men. That will help my lust for Jack fade away. Or it could make me measure every man against him and find none of them compare.

"What the fuck are we doing here?" Derek asks.

"Good question. Your buddy the mayor wanted to talk to us. That's all I know." Bill wipes the remaining sleep from his eyes.

"Do you think we're getting a key to the city? Would we each get a key?" Hank asks. "How heavy do you think those keys are?"

None of us have the energy to answer his questions. Leo waltzes through the rink's entrance in a black peacoat over a crisp shirt and slacks. A part of me wonders if he sleeps in a suit.

"Morning!" he says to us.

"Leo, what the fuck is this about?" Derek asks. Fortunately, they're childhood friends so he's allowed to throw an F-bomb the mayor's way.

"Follow me." His smile is chipper, the wheels turning behind his eyes as he walks past us to the rink. He whistles through his fingers to get the Blades' attention. They stop their practice and skate to the edge of the ice.

"I hope you don't mind that I crashed your practice," Leo says.

"It's cool. We're just wrapping up." Jack takes off his helmet, his hair thick and shiny with sweat, red lips popping against the bright white of the ice. He is just as sexy as he was the other night. I truly don't know how I'll resist him, but if I can live life without my left eye, I can make it without Jack Gross.

Our eyes meet for a millisecond before he returns to the mayor.

"I wanted to discuss an idea I had." Leo warms up his hands and stands on the bottom bleacher. Being a politician, the man can't help but always go for the best angles. "Most of the guys on the Comebacks are local legends. Over twenty years ago, they played together at South Rock High School where they won back-to-back state championships, the only time that's happened in the school's history. The Wolf Pack. You were and still are legends. And you're showing all of us that your hockey days aren't over. Far from it." Leo claps for us. He's the only one that does.

He clears his throat to continue. "And the Blades are also made up of champions. Dominick Miller and Jay Fuentes played at Briar Hills High, part of the team which also won a state championship a few years back."

My teammates and I roll our eyes at "a few years back."

"And then we have Jack Gross."

Leo points to Jack like he's the grand prize on a game show. Jack's cheeks are still red from playing, but there's a shade of blush mixed in.

"MVP at Briar Hills two years in a row. He was the force behind that championship. Number one player with goals and assists. And then of course, Jack was drafted and then played in the NHL for four seasons. He's an actual pro hockey player."

Jack looks like the acclaim is a medieval torture device on him.

"You brought us out here to run through our resumes?" Bill asks.

"I'm getting to my point."

"Could you get there already?" Bill is never one for bullshit, no matter who it's coming from.

"We have two generations of local athletes. And a professional hockey player. It's a perfect battle of young" —he points to the Blades before pointing to us— "versus old."

"Thanks," deadpans Hank.

"So what I propose is changing up the game schedule and setting what I call a Sourwood Face Off: a special charity game of the old guard vs. the new guard. The Comebacks vs. the Blades. We promote it as a big event, get the whole town out. All ticket sales can go to charity. The Wolf Pack versus the young guns. The amateurs versus the pro. What do you think?"

My teammates and I share glances of uncertainty. None of us want to lose on such a public stage, in front of everyone we know. We don't want to prove people's assumptions right, that hockey is a young man's game. And I can't help but think this is a disaster in the making for myself especially. I'm still rusty, very rusty.

"Let's do it." Jack steps forward, confident as ever. "That is, unless the Comebacks don't feel comfortable with it."

"Game on," Bill says without hesitation. He shakes Jack's hand. This time, I feel Jack's eyes on me, but I can't meet his.

Bill's determination lights a fire that spreads to all of us. We may be old, but we are still as competitive as fuck, and we play to win.

"Excellent. We'll set up the game for a month from now." Leo claps his hands in victory. Him with his darn PR wins. "This is going to be great. A charity hockey game targeting multiple demographics of Sourwood residents."

"Nothing cynical about that at all." Des raises an eyebrow.

Leo throws his coat over his shoulder and leaves. The Blades and the Comebacks stare each other down.

"We look forward to kicking your ass," Jack says, winking at us. Although that wink feels specifically targeted to me.

19

JACK

That afternoon, I take an Uber to my second interview at the airport. I'm a bundle of nerves for two reasons. One, the job, obviously. It would be nice not watching my savings dwindle like sand running through an hourglass. But also, I'm going to see Griffin again. In his gray jumpsuit. Oh, that fucking gray jumpsuit. It's like the jockstrap of uniforms.

I tap my finger against the window as the car drives down the wooded road to the airfield. The driver eyes me through the rearview mirror.

Why is it that I'm more nervous about seeing Griffin than I am about nailing this interview? Is it because I can't stop thinking about the possibility of getting nailed by him?

Griffin and I had unfinished business...which we finished in that alley the other night. I finally caught the guy who slipped through my fingers. I finally got confirmation that yes, he finds me attractive and yes, he is hung like a rhino. He made me wish I had the ability to unhinge my jaw.

I should do what I always do after I hook up with a guy. Move on dot org. Especially now that Griffin and I are facing off in this big charity game. It's been less than a day, and already the mayor had a graphic made up and posted about the Sourwood Cup across the town's social media channels.

A deep breath exhales from my lungs as the woods clear and the airport comes into view. I'm trying a calming breath exercise recommended by Miller. I want Griffin, but I need this job. Or do I want this job but need Griffin?

Single engine planes and a few private jets dot the tarmac. The driver pulls into the parking lot.

I take one more calming breath, for the job and for Griffin. Technically, I don't have to see him. I can go straight into the office. Yet I know on an instinctual level my body will not allow that the same way it won't allow me to gingerly walk off a cliff.

The driver clears his throat, my cue to get the fuck out.

"Thanks," I mutter.

I puff out my chest and stroll into the hangar, feeling cool and relaxed. When in doubt, fake it 'til you make it.

In the center of the hangar is the largest plane at this airport by far, and the most noticeable. I've never seen a pink airplane. On the side of it "Penelope Towne" is painted in big, swoopy letters. That sound you hear is every girl I went to high school with screaming in jealousy.

A burly patch of gray on the left wing stands out amid the pink.

A familiar swelling takes place between my legs.

It's just the jumpsuit, I tell myself.

"Hello up there!" I yell to Griffin. "Better make sure this plane doesn't crash. It'll be carrying precious cargo."

A slight smile curls onto his face revealing a sliver of white teeth, his beard crinkling around his lips. It's so fucking yummy.

He peers past me to the parking lot. "Did you take an Uber here?"

My driver peels away, a giant Uber sticker visible on his bumper.

"Fancy," Griffin says.

"I'm saving up to get my car fixed." I don't need to delve into that mortifying aspect of my life, a pro athlete who can't even afford new brakes. I point to the plane. "You a Penelope Towne fan?"

"Can't say I'm familiar." Griffin steps back onto the scissor lift and comes down to my level. His uniform pulls across his chest and stomach, and I don't know which is hotter.

"She's good. Like Taylor Swift but with a harder edge, but like a corporately appropriate hard edge," I inform him. "She was a constant presence on my Spotify Wrapped in high school."

"What's that?"

I bulge my eyes, wondering if he's serious. Then I realize that my dad probably doesn't know what Spotify is either.

"It's like listening to her CD over and over."

He nods and wipes his thick, strong hands on a rag, the same hands that moved me around the other night like a puppet on a stage, telling me I was his and his alone in that alley.

I take another deep calming breath in the hopes that it can also keep boners at bay.

"So what do you think about this game?" I ask.

"The Sourwood Cup?" he says as he rolls his eyes.

"Are you sure you guys want to do it? I don't want to humiliate you in front of all your friends. Though, I will if I have to." Oddly, talking shit helps level me. It's how I get in the zone on the ice, bringing the most intimidating players down to size.

"Who says we're the ones that'll be losing?" He crosses his arms, making his muscles bulge. I have to admire his confidence, even though it's ridiculous.

"Nature. Science. We're younger and faster."

"We have decades more experience than you."

"Not all things get better with age."

"You sure about that?" he asks, his voice low and deep. It sends a bolt of heat to my dick that no calming breath could abate. I can't stop thinking about the feel of his body under my fingers. It wasn't hairless and tight like guys my age, all muscle and no personality. There was an added heft, a slight sag around his pecs and stomach, mature creases in his forehead. Yes to all of it.

I take a step back, away from this fine specimen of man. "Okay, then. It's not too late to back out. I have to warn you, I'm good."

Sure, I say this to brag, but after this morning's practice, it's also true. I was on fire today. My passes were sharper. I was faster on the ice. Cleaner shots. Miller and Fuentes both commented on the improvement in my game and that I was finally shaking the rust off. It's why I was so confident to accept the mayor's challenge.

Griffin laughs to himself. He tosses the rag on top of his tool chest. "Who are you meeting with today?"

"Alan something and Allison Lembeck?" I'm amazed I remembered their names since I haven't done any research on them.

"Alan Tudor and Allison Levitt?" he asks.

"That's it!"

"Alan is Darlene's boss. He loves airplanes. Ask him about his plane and flying to Nantucket. He'll chew your ear off about it all day. And Allison loves hockey. Her sons play in the peewee league. She'll probably spend the whole interview asking for pointers." I nod and take mental notes. "My guess is this interview is a personality check. Do we want to spend five days a week around this guy? All you have to do is charm them."

"I can do that. I charmed the pants off you."

"I recommend you keep their pants on." Griffin squats down and pulls a drill from the bottom drawer. My comment rolled right off his broad back.

"Thanks again for putting in a good word for me."

"You didn't seem grateful. You, uh, pissed on my truck."

I smack my hand on my forehead. Oh, right, the part of the night before we kissed. I'd blocked it out.

"I'm young and stupid?" I offer.

"You only have a few more years to use that excuse."

"Thank you. I appreciate it. I'm going to crush this interview." I find myself mustering fake enthusiasm, saying words my heart won't back up. But Griffin went out on a limb to keep my name in the conversation. I don't want to embarrass him.

"Yeah."

Apparently, I'm not the only one mustering fake enthusiasm. I follow Griffin to the opposite side of the plane where he takes another scissor lift to the right wing. He uses the drill to tighten some bolts.

"What does that mean?" I ask over the drilling.

"Huh?"

I wait until he stops, the drilling sound carving right into my head. "I said I'm going to crush this interview, and you were just like whatever. You've doubted the Blades can kick your ass, and now you're doubting I can kick this interview's ass?"

"I think you can crush it. But I don't think you want to."

I toss my head back to look up at him and scowl my objection. "Of course I do. You don't know shit."

Griffin is unfazed. In fact, he seems to find joy in my indignation.

"Can you come down? This is hurting my neck."

The scissor lift lowers to the ground. Griffin gets out and puts the drill away. "It doesn't seem like you want this job, to be honest. You don't even know who you're meeting with."

"I knew their first names."

When people lose a sense, their other senses are heightened. Did losing half his eyesight make Griffin able to read my thoughts? I'm quickly learning it doesn't pay to lie to Griffin. He makes me want to spill the beans.

"I really appreciate you helping me get this second interview. Look, this isn't my dream job, but I don't know what is. It was supposed to be hockey. I'm grasping at straws here. I just want to make enough money to pay my bills and fix my car, then I can take it from there. I promise if I get this job, I won't fuck it up and make you look bad."

I reach for his hand, his calloused fingers sending a charge up my arm. Griffin keeps studying me, but something behind his eye softens, like whatever stoic grip he has on himself loosens a tad.

"You're a fan of Penelope Towne?" He scratches at his beard. "You want to go on her plane?"

20

GRIFFIN

I've worked on tons of private planes. The wow factor wears off quickly once you realize it's the same seats you find on a commercial plane. Sometimes, like in Penelope Towne's plane, there's even a couch. But the couch isn't that comfortable. It's only cool because it's on a plane. The only real perks are not dealing with annoying passengers and having your own bathroom.

Jack's mouth is practically on the plush pink carpet.

"Ho-ly shit." He stumbles around as he takes it all in. The plane is as pink on the inside as the outside, down to the walls. Pink leopard print pillows are splayed across the couch.

Jack opens a fridge up front and snaps a picture.

"Don't post any of this." I don't want to lose my job.

"I'm not. This is for my own private memories." He picks up a can of La Croix. "Hey, we both like peach-pear!"

I motion for him to put it back. "Since you're a fan, I thought you'd want to take a look."

Jack sinks into one of the seats. He lets out a big aahhhh, even though it's likely not much more comfortable than a regular airplane seat.

"This is amazing." He pulls an eye mask from the pocket on the side. In big letters, AT is spelled out. "This is Alberta Towne's face mask! She's Penelope's overbearing momager."

"Weren't you on private planes when you were in the NHL?" I ask. It's very cute how impressed he is by all of this; I expected him to be a bit more jaded. From what I've read, NHL charter planes are very swanky.

"We all got first-class style seats. But there weren't couches like this." Jack collapses across the sofa as if lounging by the TV, his strong body taking up all the space. "We had to wear a suit jacket and dress pants whenever we flew. It's in our contract. And that shit isn't comfortable to fly in."

Jack adjusts the suit he's wearing, the same one as last time, still a size too small for him. The few times I've worn suits, I've ripped them off as soon as I could.

"Don't get me wrong. It is nice. Really nice," he continues. "But pretty soon..."

"The magic wears off?" I ask.

"Yeah. You're still stuck on a plane for a few hours."

I sit in the momager's seat. It's best that I don't sit on a couch with him. I don't trust myself to play nice. Not when I've been daydreaming about tearing his suit off since the second he strolled into the hangar.

I check my watch. "When's your interview?"

He checks his phone. "Like ten minutes."

"It'll take you two minutes or so to get to Alan's office."

"Perfect. Setting timer for eight minutes." Jack pushes the requisite buttons on his phone.

Great. I can withstand temptation for eight more minutes. Barely. Jack's ass looks fucking delicious in those pants. *I can do it.*

I don't know why I haven't gotten Jack out of my system yet. I can't dwell on that currently.

"Can I see the cockpit?" Just hearing the word *cock* escape his lips makes my pants tighten. The horny part of me wonders if he emphasized that syllable extra hard.

Less than eight minutes. Less than eight minutes.

"No."

"Are you afraid I'm going to accidentally turn on the plane?"

You're turning me on, and I doubt that's an accident.

Jack leans over the couch to strum the guitar on the floor. "You know Penelope is dating a hockey player? He plays for the Boston Smugglers. You ever wonder if they've had sex on this couch?"

Is there a button overhead I can press so that my heart stops racing at that question? Or one to eject me from the plane?

"Maybe Penelope's been on her knees right here, giving him a grade-A hummer."

"It's not something that's crossed my mind." Although, at the moment, it's all I can think about. Shoving Jack's head into my lap, his lips stretching around my cock again.

Less than seven minutes. Less than seven minutes.

"Maybe some flight attendant comes in, gets on his knees, and they take turns sucking him off." Jack leans back on the couch, opening his legs and imagining the scenario. He turns to me, flashing a dark smile that lets me know exactly what he's doing. "That'd be kinda hot, right?"

He adjusts himself over his pants, his thickening cock surfacing through the fabric.

"You know that she doesn't travel alone. She has a whole staff."

"They can watch." Jack rubs his length, then gives it a tug. At first, I hoped Jack talked a big game to make up for shortcomings, but I've seen with my own eye that his confidence is pure big dick energy.

My pulse quickens, throbbing wildly in my neck. I will my dick to stop stiffening, but it won't listen. It is fully under the control of Jack.

"Or maybe her bodyguards secretly have sex on this couch. Big guys sucking each other off." Jack's eyes hold me in place. He glances down at my crotch, where my erection pokes against my jumpsuit. An aura of victory envelops him.

Less than six minutes. Less than six minutes.

"What are you doing? Shouldn't you be prepping for your interview?"

"Probably." Jack strokes himself over his pants.

"You shouldn't be doing that," I tell him.

"Doing what?"

"Touching yourself." My tongue is thick and heavy in my mouth, each word more unsteady than the last.

"You're right. I should be touching you instead." Jack reaches out and palms my dick, unleashing a Hoover Dam amount of lust through every synapse of my brain.

"Jack," I hiss, but I don't push him away. I get more lightheaded with each stroke of my cock. "This was supposed to be a one-time thing."

"I know." Jack looks up at me with those crystal blue eyes. "But I decided I want more."

He leads me forward by my cock, and I sink to my knees. His erection sticks up in a conspicuous tent. I've never given head before. What if I fuck it up?

"Griffin, we only have five minutes. Get to work." Jack undoes his belt and pulls his cock from his boxers. It's thick and sticking straight up, fuzzy golden hairs around the base.

The first time I put on ice skates, I didn't wobble or fall like other kids in my class. My coach noted how quickly I found my balance. I feel that same innate balance as I take Jack in my mouth, the clean taste of his cock mixed with the bitter hit of precome at the tip.

Out the window, the entire hangar is visible. The plane is high enough that nobody should be able to look in...I think.

Jack throws his head back and arches so his cock fills my mouth. I bob up and down, getting him nice and slicked up, his dick wet and hot against my tongue.

"Good, good," Jack repeats. "Just like that."

Considering I'm a newbie at this, I relish the praise more than I should. He lets out a loud moan packed with unrelenting desire. Just then, I remember that the aircraft door is still open. Anyone could hear if we don't keep it down. Anyone could walk in.

That should make me want to stop, but it only makes me want to suck him harder and force louder moans from him.

Jack pulls out and slaps his cock on my tongue before sticking it back in. He cups a hand around the back of my head and pushes me down. I cough from putting the whole thing in my mouth.

"Good," he says, lighting up another happy button in me. "I don't want to boost your ego, but you give really good head. It feels so good with my dick in your mouth."

My tongue rides up his shaft and slinks around his head, licking up more precome. Jack sinks deeper into the couch.

"I love watching you take all of it." Since Jack's hockey career didn't work out, he should be a sports announcer, because his play-by-play is setting me ablaze. My body shakes with desire. My cock is so fucking hard if I shift the wrong way, I could blow my load.

Jack pushes down his pants and boxers to his knees. "I want to try something. I want you to eat my ass."

The ask immediately revs me up like a motorcycle engine. A torrent of heat rages within me. My mouth is practically watering.

Before I'm able to nod yes, Jack lifts his legs and hugs them to his stomach. He can probably see the excitement painted on my face. His white dress shirt spills to the side, his tie flipped over his shoulder, his pants and underwear bunched at his ankles. And in the middle of that chaos, the glorious eye of this storm, is his hole. It's the only pink I'm interested in on this plane.

I press the flat of my tongue against his opening and drag it slowly up until his balls are in my mouth. I've waited my whole life to know the salty, forbidden taste of another man, and even though the timer is counting down, I want to savor this. I want to savor Jack.

"Fuck. Yes. Your tongue feels so good on my hole." Jack's normally pale face is fully red, squeezed tight with pleasure, and maybe a little pain. That sitting position can't be comfortable.

I lick another stripe up his hole, this time letting my tongue circle his opening. Jack's muscles tense under my touch. His thick, trunk-like thighs flex, the carved muscles emerging under his ivory skin. I press my hands on his ass cheeks, leaving red finger marks.

I moan against his opening as my tongue circles the rim. "So hot."

"You like tonguing my hole?"

I growl my answer into his cheeks. I press inside him, feel his hole tighten around me.

"Fuck. No one's ever eaten me this good. It's making my fucking eyes water. Now stop teasing me and make me come," he cries out, the bossiest of bottoms.

I love it. I hold nothing back. I dart my tongue in and out of his hole, lapping up his heat. Above me, I hear the swishing of fabric as Jack feverishly jerks himself.

"I'm so fucking hard right now. Your tongue is making me so hard. I can't wait to come. I'm going to fucking come everywhere."

"Tell me when," I say, not wanting him to mess up his suit or this plane.

"I'll try. God," he cries out, whiny desperation lacing his voice. Big, cocky Jack reduced to rubble.

I lick my index and middle finger and slide them inside his wet opening as my tongue works the perimeter. His hole instantly tightens around them. My cock throbs in my pants, so heavy and hard, I don't know how the fuck I'll be able to walk out of this plane.

"Griffin. Oh my God, Griffin. Your fingers feel so good inside me. Finger-fuck me."

I get fast and rough, nailing his hole over and over, my thick fingers disappearing into his tight ass. I spit on his hole to keep it lubricated, and the noise from Jack as well as the friction has to be audible in the hangar because it's blaring in my ears. But I can't stop. My hunger for Jack knows no bounds. In that moment, I forget about the plane, the game, my job. All I want is him. His touch. His voice. His heat. It is all-consuming.

"Fuck, I'm coming. You're making me come," he squeals out.

Like throwing a blanket over a raging fire, I put my mouth on his dick just as he explodes. I swallow his manly seed. I give his still-hard cock a few more sucks before he unfolds himself and collapses, fully spent on the couch.

As if ordained by a higher power, at that second, his timer goes off.

"Time for your interview." I wipe my lips.

He nods, still in a daze. His pupils continue to be lust saucers, yet he manages to pull up his pants. I look down at my jumpsuit and notice that my cock is about to tear a hole in them.

"Actually, if you jog down the sidewalk, you can get to the lobby faster. You have an extra thirty seconds."

"To do what?" he asks, grinning at my hard-on.

I stand up and unbutton my jumpsuit as quickly as my fingers will allow. I whip my dick out and shove it into Jack's willing mouth. He tugs the jumpsuit and pulls me forward, sinking my rock hard cock deeper inside him.

"Take it," I grunt. "Take it."

I'm not as chatty as him. I get to the point.

I can't get enough of him and the magic of his tongue. Something about Jack unleashes a beast within me. I grab a fistful of his golden hair and yank so my cock is all the way inside him, making him gag.

He smiles up at me when I pull out, like he just got on his favorite roller coaster.

He strokes me as he sucks, and the sight of my cock disappearing into his pretty, dirty-talking mouth sends me over the edge. My balls draw and everything goes white as I cream down his throat.

Once again, he collapses back onto the couch, which I will definitely make sure to wipe down before my shift ends.

"Shit. Sorry," I say, worrying that maybe it was too much for him.

"Don't be sorry. I'm not looking for something tender. " Jack stands and tucks in his shirt. He smooths out his pants, although he can't get out all the wrinkles.

He checks the time on his phone.

"If you're late, blame me," I say.

"No need. I'll just explain that I always try to be punctual, but your mechanic decided to finger-fuck me into oblivion." Jack straightens his jacket and fixes the collar.

"You were the one—"

Jack puts his hand to my mouth. "Flustered is a very sexy look on you." He brushes his thumb over my bristly chin in a gesture that sends a dash of warmth through my veins. "I regret nothing."

"Good luck." I lean into him with a soft kiss that manages to crank up the heat, the taste of what just happened on each other's lips.

I plop into one of the plane's seats once he leaves. We are not allowed to lounge in any of our clients' planes. And though it's not in the employee handbook, I doubt we were allowed to do what Jack and I just did, either.

I glance out one of the windows and watch Jack jog out of the hangar. I smile to myself as he goes.

21

GRIFFIN

On Sunday, I roll into Summers Rink for the Comebacks' next game, slightly more confident than the previous week. Sure, I'm still nervous as hell. But it's a good, nervous energy. I'm juiced up with adrenaline and more excited to get on the ice than I have been all season.

The lobby of the rink is scattered with people who watched earlier games and some who came to see us. There're plenty of people I don't recognize, and it's fuller than expected. Whereas last week most of our scant audience were family and friends of the players, I get the feeling there are actual strangers here.

One of them, a gruff guy in a puffy winter coat, claps me hard on the back. "Sourwood Cup! Go get 'em!"

"Uh, thanks."

"I watched you guys back in high school. Kick some Gen Z ass!" He raises a fist in the air.

I half raise my fist back and keep walking to the locker room. It's been a long time since I had fans.

When I get to my locker, I tell my teammates about the encounter. They don't act shocked, since the same thing has been happening to them. People have been coming up and wishing them luck. One guy came up to Tanner at the urinal to give him playing tips for beating the Blades.

"What can I say? People love us," Hank says with zero modesty.

"I think it's great that people are getting invested. We need to harness that momentum," Bill says. He's always the first guy suited up. "The Blades just played before us. I watched some of it." He shakes his head, fighting the urge to get psyched out by what he saw. "There's a reason Jack Gross went pro. He's easily their top player. He has a great shot and good control of the puck."

He also is brilliant with dirty talk, a fact I keep to myself.

Bill shakes his fear away. That's what makes him such a great captain. He always knows how to get his focus back. "The Blades are good. There's no denying that. But that means we have to work harder. Each Sunday game we have is another practice, another way to improve our game." His eyes flick to me for a second. "We have the goods. So let's use them."

"In other words, let's not make asses of ourselves in front of the whole town," Des says.

"Exactly!" Derek says.

When we get onto the ice, I'm able to drown out the noise and pressure that Bill's trying not to instill in us. I focus on the game, on what I love about hockey, what I've missed about playing. The thrill of the puck careening off my blade. My skates gliding through the ice. The choreography of the perfect pass to the goal.

At the top of the bleachers, I clock a familiar blond. Jack watches us warm up. Or rather, watches me warm up, because whenever I look, I find his eyes on me. Even when my head is down, I can feel his presence.

His hair is still damp and shaggy, making him look extra adorable.

Bill corrals us to our bench and gives us one final pep talk. Today's game is against the Trouts, a bunch of guys from the outskirts of town who all fish together at a local pond where they'll play hockey when it freezes in the winter. Their beards are so long they scraggle through their face masks.

By the time both teams get on the ice for the puck drop, Jack is gone.

As soon as the puck drops, I become an immovable force on defense. Pretty much nothing gets through me. I deliver a perfectly timed poke check as the Trouts' forward tries to cut to the middle of the ice, knocking the puck away and preventing a dangerous scoring chance. I smoothly recover the puck and skate it out of my zone, threading a crisp pass to Des who breaks out down the ice and scores.

I continue winning puck battle after puck battle in my zone, tying up sticks in front of the net. I can tell the Trouts' forwards are pissed off as they barely get any shots on our goal, muttering expletives at me as their breakaways keep getting rejected. I'm able to anticipate passes before the opposing forwards can even make them and intercept multiple cross-ice passes.

In the final period, the opposing forward charges to the net. I skate in front of him as he takes his shot, the puck bouncing off my shin guard with such force I worry the gear is going to crack. I quickly recover and clear the puck with a sharp pass to Bill.

The game flies by in a joyous blur. It's the same euphoria I felt on those rare times when I studied for a test and knew every answer, where filling in the Scantron was a preordained victory lap. When the game ends, I don't want to get off the ice.

We win in a shutout, four-zip.

"Holy shit," Bill says to me in the locker room afterward. It takes a lot to stun Bill. His poker face is a default expression. "Griffin."

"Good game, right?" I ask.

"*We* had a good game. *You* had a fucking incredible game. Holy shit." Bill happily wears his expression on his face this time. He's as excited as my daughters when we put up the Christmas tree.

"You were on fire," says Des behind us.

"Griff's mojo is back!" proclaims Hank.

"I knew it would come back. It just needed some time," says Bill.

"I'll be honest. I didn't know if we had an ice cube's shot in hell of beating the Blades." Des takes off his gear, chucking it into his locker. "But now, I think we actually do."

To my surprise, nobody disagrees with that statement.

Bill grabs my cheeks, his eyes wide with glee. "Secret weapon: activated."

———

"Hey, what the hell are you…" Jack stops mid-sentence.

I push myself out from under his car and rub my hands off on my rag. I've raised it using a pair of jacks, which allow me and my creeper better access to the underbelly of his car. I'm even wearing one of my work jumpsuits. I have a suspicion that it turns him on.

I stand up from my creeper. Jack looks at me, the jacks, the toolbox, his car. He can't make sense of anything.

So this is what it takes to shut Jack Gross up, huh?

"That's my car," he says, pointing at the rundown, two-door vehicle that desperately needs to go through a car wash. He points at me, but has no clue what to say.

"You said you needed new brake pads." I pull the rounded pads from my toolbox. "Sometimes we have extra auto parts at the hangar. These should fit your make and model. They're ceramic, too, which typically last longer than metallic."

"Um. Okay." Jack's index finger is still pointed my way. "You're giving me new brake pads?"

"Yeah. The brake pads themselves aren't expensive. You're mostly paying for labor." Being a mechanic may not be a very lucrative job, but the amount of money I've saved not getting ripped off by other mechanics could probably pay for an Ivy League education for both of my daughters.

"How do you know where I lived?"

"I asked your teammate."

"And he told you?"

"I asked nicely." His teammate Fuentes made me promise that I wasn't coming over here to cause trouble. I assured him I came in peace. My reason for visiting Jack would be a net positive for both teams.

"How did you know which car was mine?"

I smack the "Puck Off" bumper sticker on his car. I lay back down on the creeper. "Can you hand me the metal wire brush? Your rotor is really corroded."

I push myself underneath the car again and hold out my hand. A few seconds later, Jack shoves the brush firmly into my palm. After putting on my goggles and dust mask, I get to work scrubbing the rust off his rotor, finding the shine under the grime. I hop out from under the car and continue scrubbing.

Eventually, Jack finds the extra metal brush and protective wear and scrubs at the rotors for the back wheels.

"I was going to get my car fixed," he says.

"I know. I had the parts and the time."

"Thanks." The word is filled with genuine emotion, a hidden tiredness coming off him.

"You don't want to drain all your savings on Ubers." I maneuver the brush between the bolts. Jack finds a stubborn patch of rust and scrubs hard, his forehead reddening with exertion.

"I wish my dad had taught me how to fix cars rather than play hockey. Is that how you learned?" Jack asks.

I give a terse nod. "Fixing up his hot rod was the last thing we did together before he died."

"I'm sorry."

When I'm working on a plane, there are times when I close my eyes for a second and the smell of the machinery sends me back to our family garage with my dad. We'd spend nearly every weekend working on his car, the hours sailing by, beer for him and Coke for me, classic rock on the radio. There was no greater high than the jittery anticipation of watching him turn the key in the ignition and the exhilaration of hearing the engine come to life.

"I'm grateful he taught me everything he knew about cars. When hockey didn't pan out and I lost all my college scholarship prospects, I needed a job. Luckily, you can fix cars with only one eye. I kept learning and worked my way up to fixing airplanes."

Even though my hockey path didn't work out, I hold out a sliver of hope that my old man would be proud to watch me work on massive jet wings and engines. Or maybe it would only disappoint him, wondering about my wasted potential.

"You're making your parents proud," Jack says. "How's this?"

I come over and slide my finger over the rotor. "It needs to be a little smoother."

Jack nods and reverts to rigorous scrubbing. Any rust on the rotor will compromise the new brake pads and make them less effective.

Mom and Dad are watching me from heaven, and I can't help wondering if they're proud of what they see. Their son was supposed to be a hockey star. That's what all the struggling was for. "I wanted to give my mom the life that we never had growing up."

"Fancy cars? A big house? Fur coats? Those things are overrated. They make you happy for a little bit, but not long. The high wears off pretty fast. And I'm sure you're aware of how much of a money pit a fancy car can be."

I chuckle as I scrub around a stubborn patch. People who owned sports cars were always shocked and appalled at how much it cost to fix them. They assumed we were ripping them off, but it was actually the manufacturer ripping them off with expensive parts.

I go over to Jack and feel his rotor. Nice and smooth. Like his bare ass.

"So why the hell are you fixing my car on a Sunday night?" he asks.

"Because I kicked ass this morning. I had my best game of the season by a mile. I wasn't in my head. I was nailing all of my shots and passes."

"You were in the zone," Jack says, something clicking for him. "I was, too."

"I heard you played great in the game before us."

"My teammates had been telling me I was rusty, but that I'd shake it off."

"Sounds familiar." I slide the new brake pad into the wheel I'm working on, then do the same for the other front wheel. "We need to keep the momentum going."

"What do you mean?"

"First rule of hockey: if something brings you good luck, you keep doing it."

Players grow out their hair and beard to caveman extremes. They eat the same foods. They listen to the same song on the way to the rink. It's all about keeping the good luck streak going no matter what.

I move to the back wheels and place the brake pads in then tighten the calipers.

"Are you talking about what I think you're talking about?" Jack asks.

I nod, knowing that it sounds both insanely crazy and supremely logical. "How else do you explain why we're suddenly both better players?" I walk over to Jack's wheel, the final one left. "I thought it was just something we needed to get out of our systems that one time. Or two times. But what if it unlocked something for us? We both had big wins. We should keep the good luck going."

"By fucking each other?"

"Yes," I say with utmost seriousness in my voice and a tightening in my pants. "People are actually talking about this game between our teams. We don't want to embarrass ourselves on the ice. We need to do whatever we can not to jinx ourselves."

"By fucking each other?"

Every time he says fuck, my dick jumps.

"I mean, yes. You didn't seem to hate it." His dirty talk and desperate moans echo in my head. I want more of them.

Jack clears his throat, a patch of blush emerging on his cheeks. "This is nuts."

"Is it any worse than guys who refuse to change socks for the season to keep up the good juju? Look, I'm not asking for your hand in marriage. I'm not even asking you to dinner, Ringer. I just want to win some games."

I also want to kiss him hard and feel his body clench and shake under my touch as he explodes with orgasm.

The taste of victory will be just as delicious as the taste of him.

I hand Jack the final brake pad, my finger slipping over his.

"I guess if it'll help us, then we should keep doing it." Jack slides the brake pad into place. "For the good juju."

22

JACK

I don't believe in luck. I believe that there is no rhyme or reason to why things happen or why people behave the way they do, and that no amount of prayer or tarot cards can explain the cruel twists of the universe.

Except when it comes to hockey.

Hockey is bound by a higher spiritual code with a strict checks and balances mindset. Every action we do or don't do can impact that balance and effect our game. Hence, to appease the hockey gods, I must get it on with Griffin Harper.

I'm sorry but I don't make the rules.

At first, I don't know when exactly we'll be hooking up next. Is that part of the good luck arrangement? Do we have to knock boots at a designated time or place? Now that Griffin fixed my car, I could easily pop over to the hangar and have him rail me on top of an airplane wing. Or we could meet up in the alley again so he could have his way with me with the mallet swinging between his legs.

Even though he was the one who brought up this idea, a part of me wonders how serious he was. Having a really good game can mess with a guy's head. Maybe when he got home, he realized that he didn't need me.

That might explain why I haven't heard from him since Sunday night. Time goes slower when you're unemployed. I could text him, but I don't want to find out that he had a change of heart. I'd rather this wild idea fizzle out and awkwardly avoid him at Summers Rink.

I get to the rink early Wednesday morning for team practice. A light drizzle falls on the grounds, puddles forming in the parking lot. In the locker room, I get myself in the zone. I have my own rituals for pregame preparation. Things I chant to myself. I try some of Miller's breathing techniques.

Fuentes walks to the center of the locker room, all business. "Guys, I talked to Marcy, and we're going to double up on practice time for the next few weeks. She was able to maneuver the schedule so we can practice on Friday mornings, too."

Some of the guys groan.

"Hey!" Miller yells before forcing himself to take a deep breath. He then hands the floor back to Fuentes.

"We need all the practice time we can get. Every day, I'm seeing posts people are sharing about the Sourwood Cup and how excited they are to watch the game. A reporter from The Sourwood Gazette wants to profile us for an article. This thing is taking off, so we need to make sure we're the best we can be. So if that means you can't go out Thursday night, tough."

The groaners shut up this time. I can feel eyes on me. As the former pro that is helping to generate buzz about the event, my opinion carries substantial weight.

"No problem, baby. Count me in," I say.

Fuentes gives me an appreciative nod. We head out the locker room onto the rink, the cold steaming off the fresh ice. As I'm about to put on my helmet, I spot Griffin by the snack stand. He nudges his head toward the locker room entrance.

"Give me one minute," I tell Fuentes. "I forgot my lucky bracelet."

"I thought you lost it."

"It's a new one," I say, my pulse beginning to quicken.

"Be careful. You don't want to fuck with good luck things in the middle of a season."

"I'm not. I know what I'm doing," I say as my dick hardens in my jockstrap.

Back in the locker room, I search the rows until I come to Griffin, leaning against the row of lockers farthest from the rink entrance.

The man knows how to lean. He wears a black hoodie that fits snuggly around his stomach and muscled frame.

"Hoping to see what a good hockey team looks like?" I ask.

"Just wanted to give you some good juju before you get out there." Griffin closes the gap between us and pulls me into a deep kiss. Even though I'm nearly as tall as him, and I'm wearing all my pads and gear, he scoops me into his arms like I'm a newborn kitten.

I melt into his kiss, his warm lips and scratchy beard making me dizzy with lust. Griffin pushes me up against the lockers, his tongue sweeping through my mouth. Through all my gear, I can feel the heat of his hungry hands. My cock strains against my protective cup, aching for release.

"We need to be quick," I say between dogged breaths. "I have to get back out there. I don't want them to come looking for me."

"Imagine the position they're going to find you in." Griffin arches an eyebrow.

He spins me around so my face is pushed up against the lockers. I push my ass out, desperate to know his plan, wanting whatever he can give me.

"Someone's horny." He chuckles, his deep voice vibrating against my neck.

Griffin reaches around and unties my hockey pants, his rough fingers brushing against my bare stomach, sending a hot chill coursing across my skin. He drags them down, then my mesh shorts and long underwear. The cold air hits the bare skin of my ass with a sting.

He growls with approval at what he sees.

"Are you going to eat my ass again?" I ask in a husky whisper. I've never wanted so badly for the word "yes" to come from someone else's lips.

"Maybe. If you're lucky."

He dips a finger down my crack and taps my hole. I gasp out in pleasure.

"Fuck. I love when you play with my hole." I know I should shut the fuck up. Not give myself away to the guys on the ice. But the way Griffin takes over my body makes me want to be loud, the way you scream at the top of your lungs at your favorite concert. The echoey sounds of my teammates on the ice bounces off the locker room walls. Any one of them could walk in.

Griffin's rough finger circles my rim. He gives my cheek a hard slap.

"I can't wait to feel you inside me," I cry out.

A sigh of want tumbles out of me when I hear him get on his knees. Griffin lets out a little grunt of pain familiar to any hockey player with tight joints.

"Yes. Eat that hole." I bite my lip, willing myself to shut up as the flat of his tongue presses against my sensitive opening.

"Don't tell me what to do, Ringer." His hot breath dances on my hole, heat crackling through my body. The tip of his tongue swirls around the hole, sending every nerve ending standing at attention.

I pull my jockstrap down to free my aching cock from the restraints. I'm so fucking hard I see white spots in my vision.

"Tongue me, Griffin. Yes." I palm the locker for balance. With my other hand, I grab Griffin's hair and shove his face deeper inside my opening. The coarse hairs of his beard rub against me as his tongue goes to work.

"Give me all of that good juju," I say.

I bite my elbow pad as his tongue breaches my hole and slides inside me, spiking in and out. A cruel tease. I clench around his tongue.

"I love the way you tongue fuck me. I can't wait for it to be your big dick stretching me open."

Griffin moans against my hole. We haven't discussed sex yet, but my thought on the subject is that I want it. I want it bad. And I want it from Griffin.

He stands up and leans into my ear. "You want that, yeah?"

"Yeah," I whine.

"You want my dick."

"So bad." Griffin reduces me to a begging puddle of a man, and I'm okay with that as long as he delivers the goods.

I hear the teeth of his zipper break open. He grips my shoulder and steadies himself behind me. My legs can barely stand upright. The need pooling in my stomach rips through me with unrelenting intensity. I stroke myself faster, harder.

"Fuck me," I cry out.

"You'd like that, wouldn't you?" he teases. He drags his cock up and down my slick crack.

"No shit."

"You want this cock." His plump head pushes between my cheeks and presses against my opening. Just when I think he's going to push through and penetrate me, he pulls back. His cockhead circles my hole.

His teasing shreds my patience. Heat and lust rage in my chest.

"Give it to me," I plead with him like I'm fucking entitled to his cock.

He laughs against my neck. "You'd like that."

Again he slides his cock down my crack, pushing against my hole, and stopping just before breaching.

"I was tested recently. I'm good to go." Not even the talk about STDs can ruin this mood. I jut my ass closer to his crotch. At this point, I wish I were a Jedi so I could use the Force to move his cock inside me.

"We're not having sex. You have to go to practice." He spreads my cheeks apart and thwacks his cock on my sensitive opening. Every nerve in me pulses in response.

"We can be quick."

His breath dances beside my ear. "Not with the things I want to do to you."

Fuck. I can barely see straight. I tighten my grip around my own cock and jerk myself faster, harder, my mind scrolling through every potential scenario on his list.

He holds his hand by my mouth. "Spit in it," he commands.

I lick his hand because I need to disobey him and show him he's not the only one with a say here. Then I spit a glob into his hearty palm.

I hear him slick up his cock. He slips a finger inside me and grunts into my ear.

"Ringer, I can't wait to come all over you," he murmurs in my ear. I glance over my shoulder and catch him jerking himself off, his cockhead resting above my slick hole. "I want to watch you on the ice knowing that my come is sliding down your leg."

"Fuck. Yes. I want your come." My body tenses into a tight ball as desire fully takes hold of me. Hearing his grunting in my ear as he gets closer hurtles me over the edge.

He fists my jersey as he lets out a stifled groan and unloads down my ass. His hot seed drips down over my most sensitive areas, sliding between my cheeks. My balls draw up and I shoot onto the locker. Fortunately, metal is easy to clean.

Griffin rests his head against my shoulder as he catches his breath. "I love good juju."

"We're going to crush it on the ice this week."

He grabs a roll of paper towels from the bathroom sink and runs over. He rips off a piece for me to wipe off the locker I sullied. He's about to clean me up down there, when I push his hand away. I pull up my jockstrap, base layer, and hockey pants with his come still on me.

"You can watch me skate out there." I wink at him and enjoy that shocked grin he gives in response. "For the good juju."

23

JACK

Over the next two weeks, the juju was strong with Griffin and me. We did whatever we could to keep that good luck streak going. Whether that entailed giving each other handjobs in the Summers Rink parking lot, or blowing Griffin in my apartment garage, or having Griffin push me against a tree in the woods behind Summers Rink as he ate me raw.

Nobody could say we weren't focused on winning.

And it was working. Over the next two Sundays, the Blades and the Comebacks won their respective games. I felt myself come back into my own on the ice. I was quicker and nimbler on my skates. I was nailing shots that I couldn't make to save my life a month ago. The confidence that had eluded me when I joined the team had finally made itself known. I could proudly say that I belonged on the ice.

Even better than that, I was having a fucking blast. I tried to keep my angry game face on during games, but I'd catch myself smiling constantly. There was no overbearing dad or coach breathing down my neck. I was playing hockey because I wanted to and finding joy.

Pressure was building, though, as more people came to our games and buzzed about the Sourwood Cup on social media. Around town, I got a few nods of support, too.

The good juju was working on Griffin, too. I hung back and watched his game last week in stunned silence. I pray to God that I could be that nimble at his age. He was a bolt of thunder on the ice. Who could guess that he hadn't played in decades? It really was like riding a bike. My admiration for his skill was twinged with fear that I'd actually lose to him in the Sourwood Cup. Griffin had gotten his groove back. I really shouldn't be helping my opponent. But I can't stop.

On the ice, my mind was clear. My whole world was the game. But off the ice, I couldn't stop thinking about Griffin and when I could see him next. When I could taste him, touch him, smell him, hear him. When I could laugh with him.

"Deep breath." Miller sits on the floor of his yoga studio sitting cross-legged, his eyes closed. "And exhale."

All the Blades exhale on cue, a loud whoosh echoing in Miller's studio.

"If there is a mental barnacle clinging to your mind, now is the time to gently pluck it off and cast it back peacefully into the sea."

"Aren't barnacles technically parasites?" asks Fuentes.

"Be gone, barnacle," Miller says, and I can't tell whether or not that was meant for Fuentes.

I shut my eyes and try to cast out thoughts of Griffin. I don't need to think about Griffin. I only need to suck him off.

That gets me wondering why we haven't had sex yet. I tried initiating it in my garage the other day, but he declined and wanted to stick with blow jobs. Some guys are very strict when it comes to the good juju. Perhaps Griffin believes that having full-on sex will scramble the good luck pattern we've established. Good juju is more fragile than a wine glass.

Fuck, I shouldn't be thinking this much about Griffin and sex and sex with Griffin. Our time together is simply a means of improving our game. People I get close to have a tendency of turning their backs on me. I won't be adding Griffin to that list.

"And inhale peace and calm." Miller sucks in a breath. I follow accordingly. "And exhale stress and anger. Good."

I take two more cleansing breaths and find some degree of peace, if only for a second before Woody, our goalie, lets one rip.

"My bad," he says.

Miller holds back his anger long enough to put his hands together and wish us namaste.

"You ready?" Fuentes asks me when the class breaks.

"For this Sunday? We have it in the bag." We're facing the Overbites, a team made up of jolly dentists and orthodontists who hand out free toothpaste samples during intermission. The real win for them is improving Sourwood's oral hygiene.

"For next Sunday." A split-second of panic flashes across Fuentes's big, brown eyes.

"I'm totally ready."

"So are they," says Miller. "At their game last week, the Comebacks shut out another team thanks to Griffin Harper."

Whatever Zen Miller had is gone with the mention of the Comebacks.

"Griffin just hit a little hot streak. They haven't played us. And when they do, we won't make them forget," I say.

"Whatever you've been doing, keep doing it. You're on a hot streak, too." Fuentes rolls up his yoga map.

"Oh, I will definitely keep doing it." I hold my rolled up yoga mat over my hardening cock.

I SPEND my Friday night at home going down a YouTube rabbit hole of 1990s NHL hockey games. I stand over my sink and eat ramen with one hand while holding my phone in the other. There are countless better ways to position myself, but I'm too sucked in to move.

An email notification dings on my phone, throwing me from my algorithm-induced haze. It's from Darlene at the airport. Considering it's being sent on a Friday evening, I can only guess what she wanted to tell me.

Dear Jack, while we all loved meeting with you, unfortunately...

I exit out of the email and return to YouTube. Oddly enough, I don't have a reaction to the news. There's no crestfallen dip in my chest. It feels more like I dodged a bullet. I shove another forkful of ramen in my mouth and decide to get serious.

I click open my web browser and navigate to a job board website. I scroll down endless open opportunities and upload my resume machine gun style. This is what I'm supposed to do, right? Keep applying until someone bites. It feels like there's not much choice involved with a job hunt, which there should be since I'll be spending forty hours each week there. I wish I had some direction here, some secret talent that I could leverage. I hate feeling so lost. Hopefully, the universe has a clearer idea for my future.

After sending untold numbers of resumes into the ether, most of which will never be acknowledged, someone buzzes my apartment. My dick immediately assumes it's Griffin and gets hard.

"Hey sexy," I say into the intercom, deciding to have a little bit of fun this evening.

"It's Dad."

Awkward. His voice is the ultimate boner killer.

"Are you expecting someone?" he asks.

"Just being stupid. One second." I bang my head against my front door as penance for my dumb move. Then I buzz Dad up.

He comes with a box in hand. I recognize it from when I sifted through my old bedroom for the lucky bracelet.

"I figured you should have this. I should've asked you what you wanted to keep from your old room before I packed it up." He can't make full eye contact with me, like he feels just as awkward as I do. Dad only came to my apartment once and looked around in disgust. He probably remembered the swanky high-rise I used to live in with a walk-in closet as big as this whole studio.

"Thanks." I take the box from him. Inside are medals and trophies from my hockey days. Framed clippings. It's a sad, cluttered shrine to a guy I used to be, the one who was going to finish what his dad started.

"There's a lot of great stuff in there. Your first hockey jersey from your peewee days. A letter you wrote to yourself in crayon about how you were going to be MVP when you got older." Dad smiles warmly at the box, unable to resist the pull of memories.

"I remember that." In fifth grade, we had to write a letter to our future selves. I wrote about being a pro hockey player who drives a flying car. Half-right isn't bad. I flip open the letter. "How has my handwriting gotten worse?"

"And your bobblehead collection. I didn't throw those out."

"All three of them?" I wanted to be one of those kids who collected things, but it rarely lasted past a few items. I either got bored or forgot about it when hockey started up.

Dad laughs as I pull out the bobbleheads of the players from my favorite team. I idolized them growing up, until they passed me over in the draft. I keep eyeing Dad, the warm and fuzzy moment between us feeling like an alien experience. It's odd not having him scowl in withering disappointment.

I ride the moment rather than question it. I dig farther in the box and pull out an old picture from my first game. Mom and Dad flank me, proud as can be.

"There were some old pictures in the bottom of your old closet. Thought you might, I don't know...you might want them."

Mom is beaming, her smile taunting me.

"Why did she leave?" I ask.

Dad sighs. "We got married way too young. I was barely twenty, and she was nineteen. We'd only been dating a few months when she got knocked up, but her parents were strict Catholic."

I snort. "I figured it was a shotgun wedding." Their expressions in their wedding photo read more as panic than romantic bliss.

"In a way, I don't blame her for leaving. She held out hope that my shoulder would improve, and I could play again." He shrugs, defeated. "This is not the life she wanted."

I've thought about trying to find her, but I couldn't bear meeting her only to get rejected again.

I toss the picture back in the box and cover it with my old

uniform. I don't have the strength to rip it up, and I hate myself for that.

How could a mother beam at her son and then leave? People are complex, and they contain contradictions, but it's something I've never been able to square. In hockey, defense is the most important position, more important than offense. Same goes for life, I guess.

"You don't need to bring over Mom's stuff."

"You looked good in your hockey gear. I thought you might...well, it's up to you what you do with it."

"She didn't want me, so I don't want her. Easy as that." I close the box and place it on the floor next to my couch, one of the few places of free space. "You really came all the way over here to drop off a box?"

"I haven't seen you in a bit." Dad stands by the door, hands in his pockets, looking a little too innocent. "I've been hearing about that big game. The Sourwood Cup."

I roll my eyes. Is this thing the Stanley Cup finals? Never underestimate people's desire to root for something.

"Sounds like it's going to be quite the event. I know I was dismissive of your interest in this league, but I'm glad you signed up. I've been hearing you had some great games recently. Just like old times." His eyes twinkle with distant memories of cheering on his winning son.

"Thanks?" Hearing Dad be supportive is like walking down a dark alley in a horror film waiting for the killer to strike.

"People are talking about it. I saw the paper did a big profile on you and the team. It's good to hear your name getting talked about again."

I don't even remember what I talked to the reporter about. Fingers crossed she made me sound like an intelligent human being.

Dad smiles, more twinkling eyes, more walking down the dark alley. I get the sense of wheels turning in his head. "Because the game has been getting a surprising amount of coverage, especially around you, I decided to be proactive and make some calls."

"What kind of calls?"

"When players leave professional hockey, where do a lot of them segue into?"

"Shilling for crypto?"

Dad ignores my joke. "Coaching."

The word is a pit dropping in my stomach.

"A lot of players become coaches. They coach in the NHL, in the minors, and even at the collegiate level. All of your coaches were former players."

I remember old coaches regaling us with tales from the good ole days of hockey, when you could be *really* violent on the ice.

"I made some calls to the local colleges around here—"

"You're no longer my manager. You can't represent me."

"I called as a father looking out for his son." His warm tone makes me want to vomit. "Hudson University has an assistant coach position open. The head coach remembers you not only from the NHL but from when you played in high school. He was happy to read that you're still playing."

I hate to give him the satisfaction of being right, but I do admire the hustle on my behalf. Even though "my behalf" always means "our behalf." I'm still jobless and moneyless, and coaching sounds more enticing than restocking an office fridge.

"He's going to be at the Sourwood Cup. If you can kick ass on the ice and bring in a huge victory, it'll show him you've still got the juice."

The opportunity is enticing, but there's a weird pang that hits my stomach when I try to imagine myself coaching. It's like watching a movie and the sound isn't synched. I can follow along but it's still off. Part of the fun is that the league is recreational and only a small part of my week. I don't know if I want to make hockey my full-time job again. As stressful as job hunting can be, there's something exciting about imagining a new path.

"I'll think about it," I say.

"Think about it. Nothing's going to happen until after the game. Coaching could be a great next step for you."

There's something slightly different about his overture this time, as if maybe a small part of this is coming from a genuine place of a dad looking out for his son.

He hands me a business card. "Here's his information in case you want to talk with him more about the position."

I secure it to my fridge via a hockey puck magnet pulled from the box of old things.

"Whatever happens, I can't wait to watch you kick the shit out of Griffin Harper. Hell, I've been waiting over twenty-five years for this." A vengeance-fueled smile twists across his lips.

A pit grows in my stomach, thinking about everything I've been doing with Griffin unbeknownst to Dad or anyone else.

"Yeah, it'll be a good game," I say.

"You don't sound as confident as you should. Are you actually worried?"

"Dad, what happened with you and Griffin was ages ago. Maybe let it go."

And there's the Dad I know, the one whose engine runs on grievance and anger. His forehead crests into a hard crinkle.

"I wish I could, Jack," he says, a rare moment of self-awareness. "Your hockey career might not have gone the way you wanted, but you still got to have it. You never had a dream ripped away from you at the last minute by some cocky, bullheaded asshole. He wanted to take me out. He wanted to be the star for the scouts in the audience. He wanted all the attention. If he had it his way, he would've knocked me unconscious." His jaw tightens, the moment forever fresh in his mind. "As you get older, you truly understand that life has no do-overs. You only get one lap around the track. He took that from me. I can never get that life back. I can never get that time back."

I want to tell him that I understand, but I bite my tongue. Some cans of worms aren't worth opening. I don't want to ruin this moment we're sharing, when for once, it doesn't feel like we're enemies.

The game of hockey is unpredictable. I go into every game knowing there's a chance that we won't win, no matter how crappy the other team is. Even the Overbites could give us a run for our money this Sunday. Yet Dad's hopeful, hangdog face gets the better of me.

When Mom left, he was all I had. It created a hardened bond between us that can't be broken, no matter how toxic. His pride when I'd win a game filled me with a kind of warmth I wasn't getting anywhere else. The need for Dad's approval is a drug I can't stop huffing no matter how bad it is for me.

"Don't worry, Dad. I promise you we're going to win."

24

GRIFFIN

I have my girls for the weekend, and it allows me to forget about hockey and Jack for a bit. Friday is warmer than usual, so we go for a short hike after school and order in pizza. Saturday, we wake up to rain. I used to love lounging on my couch on a rainy day. Unfortunately, little kids don't lounge. They are like Energizer Bunnies from the second they wake up.

I toast frozen pancakes for breakfast, and they watch a little TV as the rain continues to come down. The girls play in the living room, jumping on couch cushions as if the floor is lava. My hope is this lasts all morning, at least.

I don't have them as often as Carmen does. My encyclopedia of indoor activities is slim. I text Tanner for ideas. I figure he is up to date on all kids activities. He writes back almost immediately about a new paint-your-own-pottery place that opened up downtown. He tells me to book a timeslot online.

I manage to grab the last opening for this afternoon.

"Girls, do you want to make your own pottery?" I realize there's a chance they could say no, and then I'd be screwed.

Luckily, they jump up and down with excitement.

"Can George come?" June asks.

"George the reindeer?" I don't know why I'm asking for confirmation, but she nods her head yes.

"I promise he won't chain smoke at the pottery place," she tells me.

"He's really trying to quit!" Annabelle says.

"Hmmm...I don't know if George can fit in the car. And is he able to paint with hooves?"

I also don't know why I'm bringing logic to this conversation, yet the girls aren't fazed by my questions.

"One second." June holds up her tiny finger. She and Annabelle run into the dining room and fake whisper to the wall where I assume George is resting. They scurry back a few seconds later.

"George is just going to hang out in the house today. He's had a busy week and needs to decompress," June says. I like to play a little game with myself to figure out where she learned new words that are peppered into her vocabulary.

"Fair enough. We can play here a little bit more, and then we'll go out to lunch, then to the pottery place."

The girls give me a thumbs up to this plan.

I point to the dining room. "George," I say loudly. "There will be no smoking in the house while we're gone. If you need to smoke, you can do it outside on the deck."

I hold George's non-existent eye contact for an extra second to get my point across, and I almost trick myself into believing there's a chain smoking reindeer in my house.

———

BY THE TIME we go into town for lunch, the rain's gone. The girls still insisted on wearing their rain boots; June hops into every puddle on the sidewalk as we walk from the car to Caroline's, a beloved greasy spoon diner with delicious food. It's one of the few places where the girls can find something on the menu.

"Dad, what's eggplant parma-sand?" Annabelle asks.

"Parmesan. It's an Italian dish. Have you had eggplant before?"

The girls shrug, unsure. I give myself a Dad demerit because that's something I should know.

"For breakfast?" June asks.

"Those are eggs, I'm assuming. Eggplant is different. Why don't you girls split a sandwich?" Caroline's piles their sandwiches a mile high. We're talking walls of pastrami and chicken salad.

"I don't want to share!" June protests.

"Why don't we all share?" I propose. "You can have half of my sandwich."

"We have to share your half?" Annabelle cocks her head to the side as she tries to do the math. Fractions are a new concept for her. June shakes her head no, never one to wait for the data.

"What if I get a sandwich, and you each get a cup of soup?"

"I don't want soup," June says.

"What kind of sandwich do you want?"

"Do they put mustard on the turkey?" Annabelle wonders.

"We can get it without." I study her face to determine whether that was the right answer. "Or with." I'll bet Des has less trouble negotiating multi-million dollar contracts.

"Can they put mustard in the middle of the sandwich?" June asks.

"I don't like mustard. I like ketchup!" Annabelle chimes in, panicked.

"I don't want ketchup on mine. Gross," June shoots back.

"Here's what we're going to do." I bend down their menus so I can see them, then I go in for the close. "We'll split a turkey sandwich and ask for mustard and ketchup on the side. I'll put ketchup on the bread of Annabelle's half, and I'll put mustard on the pieces of turkey in the middle of June's half. Okay?"

The girls hesitate a moment, considering the offer. I keep my fingers crossed we can avoid another round of negotiations. When they give me the greenlight nod, I let out a small sigh of relief.

"Can we get dessert?" June smiles at me, never knowing when to quit while she's ahead.

"We're eating lunch first." I look to get the waitress's attention, when I spot Jack sitting at the counter, hunched over a menu and a cup of coffee, a quiet moment to himself. There's something unguarded and tentative about seeing him in the wild like this. His typical bravado from the ice, and from the bar, isn't present.

I wave to him when he catches me looking. He nods back, another polite gesture. Funny how we're so good at getting each other off, but polite gestures feel odd and foreign. He shoves his hands in his cozy hoodie as he reads through the menu. I don't know what it is about men in hoodies that turn them automatically into cute, strong teddy bears.

"Who's that, Daddy?" the girls ask.

"That's, uh, nobody." I instantly get a twinge of guilt for lying to my girls, even if it is a little white one. They scrunch their little foreheads, adorably calling bullshit, too. "That's my friend, Jack."

"Why is he eating alone?" Annabelle ponders. Kids have a preternatural ability to ask direct questions. Getting older means gaining a filter, which has its pluses and minuses.

"I don't know. I guess he has to eat a quick meal. He probably has lots of things to do."

The girls peek over the top of our booth at Jack, and I can't help but join them. It's one of the few times where he isn't his cocky self, like an actor caught off camera.

"Girls, stop staring. Let Jack enjoy his meal in peace."

"Dad's friend Jack!" June yells across booths of older patrons. "Do you want to eat lunch with us?"

"Sit with us!" says Annabelle, emboldened by her completely filterless younger sister. The girls wave him over, their flailing, slim arms slicing through the air.

"Girls…" I try to regain control without reprimanding them.

They tip their heads back to our table, mouthing "Come on." No man can resist that level of cuteness.

"Friends don't let each other eat alone. In school, we're supposed to include other kids." June makes a fair point. I want to be a good example.

I join in waving him over. We share a bemused smile, both realizing that it's best to do what they say.

The girls scream their delight as Jack stands up from his counter stool. My stomach flops into a puddle of awkwardness as Jack approaches. Because Caroline's booths are older, it's a tight squeeze. Annabelle moves onto my booth seat, and Jack takes the other side with June.

I thought I'd be safer not having him sit next to me. No touching or brushing of legs. Yet from this position, I'm able to stare straight into his vibrant eyes, making this just as awkward a seating choice.

"Hi! I'm June."

"I'm Annabelle."

"I'm Jack. Nice to meet you." Jack holds out his hand to shake before realizing a hi-five is more appropriate.

The girls hi-five him back.

"Why were you eating alone? Where are your friends?" June asks him, no care about social pretense. I wish I could be like her sometimes.

I try to signal to Jack that he doesn't need to answer any of their questions, yet he doesn't look my way.

"I was having a rough day, and I needed a bowl of my favorite chicken noodle soup. It always makes me feel better."

His answer catches me off guard. I want to ask him what's wrong, who made his day rough for him, and what can I do to make it better, yet I smartly resist.

"Daddy's ordering us chicken noodle soup, too!" June says. A minute ago she was adamantly against soup. I don't argue.

"Good call." Jack gives her a thumbs up.

"I like the noodles more than the chicken," June says with a smile that splits her face.

"Same." Jack nods in solidarity.

"I love putting a whole piece of bread in there and letting it get all soggy," Annabelle says.

"You know what I like to do?" Jack leans in. "I take a bunch of crackers and put them at the bottom of the soup, and I cover them with the noodles. You don't want a cracker that's half-in and half-out of the soup, or only one side is in the soup. You take a bite, and you can't tell whether it's mushy or crunchy. Gross!"

June and Annabelle nod along as if they're front row at a tent revivalist.

"Putting them firmly at the bottom of the soup is the scientifically proven best and fastest way for them to get nice and soggy. They mesh together to become one mass of mushy cracker."

The girls' heads spin with new ideas.

The waitress comes over to take our order. She doesn't blink twice at Jack moving to sit with us. She's on top of it.

"What are you girls going to have?"

"Chicken noodle soup. Extra crackers!" June says.

"I want chicken noodle soup and extra crackers, too," Annabelle blurts out, worried that they'll somehow run out.

The waitress turns to me for official approval.

"They'll also get a turkey sandwich plain. Ketchup and mustard on the side."

"No! I don't want a turkey sandwich. I just want chicken noodle soup," June says, with Annabelle nodding in agreement next to me.

————

A LITTLE BIT LATER, I'm munching down on the turkey sandwich they didn't want. The girls and Jack build cracker floors at the bottom of their soups. The girls spend a bit too long playing with their food rather than eating it, but once Jack starts taking spoonfuls, they follow suit. Naturally, the girls also want some of my turkey sandwich. It's a universal rule that a child's favorite food is whatever's on their parent's plate.

And perhaps it's that Jack is great with kids. The girls regale him with stories from school and storylines from their favorite shows. He listens as though he was hearing a famous lecture from a renowned scholar. They ask him questions about his life and his favorite desserts. He answers as if being interviewed by Oprah Winfrey.

"Has George tried chewing gum?" Jack crinkles his forehead in a genuine desire to help.

"He says he doesn't like gum," June replies.

"Who doesn't like gum? He just hasn't found the right flavor. Maybe reindeer don't like fruity or minty gum. Maybe it needs to be more savory, like soup-flavored gum or hamburger-flavored gum." Jack shovels part of his cracker mushy mass into his mouth.

"George likes lettuce," Annabelle offers.

"We'll try lettuce-flavored gum!" June bounces in her seat.

"That's a winner." Jack shoots me a quick smile and wink that gets me all fuzzy inside.

"Girls, I think Jack is tired of talking about George's smoking."

"Chain smoking," Jack corrects me, surprising even June and Annabelle.

He wipes his mouth with a napkin and tosses it into his empty soup bowl. "So what do you think of your dad being a cool hockey player?"

At this, the girls get quiet. They look at each other and shrug, not used to not having an answer.

"You girls like hockey?"

They shrug again. It's wild how kids can go from super loud to super quiet depending on the topic.

"They've never been to a game," I tell him.

"They haven't?" Jack guffaws. I signal for him to drop it.

"Mom says it's too scary." June eats a spoonful of soup.

"It's not scary at all," Jack says.

"Don't the players hit each other?" Annabelle asks.

"They run into each other. It's like bumper cars. They bonk and crash, but it's all in good fun. And the players wear big, puffy clothes. They have to walk like this." He impersonates a hulking walk where he can't put his arms down. The girls laugh. "When they knock into each other, it doesn't hurt." Jack arches an eyebrow. "Do you girls know what bumper cars are?"

"Yes," they say, offended at the assumption. We ride them every year when the fair comes into town. June insists on manning the steering wheel and careening into other cars.

"Your dad is great on the ice. He's fast."

"Does Daddy skate like he's on the ice capades?" June asks.

"He does. He really does. He's magic out there." Jack winks at me, and it sails over the table like an arrow straight into my heart.

I check my watch and signal for the check. "Girls, we have to go. We're going to be late for the pottery class."

"Pottery class? Fancy," says Jack.

"I thought it'd be something different on a rainy way. Or what was a rainy day." I take the check from the waitress.

"I'm going to paint Elsa," says Annabelle.

"No, I am!" June screams.

"You both can," I explain calmly.

June throws herself back into the booth cushion. "But I wanted to first."

"What if one of you paints Elsa, and the other paints Anna?" I suggest.

"Can I paint Sven?" June asks, stopping herself just before a crying fit.

"Yes." Another successful negotiation in the books. I eat the last bite of my sandwich.

"Can Jack come?" June asks.

"Jack has things he needs to do. We don't want to take up all of his time."

"Please," they say. June and Annabelle unleash their big, doe eyes at Jack. Poor guy is unprepared and powerless against their charm offensive.

"Uh, sure. I could paint."

"Jack." I catch his eyeline, trying to convey that he doesn't need to be beholden to their whims. He's allowed to say no. Yes, they might cry, but I can be the one to handle that.

To my surprise, Jack is unfazed. Dare I say, he seems eager to join them...to paint vases...with *Frozen* characters.

"I'm down." Jack hi-fives the girls. "Between me and your dad, who do you think is the better painter."

"Jack!" The girls yell in a heartbeat before spiraling into laughter.

"I can beat you on the ice and in the pottery studio." Jack flashes me a cocky, victorious smirk.

25

JACK

I used to think being in a hockey rink was the loudest, most chaotic environment I'd been in. And then I stepped into The Pottery Palace.

An onslaught of blindingly bright colors, peppy music, and kids speaking to their parents in the highest possible volume greet us upon entry. June and Annabelle acclimate right away, running into the fray to pick out the ceramic item they wish to paint.

I can't imagine Griffin existing in a world this busy. I'm amazed he can fit inside at all. His bulky frame squeezes through the front door, whereupon his head hits a light fixture hanging from the ceiling. All of the tables and chairs are kid-sized. We are Gulliver in that land of Lilliputians.

"You okay there?" I ask.

"Fine," he grumbles. Some of the other parents turn their heads, as if they've never seen a massive one-eyed father before.

"Hi! I'm Amy and welcome to The Pottery Palace! Name?" A young woman wearing a headset approaches us with a smile as bright as the wall color. Griffin gives his name, and she looks it up on her tablet. Her aura rests somewhere between camp counselor and maître d' at the hottest restaurant in Manhattan.

"I see one adult and two children here to create." She glances at me, then back at her tablet.

"There're two adults here. We have a guest." Griffin nods at me. A slight hint of amusement perks up his lips. "Is that okay?"

"I'm not going to paint," I throw in. "Just keeping this guy company."

She drags her finger up and down the tablet, half-checking and perhaps half-wondering if she holds more power than God in this moment.

"There was only one parent on the reservation," she says, her chipper tone belying a steely edge.

"Again, I'm not going to paint. Just hang. I won't even use a chair." I bat my eyes at her and use the full force of my masculine wiles. I may be dudes only, but she doesn't have to know that. "The last thing I want to do is make your job any tougher, Amy. I haven't seen my nieces in the longest time. I promise if I cause a ruckus, you can crack one of these pots over my head and toss me into the street."

Amy giggles at that. Like tug of war, I pull her mood toward camp counselor and away from maître d'.

"Okay. I'll make this one exception. But I'll be watching you. No sitting in a chair." She holds the tablet against her chest, perhaps trying to draw my attention to her rack.

"You got it, drill sergeant!" I give her a salute, which elicits another giggle. Griffin rolls his eyes.

The girls run back to us, each holding an identical gray vase. An "artistic coordinator," a guy my age in a magenta apron that gives me Ferguson's PTSD, sets the girls and Griffin up at a table with paint. There's no Frozen-themed vase. Instead, the coordinator tells them to use their imagination, which does not go over well with the girls. Tears immediately follow.

"I thought there were specific things you could paint of Disney characters," Griffin whispers to the coordinator.

"No. I'm sorry. All pottery is a blank canvas to be filled by imagination!" he says, assuming that saying "imagination" over and over will trigger something in the girls.

"Crap," Griffin mutters under his breath. "I thought you guys did that."

The coordinator shakes his head no. The girls' cries intensify, creating a huge spotlight on us. I can feel eyes on Griffin from other parents. Big hockey man has no idea how to handle children, they're probably thinking. I turn to Griffin, about to suggest that we should go since the girls are so upset.

He squats down, rips a paper towel off the spool on the table, and wipes at the girls' eyes, ignoring every single sideways glance.

"I wanted to make an Elsa pot," June says between sniffly sobs.

"I know, sweet pea. But what about this? What if we paint a pretty vase for your ice castle?" He rests his hands on June's and Annabelle's shoulders. "You girls are going to have a massive ice castle, and it's going to be empty. It needs to be furnished and decorated. I've seen Elsa's ice castle, and she has no decorations. Nothing on the bookshelves or on end tables or window sills."

"Why *is* it so empty?" Annabelle wonders.

"Do you want your ice castle to be empty like that?" Griffin asks, his voice animated like he's giving the sales pitch of his life.

June and Annabelle shake their heads no.

"I want to paint a blue and purple pot to look like ice," says June.

"And Annabelle, what if you painted yours with yellow and orange?"

"They can look nice next to each other." Annabelle's eyes shine with possibility. And just as fast as she and June devolved into crying fits, they sit down at the table, gather their painting supplies, and get to work.

Quiet takes over the table, and I'm quietest of them all. I am stunned into motherfucking silence. Did I just watch a guy nail a shot into the top left corner of the net from the center of the rink?

Griffin stands beside me, beaming down at his daughters.

"That was...incredible. You are Dad AF."

"Thanks?"

"How did you do that? I was ready to bolt," I say.

"Parenting is the act of subtly convincing kids to do things and getting them to assume it was their idea."

It's official. This man parents as well as he eats ass.

Griffin squats down to the kid-sized chair he's forced to sit in. His big butt is no match for the furniture. It's like balancing a basketball on a toothpick. He hunches over the pottery table with the paint supplies as if he could swallow them in one bite. It becomes quickly apparent that the girls don't have the attention spans or artistic prowess to make their visions come to life. The adults will need to help out.

"Hey June, can Jack borrow your chair?" Griffin asks.

June hops off her stool and brushes it off with a clean paintbrush. She pats the seat twice.

The four of us work on painting their vases. Annabelle goes for yellow and orange stripes, while June is looking for something more chaotic, more Jackson Pollack-y.

"What's this ice castle you girls keep talking about?" I finally ask. At first, I thought it was imaginary.

"Daddy's building us our own ice castle in the backyard for our birthday," Annabelle says.

"Like the one in *Frozen*," June says.

I look to Griffin who confirms it with a nod.

"You're building them an actual castle?" Growing up, I never got anything like that. All my gifts were hockey related, no matter what was on my wish list. And here this guy is, building a freaking castle for his girls in honor of their favorite movie.

With each second that passes, it's getting harder to want to kick Griffin's ass on the ice, and even harder to pretend my attraction to him is purely for the good juju.

Griffin puts on a pair of black-framed reading glasses and rolls up his sleeves to get into painting mode. I, in turn, want to fucking melt. Beefy guys who wear glasses is an irresistible combo. And glasses over an eye patch? It hits the spectrum from nerd to badass all in one.

"You've broken out the glasses." I scoff, because I don't know how to handle his insane hotness, and so I must make fun of it.

"You'll need them one day. All those hits to the head add up."

"So far I'm still twenty-twenty." I flick my paintbrush at the vase, following June's lead.

Griffin helps Annabelle paint in a straight line, ensuring the yellow stripe doesn't bleed into the orange one. I could watch him with his girls all day.

"Dad, what do you think of this?" June shows off her vase.

"I love it."

She holds it up to me for approval. I give it a thumbs up.

"Thanks for spending your Saturday afternoon with us," Griffin says.

"I like people who are no BS." It's fun talking to a kid with no agenda except curiosity.

Someone taps me on the shoulder, and I worry I'm being too loud. Another dad with his daughter stands over me.

"You're Jack Gross."

"I am." I pray this isn't a bill collector or process server.

"I watched you play for Wichita when I lived there."

Now I wish it was a process server. A fan? I get a flash of nausea. I feel exposed in a way that's hard to describe.

"Thanks," I say quietly.

"I remember this one game, when you made this pass to Marceau, it flew across the ice right to his stick. The accuracy was amazing."

I was never sure how to handle these interactions when I was active in the NHL, on the rare occasions they did happen. "Thanks for being a fan."

"It's a shame they didn't keep you on." His comment hangs in the air as if he expects me to respond. My stomach only twists further into a knot. "Can I get a selfie with you?"

"Um, actually, I'm with my friends."

"Yeah, but it'll only take a second. Just one picture. Come on. I'm with my kid, too." He points to his daughter as leverage.

"I get that. I can autograph something for you if you want. I just don't feel comfortable with pictures being taken."

"Don't feel comfortable? What are you talking about?" He laughs it off. Fans can go from fawning to your entitled master in a finger snap. "Just take the picture."

"Like I said, I can autograph something for you, but I don't want to take a picture."

"What's your problem? You should be lucky someone's interested in taking your picture."

"He said he doesn't want his picture taken." Griffin yanks the phone out of the guy's hand. He stands above both of us.

"Why not? I said you were good until they traded your ass."

"Watch your language at The Pottery Palace," Griffin growls.

They engage in a standoff that the guy knows he can't win. He yanks his phone back and shoves it in his pocket.

"Let's go, sweetheart." He says to his daughter. "Asshole," he mutters at me as he leaves.

Griffin watches him go, his eye narrowed in barely contained rage.

"That man used bad words," Annabelle says.

"He did, love. That wasn't nice of him." Griffin returns to his little chair.

"The entitlement of fans. It's a good thing you never went pro." I sit down and laugh it off, a bit shaken.

"Does that happen often?"

"Every now and then. The fans are even more aggressive toward the star players. They feel like they have a hand in your success and are owed unlimited access to you. Usually, they don't care much about a player like me. I'm not worth gushing over."

"Why do you say that?" Griffin takes off his glasses, making me meet his eye.

"I mean, come on. I was a B-level player on a few teams."

"So? You were a pro player. That's something."

"Maybe to some people, but it's not as cool as you think."

"Hey girls. Can you take these pots to the wall so they can dry?" Griffin points to the back wall of shelves filled with projects. There's a little play area with a kiddie snack station where kids can wait until the paint dries.

Griffin scoots his chair next to me. "I didn't want them to hear you talk shit about yourself. But why do you do it? Why do you downplay this incredible accomplishment?"

"Incredible?"

"Yes. Incredible."

"I was a forgettable player for a few years. And now I'm washed up and broke." I shrug, feeling more pathetic every time I hear it said aloud.

"You got the short end of the stick in the league, but that doesn't change the fact you're a great player. I've seen you. You earned your place in the NHL." He stares at me, refusing to let me look away until I let that compute.

"Did you see the video of me crapping out with a game-losing turnover?"

"I did."

"Wait. You did?" That was supposed to be a rhetorical question. Embarrassment swarms me.

"One of my friends found it online. I was going to share it around the league after you uploaded a video of toilet papering my truck onto YouTube. But I decided to take the high road."

I nod my gratitude. I both love and hate the internet.

"It's not that bad," he says.

"Are you fucking with me?"

"Turnovers happen all the time. It's not uncommon. I had one during a game in high school. Yours simply had higher stakes."

Hearing Griffin acknowledge the moment with a shrug actually does make me feel better. The surge of mortification and frustration isn't as strong this time.

"It was a hell of a first impression," I say.

"If your coach hadn't waited until late in the season to give you serious time on the ice, you wouldn't have been in that position."

I can hear the "Hallelujah" chorus. I've always felt screwed by that freshman season. Had I been able to play more in the season, one (admittedly bad) turnover wouldn't have torpedoed my career. For the first time, someone is taking my side.

If these chairs weren't so uncomfortable, I'd hug Griffin.

"Give yourself some credit, Jack."

"Okay. What about you? Why do you crap all over yourself, huh?" I ask, wanting the spotlight off me and my career. "Why have your girls never seen you play? Why do they barely know you play?"

Griffin looks over at his daughters. "My ex-wife thinks hockey is too violent for them. She wasn't at the game where your dad took out my eye, but she's been haunted by the story ever since she heard it."

"It's a non-checking league. It's family-friendly entertainment! I don't think that's the reason, though. You think because you never went pro, they wouldn't care."

Griffin shrugs. It's one of the few things he doesn't feel like fighting.

"Maybe it's for the best."

"Why do you say that?" When he doesn't answer me right away, I dab his nose with orange paint.

"What was that for?" he asks, annoyed and also confused.

"Those girls are crazy about you! Trust me, they would love to know all about how Daddy played hockey."

Griffin shrugs, and in response, I dab his forehead with yellow paint.

"Stop," he says through laughter.

"Your girls are proud of you, Griffin."

Something changes on his face at the uttering of proud. A quick, genuine smile beams on his lips.

"You should be proud of everything you've done, too," I say. "You're a success. And maybe, despite you being a sourpuss, I kind of envy what you have. It's really wonderful."

A spark of light dazzles in his eye as he nods. He might not believe the hype yet, but I'll keep working on him.

The girls bring over fruit snacks for us. I rip open my bag and spill half into my mouth. June tries to copy me, but most of them fall onto the table.

"Are the pots ready?" Annabelle asks.

"We can pick them up in a week. They need to dry in the kiln." Griffin walks over to the holding area where the two pots and other pottery creations from today wait for their turn to glaze. We all look at our pots in wonder as if animals in an exhibit.

A pang hits my chest knowing that this afternoon is winding down.

"There's a gardening shop a few blocks down, if you guys are up for it. We can't let these great pots sit empty." Nobody says the day has to end yet. I can also put the gardening knowledge I learned at Ferguson's to use.

I look to Griffin, hoping we get the green light. A big smile stretches across his face, a face I want to kiss so badly.

"Let's pick out some flowers," he says.

26

GRIFFIN

I don't want my day with Jack to end. After pottery, we walked to My Flower of Need, each of us carrying a girl on our shoulders. When I thought we'd say our goodbyes, Jack asked to see the ice castle I was building, which immediately got the girls excited. He followed us back to our house, and I couldn't help feel a swell of pride as he admired the work-in-progress.

After that, I thought he would finally get on with his day. But then he picked up a hammer and began nailing in the last remaining planks of wood. I wasn't going to sit by and let him do all the work. The girls put on music and played in the backyard as we finished the castle, capping one of the most enjoyable days I've had in a while. Was it all because of Jack's presence? I'd like to say no, but I don't want to lie to myself.

"Whoa." I step back and take in the finished product. The ice castle sits mightily on the tree branches.

"Nice job," Jack says, nudging my elbow.

"It took the work of a lot of good friends." I've never been so happy to have handy friends. No way could I have done this on my own.

"So what's *Frozen* actually, like, about?" Jack asks, wiping the sweat off his forehead with his shirt, exposing his rippling abs. I feel a little guilty that he's spent his lazy Saturday doing manual labor and answering a barrage of questions from my daughters.

June runs up, at the ready. "It's about two sisters, and one has this scary special power, so their parents force her to stay in her bedroom and never come out. But then her parents die, and she leaves her room, and everyone gets mad at her, so she leaves and creates a new ice castle for herself in the woods..." By the end, she's out of breath. My daughter can't remember if she did her homework, but can recite the entire plot of a feature-length film in stunning detail.

"Daddy, can we watch *Frozen* tonight in our new ice castle?" Annabelle asks.

Rather than immediately say no, the spirit of the day convinces me to run with the idea. Fortunately, it's a balmy early March evening. If we bring blankets and my space heater into the castle, we won't freeze.

"Sure," I say.

"Really?" Annabelle asks, just as shocked as I am that I easily said yes.

"Really," I confirm.

"Can we make popcorn?" Annabelle asks.

"Sure."

"Can Jack watch with us?" June loops her arm through Jack's.

"Girls, it's been a long day and Jack wants to get home."

"I don't know." Jack scratches at his chin. "You ladies have been hyping up *Frozen* all day. I think I need to see it."

The girls bounce with excitement as they sense the scales tipping their way. Another kind of excitement flutters through me. The terrifying kind of excitement, like what the guy who did a tightrope walk across the Twin Towers must've felt.

"Jack, you've spent so much time with the girls. You don't need to wreck your Saturday night plans for this. Girls, Jack can watch *Frozen* on his own and tell us what he thinks."

"Watching *Frozen* is better than what I had planned," he says.

"You heard it, Daddy. He wants to watch it in our ice castle treehouse with popcorn." June stands on her tippy toes and beams in victory.

I glance at Jack, giving him the signal that he can go. But Jack pays me no mind.

"Let's make some popcorn!" He scoops up Annabelle in his arms and goes into the house.

The one guy I can't let get into my head has moved in and thrown his stuff all around.

———

A LITTLE BIT LATER, we're all set and ready to go. We set up my tablet on an extra piece of wood with the movie all queued up. We brought sleeping bags, pillows, and blankets into the tree house. Jack and I hauled up two folding lawn chairs. The girls decorated with streamers and *Frozen* accoutrement as Jack strung twinkly lights around the walls.

The lawn chair creaks as I unfold it and makes louder groans when I plunk my big ass down. The girls lay on their stomachs in front of the TV. Jack unfolds his chair right next to mine.

"Is this too close?" Jack asks.

"No. No, not at all." I cough down a flutter of excitement in my chest.

Jack collapses into his chair. "Comfy."

In the twinkly lights, his lips glow against the darkness. His stubble comes into view on his cut jaw line. He is even more handsome than usual.

I turn on the movie. The girls keep looking back at Jack to tell him what's going on in the movie. Jack, for his part, seems engaged in what's going on in Arendelle.

Me? Not so much.

Because every time I glance toward Jack, something flips in my stomach that shouldn't be flipping. He shouldn't be here. He shouldn't be this amazing with my girls. He shouldn't be making me feel this kind of happiness that is new to me, opening me up into scary places. He smiles at me in between nodding at June's commentary, and I have to look away because it causes my stomach to flip again.

My mind jumps ahead to the end of this night. How the hell are we going to say goodbye? It was one thing to bump into him at Caroline's, but then it spiraled into this truly wonderful day. All I can think about is ending things with a good night kiss, which is totally off limits. The good juju does not require a good night kiss.

This whole day has been a mistake because I'm supposed to be kicking his ass a week from tomorrow. He's supposed to be an overconfident asshole. We're not supposed to hang out, and he's definitely not supposed to endear himself to my girls.

What the hell is going to happen when he leaves? Is it just going to be a *see ya* and wave? Or do we shake hands? Will he try to hug me? Is there a tiny chance he might try to kiss me?

"Daddy, you seem confused?"

I blink and find Annabelle looking back at me. She sips from her Olaf-branded water bottle.

"The snowman is now talking. Do we need to rewind?" Jack asks.

He tries to take the remote from me, and our fingers touch, eliciting an electric response that makes the hairs on my neck stand up. I can smash into him on the ice no problem, but a finger touch threatens to knock me down.

What if I took Jack's hand? What if I brushed my calloused thumb over his bumpy knuckles and liked it? What if I admitted that today was one of the best days I've had in a long time? Being with Jack makes me believe that I'm living my life exactly as I should, that waiting for him to be my first with a guy was the right move because there is no better man than him.

Jack doesn't pretend to watch the movie. He watches for real. The girls keep looking back at him, waiting for his reaction to a musical number or plot beat, and he serves every time. And when he glances at me for my reaction, I struggle to keep my face muted when my desire to kiss him keeps gaining strength inside me like a hurricane headed for the Florida coast.

I've seen this movie enough times to know how much longer until it ends. With each second, the countdown clock pounds in my head. Because once it's over, the girls will go to bed, and Jack will go home, and we will have to say goodbye. With a head nod, a handshake, a hug, or a kiss.

It's not going to be a kiss, I tell myself. Jack is being nice to the girls. That's all.

We reach the final number. Elsa and Anna find true love in their sisterhood. Why the hell am I thinking about Jack whenever they mention true love? He's probably the conniving prince.

Everyone on screen gets their happy ending. The girls yawn. One of them may already be asleep. The credits roll. It's over. This incredible day and night are done.

I stop the movie mid-credits, an exciting panic flinging itself around in my chest. I imagine this is how people feel while on a good first date.

I sit in my seat for a few extra moments, admiring how peaceful the girls are, afraid to look at Jack.

The quiet, the darkness, the twinkly lights. It's all too romantic, and I need it to go away.

I stand up and clean up the popcorn kernels from the floor. The more I can focus on the task at hand, the better. Jack squats next to me. I can smell his woodsy cologne.

"I'm going to have half of those songs stuck in my head, won't I?"

"Oh, no question."

His laughter sends a warm and fuzzy bolt down my spine.

"I'm going to get them into their beds." I nod down at the girls, fast asleep in the pile on the blankets.

"I'll help." Jack gives me a thumbs up.

I carry Annabelle down, while Jack carries June. Their tiny chests move up and down with each breath. There is nothing more peaceful in this world than watching your child sleep.

They don't fight us when we tuck them into their beds, instead rolling over into a continued slumber. I won't tell their mother that they didn't brush their teeth. One missed night won't destroy their oral hygiene.

I watch them from the doorway, thanking God I get to be their father. I can't be mad about being in the closet until I was in my forties because I got to have them. I turn and find Jack watching me.

"They're the best," Jack says. "And they have a great dad, too."

I worry one more compliment will make me want to pull him into a kiss. I sidestep Jack and head downstairs to the front door. Jack follows a second later.

"I guess it's that time. Thanks for letting me crash your day with your girls."

"It was fun. You're good with them."

"They're good kids. It makes it easy. It's fun seeing the world from their point of view for a time."

"They keep me young," I say, a generic line I heard many a parent say.

Jack takes a step closer. My breath hitches in my lungs. I feel behind me for the doorknob and open the front door.

"Well, thanks for…" I start.

"Yeah. I guess you're not the miserable asshole I assumed," he says.

"And maybe you're not the cocky piece of shit I thought."

"Oh, I am. I mean, I think your girls liked me better than you."

My face drops, ready to call bullshit. Jack breaks into a laugh.

"Kidding. It never gets old watching you make that face, Griffin."

"Fuck off, Ringer."

He steps forward, stretches out his arms, a signal that he's about to hug me. I jab a hand forward that almost stabs him in the stomach. He looks down, and without hinting at any confusion, he gives it a nice, hard shake.

"I'll see you on the ice," I say.

"Likewise." He turns to go fast and shuts the door behind him.

I exhale a massive breath and lean against the closed front door. That was close. A tsunami of relief floods me. Awkwardness averted.

But just as quickly, regret and anger course over me. The regret burns like tequila down my throat.

"Fuck," I mutter to myself.

In the quiet of the house, I hear footsteps outside. Climbing my front stoop. Then a knock at the door.

I shut my brain off before it can chime in with thoughts.

When I open the door, I don't think, I don't hesitate. I pull Jack into my arms and plant a heated but soft kiss on his lips. One that he doesn't fight. His body melts into my arms. Strong and sinewy, it's everything I feared and dreamed of and wanted. It's better than all the times we hooked up because I get to savor it. The way my arm curls around his side, the curve where his hips meet his ass. The slightly chapped feel of his lips.

Jack moans against my lips. He dips back, cold air between us. And then he reaches past me and grabs his coat off the coat rack.

He holds it up. "I forgot my coat."

Fuck.

He slips it on one arm at a time and folds down the collar. He checks himself in the front mirror that my wife made me put up. She says people need to have a front mirror to check themselves before leaving the house. It also comes in handy when you need an extra angle for witnessing your mortification.

"Took you long enough." That signature smirk slides onto his face, only this time his lips are redder. Swollen. "I knew you've been wanting to do that all night."

"No, I didn't."

"Oh yeah, you did." He shoots me a wink. "You think you're stone-faced, but you're actually very readable."

"You know what—"

Jack puts two fingers to my lips. "Don't worry. So did I."

He pulls me against him and continues where we left off. It's like the music gets raised again, and the party can continue.

Right away, I can tell this kiss is different. There's no rushing. No urgency to get to the next step. We could stand in this doorway making out all night, and I'd be happy with that.

I take in more details of Jack. The heat of his tongue, the way his nose feels pressed against mine, the little gasp intake of breath he takes because he's not as suave as he thinks he is. I want every detail.

He dots my lips with pecks, caressing his hands through my beard. I press my tongue to his teeth.

"Slow," he says. His hands shift from caressing my beard to directing my mouth. "This isn't a game. There's no buzzer. Slow."

Jack demonstrates, sliding his tongue into my mouth, rolling it around, massaging my tongue, then slipping it out, a fish I can't catch. Our mouths open and close as his tongue gently slips in, his fingers sliding over my beard, moans coming from deep within him. The result is hypnotic and relaxing. I didn't expect to be relaxed while kissing Jack. The methodical movement of his lips and hands and the circling of his tongue send me into a blissed-out daze where time stands still.

"Like that," he says, pulling back, his cheeks flush and eyes so black I hardly recognize them. But I recognize that smirk, softer, staring back at me. "You try."

I touch my lips to his, savor their saltiness. Our mouths open and close in sync. My tongue slides into his cavernous space and swims around, sending tingles down my neck. The effect is pure magic, like that feeling of careening down the ice, wind whipping across my visor, blades gliding through the ice, rhythm perfectly in sync. I rake my hands through his hair, letting myself savor the roughness of each strand. I brush against the prickly hairs on the back of his freshly buzzed neck. I pull him harder against me, my soul feeling freer than ever in my life.

Even though we're not sharing our biggest secrets, this feels scarily intimate, but I'm not scared. I feel a trust with Jack. He may have more experience with guys, but I doubt any of them have been as magical as this.

Jack moans against my lips. His fingernails dig into my back.

"That was good," he says, gasping for air. "Really good."

He throws his arms around my neck. I go in for round three. His moans gets louder and more instant as our lips touch, and I get more confident with my kissing.

"You're a fast learner," he says into my mouth.

"I'm not a newbie," I say defensively.

"I get the sense you haven't done this with other guys."

My protectiveness over my sexual history comes out. He presses a finger to my mouth to stop me.

"I'm not judging." Kindness shines through in his dark eyes. His eyes plead with me to lower my defenses.

I push him backward against the doorframe and close the gap between our lips, the smacking sound our mouths make is a most delightful melody. That's when I remember the door is open. It's not like Sourwood's never seen two guys kiss, but they don't need to know my business.

I rake a hand through his hair and stare into his eyes as our lips part.

"I like kissing you," I tell him. I rub a thumb on his stubble.

Jack pulls back, and we gaze into each other's eyes, no fear, no wondering about what happens next. Just enjoying the moment. Just being with him.

This is nice. Just as nice as our sexual escapades, but in a different way.

He brushes his hand against my fly, sending a wild burst of heat through my core.

"Shall we take this somewhere more private? Like your bedroom?" he murmurs.

I pull back, the cold light of reality hitting me. "My bedroom shares a wall with the girls' room. I don't want to risk waking them."

"Agreed. That'd be a future therapy session waiting to happen."

"Especially with the things you like to say." I shoot him a wink. "Not that I'm complaining."

"So what do you want to do?" Jack asks, waiting on me to come up with a plan.

"I don't feel comfortable fooling around in the house, especially with the way sound travels in here. But we can't leave them in the house alone."

"Now I get why parents are so sexually frustrated." Jack leans against the door. My cock strains against my pants, begging for a solution.

But it's Jack who seems to have the lightbulb moment. He tugs at my shirt, pulling me flush against him.

"Your truck is in the garage, right?" he asks.

"Uh huh."

"And even though your garage isn't connected to the house, it's still considered part of the house, right?"

"Uh huh."

"Then Griffin, I want you to fuck me in the back of your truck."

JACK

Call me old-fashioned, but there's something about a man with a pickup truck that's hot. I won't lie; it's a bucket list sex fantasy to do it in the back of one.

I climb into the bed of Griffin's truck. The metal is cold, but Griffin's arms warm me right up when he joins me. I've had sex in more uncomfortable places. He pulls me onto his lap and delivers another exquisite kiss, learning all of my lessons and excelling perfectly. The glow of the moon and far-off streetlights streak through the garage windows.

"Good idea coming here," he says while kissing my neck.

What can I say? Being horny and resourceful is a potent mix.

I trace my finger over the border where his beard meets his bare cheek. I want to be a cartographer mapping every detail of this gorgeous face.

"You're really cute, you know that?"

"I do, but it's always nice to hear." He smiles.

I think about how fucking good he is with his daughters, how much they adore him, how much he adores them. Who knew good parenting could be a turn-on for me?

I whip off his shirt, letting my hands glide through his hairy chest.

I breathe in his scent, muzzle my face into his muscles. Things I never got to do in our previous instances. There was always a rush. Now we could settle.

I raise my arms and let him undress me as I grind my ass into his poking erection. Our chests grind together in harmony, mine smooth and his a beast. Griffin won't stop kissing me, touching me, every move bursting with tenderness.

"Stand up," Griffin says, his voice choked and husky.

I do as I'm told, getting on my feet, holding onto the cab of the truck while Griffin undoes my pants. His thick, hot hands graze over my crotch then my legs as he pushes down my jeans, then my boxer briefs.

He takes me in his mouth, sending waves of pleasure through me.

"Your mouth feels so good. So damn wet. I can't fucking wait to have you inside me."

His beard rubs along my shaft, making me shiver. He takes me in his mouth, teasing the tip. Within seconds, I'm so damn close to the edge, my body tight and coiled with pleasure ready to spring out. I want nothing more than to blow my load down his throat. My balls are begging for it. But I must hold out because I know what's coming. Griffin's thick cock fully inside me.

"Swirl your tongue around my shaft. Just like that."

Griffin goes to town on my dick, taking it all in his mouth, making the ability to stand up really hard right now. He is playing me like the world's most turned-on fiddle. I want every part of me electrified by him.

I turn around and shove his face against my ass. Sex is about give and take, and I am in the mood for taking. I demand that glorious tongue in my hole. His strong grip holds me in place as he eats me out.

"Tongue that hole. Fuck, you are so goddamned good at this." I bite my lip, wanting to scream in pleasure.

His prickly beard adds a new layer of pleasure to the process as I feel his tongue flick in and out of me. His thumb circles my hole and dips inside, making me shudder with want.

"I didn't think of myself as an ass man until I met you," he says, giving my ass a slap. "But watching you in your uniform. Damn."

"All that hockey playing. It's good for the legs."

"That it is." His hands skim down my legs, making the hairs stand up. Griffin kisses down my thigh behind my knee, making me laugh with ticklishness. He smooths a hand over my calf muscles and kisses them, too.

"What are you doing? You're into calves?" I laugh. I'd never been with someone who gave a shit about legs or calves.

"I'm into yours." Despite a snarky tone, there's a seriousness to what Griffin says, a warmth that coats his words. "They're beautiful."

"They're fucking calves."

"I like your muscles. I like how strong you are." Griffin's hand rides up to my quad, pulsing and tense to keep me up. My ass twitches, greedily wanting more. But as Griffin's fingers circle through my leg hair, eliciting goosebumps, I realize he's discovered a new erogenous zone.

"Griffin," I squeak out as his hand goes higher on my thigh, squeezing it until it reaches my ass. I cry out in want. His tongue goes back inside me. "Yes. Yes."

I stroke my aching cock, delirious with lust. Wanting Griffin. Not wanting this night to end and wanting him inside me so bad it hurts.

He spreads me wider, plunging two fingers inside me. I imagine his thick, rough, calloused hands, spending all day fixing planes and playing hockey, his manly hands plowing inside me, making me his. I rock back and fuck his fingers.

I nearly collapse when he pulls his mouth back. I'm not sure how I'm supposed to function after that.

"If I ever become a millionaire again, I'm hiring you away from the airport to do that to me full time." I sink to my knees. His dick tents his pants. "My turn."

Griffin stands up and leans against the truck bed as I take his fat cock in my mouth. Tasting his musky scent on my lips. I can't wait to feel him inside me. Griffin pushes me down, then pulls me back, controlling me by my hair. He's rough but gentle at the same time, my trust completely in his hands. I want to be his toy.

He gazes down at me, and I get the feeling he's been looking at me this whole time. There's a purity to his smile, like he's watching something of beauty, and not some horny jock slobbering all over his dick.

I stroke him while playing with his balls in my mouth, loving the unmistakable scent of Griffin.

"You better have lube in this garage," I say.

I stop mid-suck when a dog-ate-my-homework look crosses his face.

"What about lube in your bedroom?"

He shakes his head no.

"Lube in your secret doomsday shelter?"

"No lube." Griffin sits up, the lust vanishing from his eye. "I need to tell you something."

Oh shit. Guys who need to tell me something during sex is never good news. This is where it happens. The flip. Again, I let myself trust someone, and then they do a one-eighty and cast me aside.

"What is it?" I ask.

Griffin exhales a deep breath. "I've never had sex with a man."

My reaction is the obvious one. I laugh. Because this has to be a joke. Something to lighten the mood before bringing down the hammer.

"Right." I pull up my pants. "Okay, what did you actually want to tell me?"

"It's true. I've never had sex with a man." There's a sheepishness to him in that moment, something innocent and almost childlike that informs me that yes, this was the something he needed to tell me.

"You're a virgin?"

"No. I've had sex with a woman."

"Right, right. The kids." I scratch my head. "But you're like in your forties."

"I came out later in life." He shrugs.

I feel like an asshole. Griffin is being real with me, and I'm still in disbelief. Everyone has their own journey. I squeeze his hand, bring it to my mouth for a supportive kiss. "Well, I'm honored that I get to pop your gay sex cherry. The good news is that you won't have boobs smacking you in the face during it."

He lets out a small laugh, but I can tell he's still embarrassed by the admission.

"There are guys who've had lots of sex and are still terrible at it. If you can fuck half as good as you can rim, you'll be okay." I clap his shoulder, trying to think back to how a coach would give me a pep talk. "Thank you for trusting me with that."

"That's why I pushed you away on the rooftop the night we met. I wanted to keep going. I was so into you, but...I was scared. Things were moving so fast. I panicked."

"It's on me, too. I was going really fast," I admit. "I was feeling things for you, which freaked me out because that never happens with guys. Even though we barely knew each other, the vibe between us was *real*, and real shit scares me. So I wanted to cut to sex ASAP so we could come and never see each other again. Obviously, that plan backfired."

"We both suck at this." Griffin cups my cheek, massages it with his thumb, helping to settle the nerves in my stomach.

"You never wanted to have sex when you were closeted? Not even on the down low?" I ask. I sit next to him, thread my fingers through his. No matter his sexual history or non-history, I'm not going anywhere.

"Of course I thought about it. On some level, I've always known I was gay. But I didn't think you could be gay and a hockey player. I told myself that I'd come out once I became a hockey superstar. I'd make history."

I had that same thought when I got drafted, and I still kick myself for not trying to be more vocal. A part of me wanted to be really successful before I came out, so that nobody could criticize my performance based on my sexuality. That obviously didn't pan out.

"And then I lost an eye." He laughs to himself. "I let down my mom by ruining my hockey career. I let down my teammates and coaches. I didn't want to disappoint them any further. I pushed it down and tried to live as respectable of a life I could. I got married, had a family."

"What made you finally come out then?"

"I thought of Annabelle and June. I didn't want to spend my life lying to them. I didn't want them to believe that that was okay."

"All through your twenties and thirties, you didn't think of experimenting with a guy? Getting your gay ya-yas out?"

He shakes his head no. "I think I felt more comfortable being closeted and married to a woman because I was giving a performance. It wasn't the real me. It was Griffin the straight family man."

I nod along. It was easy to play Jack the flirty athlete who hits it and quits it. I could play that part forever.

Griffin continues, "But being with a guy meant showing my true self. And what if a guy didn't like what he saw? What if he saw the same thing I did: a failure. A guy who was washed up at eighteen. No college education. No left eye. Who wants to sleep with a failure, let alone fall in love with one?"

"Griffin." My heart breaks hearing him talk like that. How dare anyone say those things about this great man. There is no worthier person than Griffin Harper. I hold his head in my hands, force him to look at me. "You are none of those things. You know what I see? I see a man who's had a rough hand dealt to him but powers through. A man who wants to be a loner but has such a big heart that he's beloved by his friends and kids. You may not have won the Stanley Cup and gotten endorsement deals, but you do what every professional athlete should: you inspire people."

It happens so fast, I don't even realize it, like the overnight temperature drop initiating a new season. I am in love with Griffin Harper. I wish it weren't so. I wish I could say it was just for the good juju. But no can do. I am a goner for him.

I kiss him because I have no fucking idea what to say next, because the fear and exhilaration of this realization is choking the air out of my lungs. I love Griffin. It's something I want to keep to myself while also shouting from the rooftops.

"Would olive oil work?" he asks.

"Hell yeah. It worked for the Greeks."

He hops out of the truck and walks over to a pantry shelf, grabs a bottle of unopened olive oil.

"It's extra virgin," he says.

Back on the truck, we get back into it, hot and heavy. He massages oil into my hole, and I'm so fired up.

I get on my knees, my ass sticking out for him. It's a position that always makes me feel vulnerable, but I am comfortable with Griffin. I want him to pound into me.

Yet he doesn't move.

"Is there a problem?" I ask.

"I don't want you like that. I want you to ride me."

My mouth goes dry at the hunger that instantly builds inside me, the sheer delight of getting to bounce on his lap.

I love that as inexperienced as Griffin might be, he knows what he wants and he's direct. He balances me on his lap. Our eyes meet, a million things said between them. I've never had sex this way, but for me, sex was always a means to an end, a way to feel pleasure and nothing else.

I sink onto his cock. It pushes past my tightness, and I exhale tight breath. I put my arms around his belly to balance myself. Griffin rests his hands on my hips, steering me up and down. His biceps swell as he lifts me and puts me down. I feel weightless in his arms.

My fingers dance over his eye patch. I want to remove all layers between us. I can tell Griffin anything, be anything with him. I want the same for him.

He puts his hand over mine and together, we slide the eye patch off his face and toss it onto the truck bed. I graze over the scarred, puffy eye. It's beautiful. He's beautiful.

"Ringer," he says, a deep well of hope in his voice, as he pulls me into a delicate kiss.

I throw my head back, falling into ecstasy as he fills me up. When I pick my head up, he's still staring at me. He hasn't looked away.

I dip my head down, then to the side. The intensity of his stare is almost too much. He stares at me like I'm...like I'm valuable.

"Jack," he groans. My name on his lips. Nothing better.

He takes my chin and forces me to lock eyes with him. Instinctively, I try to pull away, but he won't let me. We are connected. I bounce up and down, fucking him harder, hoping that I can fuck him into such bliss that he has to look away.

Why won't he look away? What does he see in me?

Each second more is like stripping away another layer that I don't want him to see. I'm turned on and I'm terrified.

"Jack," he utters again.

"Griffin. I..."

I lean down and press my forehead against his. He tips my chin up so our eyes can meet. Our lips connect as he grabs my ass and jackhammers into me, grunting with each thrust.

I push back so I can better meet his gaze. In between our eyes, there is nothing. No universe. No real world. Just us two.

Griffin keeps looking at me like I could be somebody. I want to believe it. And in this moment, I do.

I squeeze my fingernails into his back as I shoot my load. Come hits his furry stomach. He grunts his approval and smiles. His strong hand massages my neck, then sinks to my chest. I lean back and hump against his dick as the last drops of orgasm empty out of me.

"I'm so close, baby," he says.

I'm baby now? I should hate that, but I don't.

I assume Griffin needs to close his eyes to get into the zone to come. But no. He keeps staring at me, as if my face is the Mona Lisa meets the hottest gay porn in existence.

I nod, silently telling him how bad I want it.

He contorts as he empties himself inside me.

I fall into his chest, and we kiss again, each of us still catching our breath.

It's not the juju.

It's him.

It's always been him.

28

GRIFFIN

My phone alarm jolts me out of a deep sleep. Jack whips his head up from my chest, his bedhead sprouting in all directions. He wipes the sleep from his eyes. Somehow, with the help of some warm blankets, we drifted to sleep in the truck bed. Whatever discomfort I felt laying on an unforgiving surface was canceled out by having Jack's body against mine.

I shut off the alarm and rub a hand through his hair.

"What time is it?" he peeks through the garage window, where moonlight and streetlights illuminate the darkness.

"Three-thirty."

"In the morning?"

"Uh huh. I wanted to make sure I'm up before them."

"What time do they get up?" Jack rolls off me, and my body instantly craves his warmth.

"June sometimes gets up at five, maybe four-thirty if she's having a rough time sleeping. And that usually wakes up Annabelle, too." I want to be certain that if they wake up, they can find me in my bed. Alone.

I'm not ready to explain why Jack was sleeping over. I'm still figuring out what this means. My heart is all over the place.

"The last thing they need is to see my bare ass when they wake up," Jack says, and I'm grateful that he gets it.

He wipes a hand through his hair trying to smooth it down. One piece in the back insists on sticking up. I push it down, but it springs right back to its upright position. Not unlike my dick right now.

He rubs an arm across his eyes.

"Are you okay to drive?" Even though he understands, I can't help but feel like a jerk for asking him to go. "And for the record, if I had my way, I'd lay in bed with you all day. A real bed."

"That sounds nice." He yawns into my chest. "I'm going home and crashing before the game."

Shit. Today is Sunday. We both have games. Jack can play on a few hours of sleep. I'm going to have a tougher time. At least Carmen has the girls today, so I can crash this afternoon.

Jack sits up for a moment, then flops against me, mashing his face into my chest. I could get used to him living permanently in the crook of my arm. "What a night, huh?"

"You said it."

A far-off look clouds his face, dimming my enjoyment. His eyes are a thick curtain I can't pull back. "This was...nice."

My heart lifts, thinking about us playing with the girls, about us kissing tenderly. I didn't think of myself as the guy who would ever get Hallmark moments. Nice is nowhere near as strong a word to describe the past twenty-four hours.

"I guess I should get going." He searches for his clothes, thrown about somewhere in the truck bed.

I reach for his arm, stopping his hurried pursuit. "Hey. What's going on?"

"I'm trying to find my clothes so I can go."

"Jack, I wish you could stay. I want you to stay. I just think if the girls saw you this morning...it'd be a conversation I don't know if I'm ready to have. But I want to, eventually. I don't see this ending anytime soon."

I surprise myself as well as Jack with the admission. It's probably bad form to mention anything serious in the afterglow of sex, but time waits for no man. I spent the first forty years of my life not letting myself feel these feelings.

"I like you, Jack. I really like you."

He nods, his jaw tight, emotion welling behind his eyes.

"Is it crazy that I want to be with you?" I ask.

"A little. But I'm just that good in the sack."

"It's not that." He's trying to deflect. I won't let him.

"Griffin, maybe we should just leave it as some hockey season fun," he says, his voice detached. He finds his boxers in a tangled ball against my leg.

"Is that what you want?" Did I completely misjudge the chemistry between us? Because what we had last night was not just sex.

Jack licks his lips, but stays silent.

"Is it because of your dad?"

"I mean, I doubt he'd be a fan of us fucking, to put it lightly. But come on, Griffin, we had some fun and maybe it's best that it doesn't go any further and ruin things. Our big game is in a week. Don't mess with the juju."

I don't know what changed with Jack, but the wall between us went up fast.

He puts on his boxers, then finds his jeans. His dexterity at dressing himself while laying down is impressive and suggests that this isn't the first time he's snuck out of someone's bed. I'd been using his shirt as a pillow.

"Can you lift your head?"

I do not. I shove the shirt behind my back. Immature, yes, but I had no better ideas. Looking into those crystal blues would make any man do crazy things.

"I know I should give you back your shirt and let you go and let that be that. But dammit, I can't." I cup his determined chin in my hand. "You're the first guy who makes me feel like I didn't completely fuck up my life, that all of these setbacks and hardships were all put in place for a reason, because they led me to you. When I came out, I did it to be honest with myself and those around me. I didn't expect to feel this kind of hope. Like maybe I'm actually doing something right in my life for a change."

"Griffin..." I feel his chin tremble in my grip, quivering with barely contained emotion. If I let him leave this garage, then this connection will be lost forever.

"And I know you're supposed to be the cocky one, but allow me to indulge for a moment: you feel it, too. You're into me."

He softens a touch, but it's very short-lived. His face hardens, a flash of anger bolting across his vision before he breaks from my grasp.

"Of course I am! But who says you're not going to push me away like the rest of them!"

"Who would ever push you away?" I don't mean to sound aloof. I'm confused as to why that would ever happen to someone as wonderful as Jack.

"Oh, let's see? I thought I had loving parents, but my mom bailed without saying goodbye. And as soon as I stopped being a hockey star, my dad stopped being my number one fan."

Red clouds his face. All I want to do is hug his anger away. He looks away, as if considering what to say next. He suddenly whips his head back to me.

"You know, before I became this big slut, I did try to do the relationship thing," he says. "Guys loved the idea of fucking a professional athlete, and once the excitement faded, they bolted, too. So I figured it was smart to just leave things at one night only. Keep up the mystique, get my rocks off, and onto the next. I was good at that. You don't get hurt that way. People don't leave you if you leave first." He shakes his head, his jaw incredibly tight. "And then I had to meet you."

I put a tentative hand on his shoulder. His muscles are incredibly tense, like he's always poised to run.

"I would never do anything like that to you," I say. I've never been so angry in my life. Rage boils inside me at what's been done to Jack. "You know I'm not like that."

"They all say that. They all say they love me until they don't."

"I will never hurt you," I whisper in his ear. "I would take the most brutal check on the ice every day for the rest of my life so you'd never have to feel this way again. I'm not going anywhere." I kiss his forehead, waiting for the moment he shoves me back, but it doesn't come. "I want you to love me. But more than that, I want you to trust me."

Shit. Did I just use the *L* word? It was something that had been percolating inside me over the past day. Listening to Jack bare his soul pushed it to the forefront for me. There may be a big age gap between us, but Jack has lived more life by twenty-four, a life filled with ups and down and victory and hurt, than most people have by fifty.

"Jack."

Slowly, he curls his hand around mine. A sliver of light at the end of this tunnel.

"I..." he croaks out, his voice stifled with emotion. A tear falls down his cheek. "Just kiss me already, Griffin."

Will fucking do.

I pull him into my lap, kissing him with all my love, all my heart, telling him everything I can't say with words. I will give him all the love he deserves, and I'm not going anywhere.

"But keep in mind if you do turn out to be an asshole, I will gouge out your other eye."

"The people in your family sure do love coming after my sense of sight."

"It's genetic." He laughs and presses his mouth to mine again, the salty taste of his tears hitting my tongue.

We pause, though, both coming to the same realization.

"Are you going to tell your dad about us?" I ask.

"Eventually. I think if I win this game next week, he'll be in a good mood, so maybe that'll be my opening."

It wasn't something either of us wanted to dwell on.

"Speaking of openings." I drift my fingers into his boxers and down his crack. He pulls them back.

"I should go, and you need to sneak back to your bedroom." He kisses me one last time before hopping off me. He finds his pants and leaves the truck bed.

This time, when I watch him walk out that garage door, I know he'll be back.

29

JACK

Despite running on very little sleep, I powered through our game with the Overbites, and I received a free pack of floss. I made a beautiful pass to Fuentes in the second period for a goal that put us over the top. It was good practice for the big Sourwood Cup game in one week.

After the game, we went to Easter Egg but made sure to keep Miller away from the pinball machines. The owner made us promise after he almost smashed his fist through The Addams Family game. Fuentes informed the team that we'd be having two extra practices this week to prepare. The guys groaned in response.

"Do you really think we need it?" Miller asked.

"Yes!" Fuentes slammed down his beer. "The Comebacks demolished their opponents today. I heard that Griffin Harper scored two goals and barely let a forward through his line. He is on fire, and he's barreling right into us."

He barreled into me last night, again and again. A flush of red creeps up my back as I remember the highlights.

"All eyes are on us next week," continued Fuentes. "People are reaching out to me every day on social media to tell me how badly they want us to lose. We're the big, bad, younger team, not the lovable underdog. If this were an '80s sports movie, we'd be the villains. I don't want to be the villains. I'm nice!"

He plunks down on his barstool and drowns his anxieties in his beer.

"We're gonna win!" I say to the team. "This isn't a movie. We are better, stronger, faster. Griffin and the Comebacks can barrel into us all they want, but we will push back."

Just like a good power bottom.

We break off into different conversations as guys eventually leave. Fuentes, Miller, and I grab another drink.

"So how are you feeling about next week?" Fuentes asks me.

I take a sip of my beer and shrug. "Whatever happens, happens."

"You sound chill," Miller says.

"Maybe I am."

"Really?" he asks. "Most eyes will be on you. People will want to see if the pro hockey player chokes against the locals. And on top of that, your future career prospects hinge on pulling out a win."

"Wow, Miller. You really know how to make a guy feel calm." Fuentes smacks him in the chest. "Excellent yogi skills, fucker."

"I was just pointing out facts." He turns to me, his big eyes getting even wider. "Do you want to do a breathing exercise to chill out?"

"No."

"Okay. Do you want one of my edibles?"

I had told the guys about the potential coaching job at Hudson University earlier in the locker room. I still can't believe it's a real possibility, and I don't know why it isn't making me more nervous. This whole weekend has been a fucking blur, and it's messing with my head.

"I want to win. I'm making no bones about it," says Fuentes. He spins the coaster like a top. "I don't want everyone in this town thinking we can't beat a bunch of has-beens."

Miller nods along with him, and for the first time, I can tell how much this game is weighing on them. I'm not the only one who should be feeling nervous. No matter the stakes, no hockey player wants to lose. We play sports not to learn good sportsmanship, but to dominate. I don't want to let them down.

"They're not has-beens," I say. "They still got the goods. But so do we."

Familiar nerves rumble in my stomach. I'm most scared about embarrassing myself in front of the whole town, proving to everyone that the NHL was right to cast me aside.

"It's an amazing opportunity, getting to coach at the collegiate level," says Fuentes.

"It is," I repeat. "It would be the most logical path for me to take. All I know is hockey." I take a swig of my beer, a curious crestfallen pang hitting my chest.

—————

OUR WEEKDAY PRACTICES ARE GRUELING. The guys are in it to win it and nothing less. I want to win this game to show them that they made the right choice in bringing me onto the team.

On Thursday night, I take an ice bath when I get home. I close my eyes and think about the coaching job. What would it be like to work with college athletes? What would it also be like to deal with administrative bureaucracy? I recall my old coaches complaining about red tape with the franchise owners. I think about the chance to live and breathe hockey again.

I try to get myself psyched up about the opportunity. Yet like a guy attempting to have sex after too many whiskey sours, I just can't get there.

A knock at the front door startles me. Because it's such a small apartment, the sound reverberates against the bathroom walls.

I throw a towel around my waist and run to the door.

"And here I thought I was going to have to seduce you." Griffin arrives wearing a flannel and jeans. Does this guy ever not look drop-dead sexy?

"What are you doing here?"

"Seeing you. I was on my way home from dropping off the girls, and I realized that I drive by your apartment building every time I make the trip."

"Don't you love geography?"

"Not as much as I love checking you out." He scoops me into his arms, and I'm pulled into his chest, inhaling his musky, fresh scent.

I tiptoe us backward into my apartment. The last thing my neighbors need is a free sex show. We stumble backward onto my couch. My towel falls off somewhere along the journey.

"Maybe we take this to the bedroom," he says as he kisses down my neck.

"You're in it."

He looks around and clocks the minimal square footage.

"You sleep on a couch?" he asks.

"It's a pullout."

"Fuck, you really are twenty-four." He laughs into my lips as he plants another deep kiss, unleashing a torrent of goosebumps across my naked flesh.

My hard cock rubs against his jeans. He gives it a gentle stroke, like a handshake for an old friend.

"You're freezing." He wraps his arms tighter around me.

"I was taking an ice bath. We had a tough practice tonight." I unbutton his flannel and smooth a hand over his chest and stomach, wanting every inch of it.

"Bill's made us practice every day this week. We finally convinced him to give us today off."

"Good. You don't want him overworking you guys and wearing you out before the game."

We talk between kisses. Griffin jerks me off at a leisurely pace. It's a very domestic situation of two lovers asking each other about their day...only with less clothes on.

"Des's shoulder has been hurting because of all the extra shooting practice."

"Tell him twenty minutes of icing it every other hour. The doctor on one of my teams said that when you over-ice it, it slows recovery." I pinch his nipple, making him grunt as he tongues my ear. "That with some ibuprofen should get him healed by Sunday."

I break my train of thought with a gasp when he lightly tugs at my sack.

"You okay?" he asks.

"Yeah. That was a good gasp." I shove his shirt off his broad shoulders. I flick my tongue over his nipple, eliciting a pull on my cock in response. We are a tangle of arms and hunched backs trying to make this position work. We collapse onto the couch.

I straddle him, letting my bare ass writhe on his tented jeans. "So how are you feeling about the game?"

I throw my arms around his neck and kiss him hard before he can answer. He gives my ass a slap and pinch. He leans back slightly so his crotch has more of a thrusting radius.

"Aside from Des's shoulder, we're in great shape. All of these lead-up games have been great practice." Griffin kisses down my chest, nuzzling his beard against my abs.

"Have you worked with Hank on his positioning in goal?"

"What?"

I lift myself so I can unzip his pants. His underwear-wrapped cock shoots out. He sits me back on top of it, teasing me with the thin cotton layer separating his dick from my ass.

I bounce against his thickness, praying that his underwear rips and he can plunge inside me.

"Hank's angle is off when he tracks a puck. He's going for ninety degrees, but he winds up like eighty degrees. And he could move a little farther out from the goal to better cut the angle and improve coverage."

"He stands square to the puck." Griffin pulls me against his chest. He yanks his boxers off and thwacks his bare, hot cock against my hole. "It's better than standing at ninety."

"It's not. Ninety gives you more flexibility to pivot." I nibble at his ear, fantasizing about getting impaled on his thickness. Being in his arms instantly throws me to the brink of orgasm. "Hank is jerking around a lot in goal. Standing at ninety would let him be faster to block pucks."

"Well, since we're giving advice, your boy Miller is too fancy with his stick handling. Likes to show off. Makes it easy to strip the puck from him."

Looking back, I can see his point. Miller can too often be a target of steals, and now I get why.

"I'll let him know. You know what's great about my couch also being my bed?" I press my forehead against his and gaze into his heavy-lidded eyes. "The lube is close by."

I reach a hand to the side table and fish around for the lube in the drawer. I throw it against his chest, a silent plea to fuck me as fast as he can.

"Do you have any other tips for my teammates, or can I fuck the shit of you now?" He doesn't wait for my answer. He lifts us up from the couch and presses me up against the window, the cold of the glass stinging my back. I hug my body against his big torso as his tongue ravages my mouth.

"I want you so bad, Griffin."

"That's fucking obvious." His greedy finger circles my hole, making my body clench with dizzying anticipation. "I've only had sex with a guy once. I have a lot of catching up to do."

I want this man to stretch me out like the collar of his favorite T-shirt.

He unlocks my legs from his waist and puts me down, then spins me around. He presses my face against the glass. I jut my ass out, wanting him to take me from behind.

"Eat my hole and then fuck me until I scream."

"You got it."

I close my eyes, fully embracing this heaven-sent moment. I heard if you close your eyes during sex, then it heightens your other senses. Yet I don't feel him spread me open or flick his tongue on my hole. In fact, he hasn't moved at all.

"What is it?" I open my eyes and crane my head back at him.

Panic takes over his right eye as he stares out the window. I follow his eyeline to the parking lot, and all at once, my body goes numb.

A man in a heavy coat glares daggers at us, his familiar scowl even more venomous. A purple apron is bunched in his fist.

30

JACK

I race to my closet and find the first available pair of pants. Usually I'm not one for freeballing it, but there's no time. I need to catch Dad before he drives off.

I thank the construction gods for making the windows taller than usual. Dad could only see chest up. So yeah, what a relief that he didn't see me getting my ass tongued. But he still saw Griffin standing behind me, shirtless.

Speaking of shirtless Griffin, he's already dressed by the time I return to the couch. Bless him for getting the severity of the situation.

"You're fast," I note.

"When you have little kids, you don't get much time to yourself to get dressed in the morning, so you need to be quick."

He tosses me a pair of flip flops he presumably found on the floor.

"Thanks. Shit." Mortification hits me. I'm wading through high-tide of this ocean of embarrassment.

"We're high up. It's dark. He probably didn't see anything," Griffin says, not even convincing himself.

I may never forget the awful look on his face down in that parking lot. I worry it'll be the last time I ever see his face. Dad and I don't get along, but the possibility that he'd cut me out of his life sends a sharp pang of fear stabbing through my heart.

"I'll be right back." I kiss him goodbye.

Turns out, I'm not going anywhere. Dad bangs at the door with such force that it shakes the cabinet doors and causes a framed poster from my hockey days crashing to the floor.

Griffin leaps up and throws a protective arm across me.

I give him a nod that it'll be okay, even though my pulse is racing so fast it's bound to go sonic boom.

Dad bangs at the door again, sending another framed poster to the floor.

"Open up!" he yells.

Griffin squeezes my hand. "I'm right here," he says.

A beat of quiet takes over the apartment as I unlock the door. It's so silent, I can hear the click. And then all hell breaks loose.

Dad bursts through the entrance, shoves past me, and takes a swing at Griffin, getting him in the eye patch. Did Dad aim for that spot on purpose, or was it a twist of fucked-up fate?

Griffin stumbles back yet stays on his feet.

"Dad! Stop!"

"What the hell are you doing with my son?" he yells at Griffin, seething with a rage I didn't know he had in him.

He doesn't wait for an answer. He lunges at Griffin, who avoids his punch this time. Griffin pushes him into the fridge. Cereal boxes and bags of chips fall to the ground.

"Dad, I can explain!"

He barrels into Griffin, sending him into the island. More of my shit falls to the ground. Griffin yowls in pain and grabs his lower back where he made contact.

"Stop!" Griffin yells.

"Is this some kind of sick revenge?" Dad heaves air through his nostrils like a bull, and to him, Griffin is a wall of red. "You ruined my career, and now you're out for my son, too?"

"I didn't ruin shit. You ruined mine!"

Dad charges at Griffin, bum-rushing him onto the couch. Fortunately, that's the one thing in my apartment that can't break.

"Stop it!" I yell at the top of my lungs. I grab a plate from the sink and throw it against the wall above the couch. The shattering break gets Dad to stop.

"Get off me!" Griffin says, pushing out of Dad's grip.

Dad paces by the window and smooths out his sweater. We have a brief window before he can be detonated again. For the first time since he barged in, he acknowledges I'm in the room. Behind his glare is something resembling heartbreak.

"What the hell are you doing with him?" he asks me.

"We were...we..." The beginnings of sentences tumble out of my mouth, but I can't finish any of them. While I'd be happy to proclaim my feelings for Griffin to almost anyone, I don't know how to thread this needle with Dad.

"Dad, it's not what you think. Griffin isn't here out of revenge."

"Are you two..." Dad points between us. His face drains of color. "I can't even say it."

"We are." Griffin stands up and straightens his shirt. "I like your son."

"What? You're...no." Dad looks like he wants to vomit. He turns to me. "Jack, you've made a lot of bad decisions in your life, but this has to be one of the worst."

"It's true, Dad." His dig at me makes me find my backbone. I'm tired of him looking down at my life. "Griffin and I are together."

Griffin holds my hand, which threatens to send Dad back into bull mode.

"Jack, this man cannot be trusted. Look, what you do in private is your business. I've never asked. I respect your privacy. But him, of all people? He took me out like an assassin in the middle of a game and destroyed my career. I know our relationship isn't as strong as it used to be, but why are you trying to hurt me?"

Dad's eyes are big and round, puppy-like, a new low for him. His silent ask for pity only makes me angrier, and I find I'm the one becoming the bull. All of my pent-up anger at Dad spirals out in a tornado of fury. He drilled into me and finally hit a gushing geyser of oil.

"It's not about you!" I yell at the top of my lungs with such ferocity it actually takes my breath away. It takes both Dad and Griffin aback. "You want to make everything in my life about you. What you didn't get. The future you want for me. Your rival. But I'm with Griffin for me. Because he makes me happy. He actually cares about me."

"You think I don't care about you?"

"You care about what I can do for you. I'm just your puppet that you can maneuver to get what you think is owed to you. You don't love me, and I'm fine with that. I've come to terms with it. And guess what? I don't love you either." His face goes even more wounded puppy dog, which only drills deeper into my oil well of rage. "You don't get to storm in here and tell me who I can and can't be with. And you definitely can't throw a punch at the guy I'm dating."

Dad shakes his head, as if he took a really bad punch. Where I thought I'd hit another nerve of anger and disappointment, there's a more subdued reaction from him. I turn to Griffin, who gives me a supportive nod, but even that gesture seems more subdued.

"You really think all that?" Dad asks quietly.

I stalk to the front door and gesture out into the hallway. "It would've been nice if you asked about my private life. Maybe I wouldn't have felt so alone. It was you who made it a secret."

Dad shuffles into the hall. "If you only knew how much I sacrificed to give you a good life. Everything I did, it was out of love."

He has the gall to sound genuine.

"Why did you even come over here?"

Dad pulls my lucky bracelet from his coat pocket. "I searched the whole house. Found it in a shoebox in my closet of all places. Thought you might need it for Sunday's game. I was really looking forward to watching you back in action. I feel like I'm watching magic when I watch you on the ice."

He tosses the bracelet into my hand. I stare at it, but don't react.

"Okay then." He shuffles down the hall, out of sight, perhaps for the last time.

I close the door. The silence in the apartment lets me hear the lock click back into place.

Griffin puts a hand on my shoulder, and it's the drop of rain that makes the levy break. I collapse, sobbing into his arms.

31

GRIFFIN

Bill wanted us to rest before the big game. I've done anything but.

I stayed with Jack all night on Thursday, doing whatever I could to make him feel better after the fight with his dad. Despite hating Ted Gross, it was hard to watch as a father. I can't imagine Annabelle and June saying they hated me, that they don't love me. Jack has a valid reason, and Ted is no saint, but it was still hard to watch. I felt bad for both of them.

I checked on Jack on Friday after work, and he was still torn up about what happened. All of the good juju we had accrued leading up the game couldn't turn his spirits around. He even mentioned skipping the game altogether. I talked him out of that, thank goodness. But how can a player go into a game with an attitude like that?

My juju was fading, too. Guilt ravaged me over Thursday night. While I know that Jack and Ted have major problems that go back years, I hate knowing that I was the one who came between them and broke the relationship permanently.

I wake up Sunday morning determined to have a good game. This is the Sourwood Cup. There's going to be an arena full of people watching the Comebacks do their thing. We've been working so hard for it. I didn't want to let my team down, and I didn't want Jack to let his down either.

My teammates and I are meeting up for a pregame breakfast at Caroline's. The guys erupt in cheers when I walk into the joint. The sharp smell of freshly brewed coffee and eggs sizzling on the skillet welcome me. There's no scent better than a diner during breakfast.

Two tables have been put together to fit all of us. Despite it being a huge game with tons of eyes on us, the guys are lively and shooting the shit like it's any old Sunday morning.

"Get this guy some coffee!" Bill yells when I sit down. I'm not used to seeing him in such good spirits. He seems happy, an odd look for him. "How are you feeling, buddy?"

"I feel great," I say.

"I'm nervous," Hank says.

"Don't say that," Des says, easily the best dressed of the team. His T-shirt and sweatpants look freshly pressed. "When you get nervous, you get gassy."

The guys break out in laughter. Hockey players are closer with their teammates than their spouses.

"Save it for the Blades. That can be a secret weapon," says Bill. "What do you want to order?"

I look at the menu and see chicken noodle soup. My heart dips.

"I'll just have some oatmeal," I say.

"You sure?" Tanner asks. "You should have something more filling."

"The man knows his own appetite. You can turn off dad mode, Chancey," Des tells him.

"You don't want to eat just before a game. You could get sick," he says back.

"Once I folded a pancake and stuck it in my sock during a game." Hank shrugs.

"Well, if you didn't have an appetite already, that'll definitely kill it," says Des.

"I'm still thinking." I scan the menu, but the letters jumble together. I can't enjoy this moment because my mind is elsewhere. And I realize it's going to stay elsewhere.

The guys all turn to me when I stand up and put on my jacket.

"Where are you going?" Bill asks.

"I gotta do something before the game." I push my chair in. "I'll see you at the rink."

———

According to Ferguson's, it's the heart of summer. Outdoor furniture displays and grills are showcased at the front of the store, even though it's cold and gray outside. Seeing it makes warm weather seem even farther away.

Something that isn't farther away is the man who blinded me in my left eye. I find Ted Gross showing a young couple a washer and dryer set. The husband opens and closes the dryer door multiple times in a row as if checking for...something. Ted is just as confused as I am.

He looks up and catches me observing the scene. He fights like hell to maintain his polite salesman grin, but the laser-focused hate radiates from his eyes.

The husband doesn't find what he's looking for and continues down the row of appliances, his search unfulfilled. His wife thanks Ted and shoots him an apologetic look before catching up to her spouse.

Ted flings one last glare in my direction and heads to the row of refrigerators, putting a wall of massive kitchen appliances between us.

"Ted," I call after him.

The kitchen department of Ferguson's is one big maze, and I am a rat going after my cheese. I chase after Ted through paths of fridges and stoves that lead to walkthrough kitchen design models. I enter a kitchen model in the back of the department with sleek marble countertops and top-of-the-line cabinetry, neither of which I could ever afford.

Ted stands at the end, next to the kitchen island, blocking my path. He crosses his arms. No polite salesman grin for me.

"What do you want?" he mutters.

"I want to talk." I hold up my hands to show I'm serious.

"Fine. Talk." He doesn't relax his stance one bit.

"We can't keep trying to beat the shit out of each other. We're too fucking old." My back still hurts from where he slammed me into Jack's kitchen island. The corner of his forehead is puffy and red from where I got him. "We need to end this."

"We can't change the past."

"We can't live in it either." In that moment, it hits me just how tired I am of looking in the rearview mirror. I lost my shot at a pro hockey career. I can't keep holding onto that anger and resentment. I can't keep viewing myself as a loser unworthy of good things in life because of one bad game.

"This isn't how my life was supposed to go," he grumbles.

"Same. Life doesn't always give us what we want, and at some point, we need to move on," I tell him, but I'm speaking to both of us. It takes two to brawl.

"You never apologized to me."

I bite my tongue, holding back the guffaw of anger surging up my throat. "You should be the one apologizing to me." I point to my eye patch.

"I can do that, too." He mockingly points to his shoulder. "Permanently fucked up thanks to you barreling into me like an asshole."

"You came at me with your stick pointing like a spear!"

I feel us begin to go in circles. I can recite our arguments verbatim by this point. Round and round we go. This is not the way.

I take a breath and muster all of my strength to utter two words.

"I'm sorry."

Ted seems flustered by my apology. He blinks a few times, trying to process.

To my surprise, I find that I don't want to throw up in my mouth after saying I'm sorry. I feel a lightness inside me, like the weight of this rivalry can finally lift off my shoulders.

"I'm sorry, Ted." Heavy chunks of anger break off me and float away into the wind. "I'm sorry about your shoulder and your career. I'm sorry this happened to both of us."

Our collision on the ice appears in my memory as fragments of a puzzle that can never be fully put together. "I remember you and your stick coming at my head, but I don't remember much else. I might've charged at you. I honestly don't remember."

Ted drops his crossed arms, perhaps a similar weight breaking off him, too. "I remember the panic I felt as we were colliding. Neither of us could stop. I thought you were going to smash into my shoulder first, but you turned your head at the last second."

"Why did I do that?"

He shrugs, just as clueless about my teenage self as I am. "Why did I hold up my stick?"

"It was our fight or flight response, I guess."

"My arm jammed back when my stick made contact with your face. It tore my rotator cuff."

We're trying to make sense of the past, a fool's errand.

"I wasn't trying to take you out," I say. "Not consciously, at least. I wanted to win. I wanted to impress the scouts in the stands."

"Me, too." Ted leans against the model kitchen counter and rubs his bald head. "One moment changed everything, didn't it?"

"Why didn't you come to the hospital to see me?"

"Because I was an asshole." His eyes, blue like Jack's, shine under the harsh light of the store. "I thought if I went, it meant I was admitting it was my fault. I'm sorry, Griffin."

My soul lifts at those two little words. I didn't realize how badly I wanted to hear them. But now that he apologized, I quickly want to move on. Holding onto this anger did nothing for either of us.

"How's your eye?" he asks.

"Completely non-functional, but aside from that, totally fine."

We break into a soft chuckle, a chip at the thawing ice.

"I really wanted to go pro. I really fucking wanted it," Ted says, a curdled wistfulness enveloping him.

"Me too."

"I thought if I could get Jack there, then it'd mean that…"

"That you didn't fail."

"Guess that didn't work." He pulls at his purple apron. He looks my way, a suspicious glint in his eye. "Are you serious about my son?"

I gulp back a lump in my throat. I wasn't ready for this to become a meet the parents situation.

"I am."

"What's he like?" There's a genuine curiosity to his voice that breaks my heart a little. As parents, there will always be a side of our kids that we'll never see.

"He's funny, inquisitive. He's a damn good hockey player. He's lost, but he's finding his way. He's cocky as shit."

Ted snorts a laugh.

"Our game is at noon. I think you should go and watch your son."

"Did Jack send you here?"

"No. Father to father, I think it'd mean a lot to him."

Ted considers it for a second before shaking his head no. "My shift goes until three."

"Can't you switch with someone?"

He shoves his hands in his pockets. "You heard him the other night. Jack wants nothing to do with me. I don't want to mess up his game by showing up."

"I think he'd appreciate it."

Ted tips his head, seeing right through my tenuous statement. "I've intruded enough on his life. I should probably stay back." He gives me a smile that I can only describe as sad. He's made his bed, and now he must lie in it.

"Okay." I hold out my hand. Ted gives it a hard shake.

"When you're on the ice today, make sure to give my son hell. That way, when he kicks your ass, the victory will taste that much sweeter."

———

THE PARKING LOT at Summers Rink is fuller than I've ever seen it. It's transformed into a full-blown tailgate. People mill about, going from car to car, some decorated with signage to support the Comebacks or the Blades. Music blasts from phones plugged into stereo speakers. Small grills and coolers are set out, the sizzle of hamburgers and hot dogs swirling through the air. It's nothing compared to what you'd see for a professional game or even a collegiate game. But for smalltown Sourwood, it's quite a showing.

Above the front entrance to Summers Rink is a big painted sign that says "First Annual Sourwood Cup" with a gold trophy as exclamation point.

Seeing the crowd and the sign makes the adrenaline rise in my system. I signed up for a fun beer league with old friends, and now we're front and center, less than an hour from having the whole town watch us. The last time I played hockey for a full, roaring crowd, I lost an eye.

I press my fingertips to my eye patch, proud of my scars. No matter what happens today, I remind myself that I came back. I gave hockey a second chance. I gave myself a second chance. And I can play a damn good game with one eye.

In the locker room, there's a nervous energy among my teammates. We're not rambunctious. Hank isn't cracking jokes. Tanner isn't whistling his lucky song.

Bill paces up and down the aisle of lockers, the first one dressed.

"Are you trying to hit ten thousand steps?" Des asks him. "Thinking of new ways to bang your assistant?"

Bill flips him the bird.

"Guys! Come in." Bill motions us to join in the middle of the room. His face is stone cold serious. He was built for moments like these. "Whatever happens out there, I'm proud of every guy on this team. Nobody thought a bunch of fortysomething guys could keep up with guys half their age. We're about to prove they're all wrong. There's a reason we're the Comebacks. Life might've kicked our asses at one point or another. Cancer, divorce, death, bad accidents." Bill glances at me for a second. "But we didn't let it keep us down. We got back up and said, 'Is that all you got?'"

The guys and I cheer and pound at the lockers. I think about how much time I wasted hiding after the incident, retreating. This team and Jack have shown me there's no safety in shrinking away. Life is about taking chances.

"These Blades want to tussle. So let's fucking tussle!" Bill yells, eliciting more cheers from us. He squashes each of our nerves. We are revved and ready to go.

Bill cranks the music. The pump-up song from our South Rock days, classic '90s jam "Let Me Clear My Throat" fills the locker room.

I keep thinking about Jack and how he's doing. I texted him good luck this morning, and he sent back a heart emoji. Sweet, but it still has me a little worried. I hope all this stuff with his dad doesn't get in his head.

"Hey Griff!" Marcy yells from the hall before barging into the locker room. Her big hair could be its own padding.

"Marcy, this is the men's locker room," Bill says.

"Eh, you don't have anything that I haven't already seen." She turns to me. "You have visitors who want to wish you luck."

"Visitors?" I arch an eyebrow. "Who are they?"

"I'm not your receptionist. Go out and see for yourself."

I know better than to disobey Marcy Summers. I follow her back to the hall, and fireworks immediately go off in my chest at the sight of Annabelle and June.

"Daddy!" they yell.

I can feel the smile take over the full bottom half of my face as I squat down and pull them into a hug.

"Your costume is really puffy," June remarks, pushing at the padding.

"It's a uniform, Junie," Carmen says above me. She gives me a supportive nod.

"I wear all this padding because it keeps me safe."

"Is hockey dangerous?" Annabelle asks, and I swear she's staring at my eye patch.

"Not this game. In this game, we're not allowed to hit each other, just like at home. And if a player does hit someone, they have to go into time-out," I say.

"There's a time-out?" June asks.

"There is. It's a box they have to sit in."

June laughs, a little too intrigued at a penalty box for my comfort. If she ever plays hockey when she's older, the other girls better watch out.

"If it looks scary, just remember that we're all friends in the end. We're playing. Having fun. Kind of like you girls will roughhouse on the couch, we're roughhousing here."

"Okay, Daddy has to go onto the ice," Carmen says.

I mouth thank you to her. She gives me a wink.

"Can I get one more good luck hug?"

I squeeze the girls tight in my arms, wondering if any part of the game can come close to this moment.

"Daddy," Annabelle says. "Kick some butt!"

32

JACK

I step onto the ice knowing it's not going to be a good game. I've played enough hockey to know when I'm in the zone. And I am not in the zone. I'll play well, maybe even good. That's what being a professional is mostly about: being able to turn it on with discipline, not motivation.

But will I be great? Will I be epic?

Doubtful.

I can't get my argument with Dad out of my head. I'm still angry at him for barging into my apartment and trying to tell me who I can and can't date after showing no interest in my personal life. I tried to make our relationship work for the longest time because he's the only family I have, but I don't think I can do it anymore.

"Hey, you good?" Fuentes asks over the pumping music. We're skating around the rink to warm up, stands full of spectators watching us. It's a packed arena.

I find the coach from Hudson University watching with a trained eye on me. A pit grows in my stomach. In my high school days, when I knew a scout or coach was coming to check me out, it added fuel to my fire. Now I only have nausea.

I look away and to my surprise, my sightline lands on June and

Annabelle with a woman who must be their mom. They wave little flags for their dad, their tiny bodies balancing precariously on the bleachers. They spot me and flail their arms in a wave. It's so sweet that it nearly lifts me out of my funk.

"I'm good," I tell Fuentes and skate off.

The crowd erupts into cheers when the Comebacks join the ice. Griffin does a lap around the rink. He shoots me a smile through his face shield.

I clock June and Annabelle going nuts for their dad. It makes me wish I had that kind of parental relationship.

The mayor makes a short speech, something about the power of community. I zone out and try to get my mindset right.

Once he's done, we get into starting position. I face off against Bill Crandell for the puck drop. Griffin's in back as defense, his eyes on me. I force myself to get my head in the game, but all the good juju has melted away. When I look at Bill, I see Dad's horrified expression from the parking lot. I see my old NHL coaches telling me I'm being traded. I see Mom's face one last time before she's gone.

Bill gets the puck and skates right past me. It's an embarrassing start to the game, and sets the tone for my wobbly performance. I struggle through the first period with missed passes and poor positioning that disrupt the flow of our team's offense. I whiff several key faceoffs, leaving the defense scrambling to recover. On a crucial power play, I mishandle the puck, leading to a turnover that results in a shorthanded goal. At the end of the first period, the Comebacks are up two-zip. I skate back to the bench, head down, unable to look at my teammates.

"Hey, what's going on out there?" Miller asks.

"Having a rough start," I mutter. I shuffle to the opposite end of the bench, away from him and everyone. I want to be alone so I can hopefully work through my shit before the next period. But I keep thinking about how I'm a guy with no family and no job. I'm sure after this game, my friends will probably drop me, too.

That crappy mindset naturally leads to a nightmare of a second period. I can't connect on a single pass, and every time the puck comes to me, it feels like I was handling a live grenade. I have two golden chances to bury it, wide open, and I whiff on both. My timing is off, my positioning is off, and I can feel the frustration from my teammates with every shift. I can't stomach looking into the stands at the Hudson University coach, if he's even still here.

Worse, each time I get into his zone, I can feel Griffin's concerned eyes on me. With a minute left, I have a clean one-timer set up, and I still miss, leading to Griffin's fellow defenseman scooping up the puck and scoring. I want to sink through the ice.

With one period left, the Comebacks are up four-zip.

"Dude, what the hell is going on?" Arturo asks. I skate past him without an answer. I keep my distance from my teammates on the bench. When the third and final period starts up, I'm essentially a zombie on the ice. My teammates have realized I'm useless and are avoiding me for plays, acting like I'm not even there.

"Time-out!" Griffin calls. The ref blows his whistle.

I skate to the bench. My teammates look at me like I'm crazy.

Fuentes grabs my shoulder. "Buddy, talk to me," he pleads.

I don't have an answer for him. I go to the bench, drink water, and sulk. I feel myself spiraling deeper into this hole.

"Gross."

I look up and find Griffin at our bench.

"Come with me," he says.

"You can't call a time-out with the other team," Fuentes says.

"I need to speak with my boyfriend," Griffin says, shutting everyone up. He holds out his hand to me, and we skate to the center of the ice. The whole crowd murmurs, wondering what the hell is going on. I'm right there with them.

"Griffin, what are you doing?" I take off my helmet.

"Babe, what's wrong?" His face is etched with concern. He's not my opponent. He's in full boyfriend mode.

The way he gazes at me with that penetrating dark eye quiets all the noise around us. It's like we're in his truck bed at night again, the world a far-off place.

"I'm in my head, and I can't get out."

"What are you thinking about?"

I glance into the stands, and the Hudson University coach watches with the rest of the crowd. I'm surprised he's still here.

"I don't want to coach," I blurt out.

"Okay."

"Okay? It's not okay. There is a coach in the stands who could offer me an assistant coaching job. And that can lead to head coaching jobs, and it can get my shitty life back on track."

"Is that what you want?"

I laugh at such a direct question. In all my wondering about my future and this opportunity, it's something I've never been asked. Something I never asked of myself.

"Of course it's what I want. It's a path to a coaching career. There are tons of former hockey players who successfully segue into coaching."

Griffin clamps his hands on my shoulders. "Is that what you want?"

He won't let go until he gets a real answer out of me, not some pre-rehearsed drivel I'm spouting off. His eye is a truth serum I can't fight.

"Why don't I want it, Griffin?"

"You've been playing hockey your whole life. Maybe you want a change."

"Whoa. I *have* been playing my whole life." Ever since I mastered balancing on two feet, I've been playing hockey. Dad took me on the ice when I was four, and I basically haven't gotten off. Imagine working in the same career since you were a toddler. No wonder why so many child stars go to rehab.

"I never went trick-or-treating as a kid. Each year, Halloween fell during a practice."

Griffin tips his chin up to me. "Jack, you are young, you are smart, and you are hard working. You can do anything."

"Anything?" I scoff.

"Yes, anything. You're too young to settle for a job you don't love.

Sometimes, I wish I'd let myself explore my options after leaving hockey."

"What if I suck at everything?"

"Only one way to find out."

I give the coach one last look and then put him out of my mind. "I'm kinda scared. But a good scared."

"You have an exciting future ahead of you, I promise you that. Everyone here is rooting for you, even the people rooting for the Comebacks."

But there's one person missing, and it digs into my heart.

"Griffin," I begin, my voice cracking. "Will I ever talk to my dad again?"

I exhale a tight breath, hating myself for admitting this. He's an asshole, but he stayed up with me all night when I got sick. He gave me pep talks when I had a bad game. He hugged me so close and told me we'd be okay after Mom left.

"I wish there was one game he could watch of mine where he wasn't thinking about my career, where he could just watch me play."

"Jack." Griffin points to the double door entrance. Dad strolls in and walks up to the glass. A knot in my chest begins to loosen.

My throat goes dry, and I swear, if I weren't surrounded by a full arena, I might start crying. Gone is Dad's scowl, and in its place, for the first time, is a face that beams pure pride.

He looks at me and taps his heart twice.

How did he decide to come? I turn to Griffin. He winks at me.

"I love you, Ringer. And I'm not going anywhere."

A bolt of confidence surges through my system. My muscles flex, ready to get back to action.

"Game on," I say to Griffin. "Let's show these fans a real hockey match."

We skate back to our respective teams. My teammates openly gawk at me, likely full of questions. But this isn't a cracker barrel session. We have a fucking hockey game to win.

"All right. Let's get back out there!" I yell, suddenly finding myself overcome with all the good juju. My teammates cheer back, our energy going through the roof.

We charge onto the ice with renewed vigor. The ref blows the whistle, and we're back. We are so back.

The rest of the period is a rush of excitement. Every player, Comeback and Blade, is firing on all cylinders. I fire off a crisp pass to Fuentes who gets the puck in the slot and nails a shot right past the goalie. A few minutes later, Miller and I set up a give-and-go that leaves the defender flat-footed, and Miller buries the puck on the resulting shot.

With five minutes left, I crash the net, scooping up the rebound and jamming it into the open side before the goalie can recover.

"Someone's gotten their mojo hack," Fuentes says. "If we can score one more goal, we can tie this thing and beat them in overtime."

In the final minutes of the game, it quickly becomes the Griffin and Jack show. The rink is electric, Griffin and I going head-to-head like gladiators on ice. Every rush, I'm blazing down the boards, only to be met by Griffin on defense, who anticipates my every move, shutting down lanes with precision. When he manages a clean break, I chase him down, forcing a turnover with a perfectly timed poke check. We push each other to the brink—one setting up brilliant plays, the other thwarting them with sheer will and skill. Each moment is a showcase of grit, talent, and unrelenting determination that has the arena on the edge of their seats.

This is the best hockey I've ever played in my whole fucking life. Griffin and I are playing on a different level, turning this grizzly sport into a beautiful ballet.

I spin past Griffin, raise my stick, and take my shot just as the buzzer goes off. The puck launches through the air, straight at the goal, hurtling like an asteroid about to wipe out the dinosaurs.

Instead of the satisfying ding of the bell, I hear the snap of the Hank's glove closing shut. Even he looks at his glove in shock. The arena goes dead silent. He slowly opens his hand, revealing to everyone the puck.

The crowd goes wild. The Comebacks scream and race past me.

They raise Hank and carry him around the ice. Pure joy radiates off them.

I skate back to my team, not feeling as dejected by the loss as I thought. By the end, I gave it my all as did every man out there.

"Hey, we played like fucking kings," Fuentes says. "That last quarter was some of the best hockey I've ever seen." He pounds my fists. "Thank you for bringing it."

"Glad you could get your mind cleared," Miller says, eyeing Griffin.

"Can't wait to meet your new guy." Fuentes nudges my elbow.

I skate onto the ice where the Comebacks continue to gush over their victory. They immediately skate up to us and begin shaking hands, telling us what a great game we played and meaning it. The Comeback wingers gush to Miller and Fuentes about their plays. It's a mutual love fest.

I skate over to Dad, his eyes misty.

"That was incredible, Jack," he says. "Fuck the NHL for dropping you."

"Thanks." It's odd hearing Dad be so effusive. "Hey, I didn't mean what I said the other night. About not loving you."

He gives a nod, his jaw tight.

We have a quiet moment, not sure where to go from here. But I hope this is step one in a new era of our relationship.

"I think someone wants to congratulate you."

Griffin comes up to me and holds his hand out for a shake. I take it and skate us to center ice. His skin is red with sweat. The white of the ice gives this an ethereal moment.

"Good game," he says. "You almost had it."

"It's okay. I still feel like a winner."

I pull him to my lips for a hot, victorious kiss. Losing has never been this triumphant.

33

GRIFFIN

We celebrate our victory at Stone's Throw Tavern. The Comebacks take over two big tables by the window, the snowy mountains just beyond us. People keep coming up to congratulate us. It's even better than a victory in our high school days because we could go out to drink rather than sneaking alcohol in someone's basement.

But rather than going over the game, relishing highlights from our thrilling match, my teammates only want to talk about one thing.

"So you're dating Jack Gross?" Hank asks. "Like dating, dating?"

"We haven't defined it, but we are together, yes." I don't need labels. Jack Gross is staying in my life for a long-ass time. As long as I get to wrap my arms around him on a daily basis, people can call it what they want.

"Have you been slipping him secrets about our team?" Bill asks. Even with a big victory, he can't get into full celebratory mode.

"No. The opposite. He was the one who remarked on Hank's positioning outside the net."

Hank sits up straighter. "Shit. In that case, I should be the one making out with him."

"I'll handle that," I tell him. Those lips are mine and mine alone.

"So since you guys are together, that means you've been able to finally pop your gay cherry, I hope." Des drinks the last of his martini. While he usually dresses much nicer, we finally wore him down and got him to come to the bar in a matching Comebacks hoodie. But he's still wearing fancy sneakers that probably cost a fortune.

I find myself blushing. "None of your business."

"All the blush on your face tells me that's a resounding yes." Des claps me on the shoulder and bites the olive off its toothpick. "You should've come out sooner."

"Everyone is on their own journey," Tanner says.

"Exactly. Derek found love with his real estate agent. Bill found it through banging his assistant." Des snorts a laugh.

"Bill's banging his assistant?" Tate walks up behind us and puts his arms around his boyfriend. "Mavis? The kindly grandmother? Didn't think she was your type."

Where Bill is beefy, Tate is slender with a boyish smile and big eyes.

"Des has a preoccupation with how we got together," Bill says, kissing Tate hello.

"Does he want to see video?" Tate arches his eyebrow Des's way.

"I just love how much of a cliché it is. It's sweet." Des chuckles nervously.

Tate leans in, a gleefully dark smile on his lips. "Oh, Des. It was anything but sweet. It was raw, and hot, and epic. You would melt into your martini if you ever knew what happened on that snowy night in Chicago."

Fuck. We sit around the table stunned into silence, mouths agape. The world around us pauses. Bill's face is bright red, while Tate remains composed. He stands back up; the world presses play again.

"Great game, guys! I'm going to grab a drink." Tate rubs Bill's head and is off to the bar.

"I need to find an assistant like that," Hank says.

———

A LITTLE BIT LATER, we haven't moved from our seats. We feel like kings, people continuing to come up to congratulate us.

"Crap. I need to check in with the babysitter." Tanner checks his watch.

"Chancey, you're too nice. You're not with the kiddos. You're allowed to say fuck." Des barks out a laugh. "Can you please use some type of profanity? Please? Early birthday gift."

"Buzz off." Tanner winks at him.

"You two...that cross-crease pass to goal in the first period was a thing of beauty," I say. They never lost their mojo. They always had it.

"We make a good team." Des says. He and Tanner bump fists. "Who wants to play Jenga? I gotta move. Gin martinis make me a little hyper. Chancey?"

Tanner holds up his phone.

"Chancey." Des pets his hand. He might be more than a little buzzed. Martinis are strong. "The crotch goblins won't fall into a well if you stay for one game of Jenga. Live a little."

"I can squeeze in a quick game." Tanner glances down at their hands touching.

He hops up. They go to the giant Jenga set by the wall.

"How's Jack taking the loss?" Derek asks.

Speaking of the extremely cute devil, Jack strolls into the bar. As soon as he finds me, a smile breaks onto his face. I am one lucky dude.

"Congratulations," Jack says to our table.

The guys give him a round of applause. Bill shakes his hand.

"Great game out there. Truly," he says. Bill may be competitive, but he respects hard work and playing against worthy opponents. A lopsided game is a waste of time in his mind.

"You guys should come to the arcade bar. They have games," Jack says.

"We have games, too!" Des yells from the Jenga table.

Tanner slides a Jenga rectangle out of the tower. Des blocks him from putting it at the top.

"You sure you want to do that?" Des asks. "It'd be a shame if you were the one who made it topple."

"Des, I know where all of your tickle spots are. Scooch." Tanner signals for him to step aside. Des puts his hand up in surrender and moves.

"Get a room!" Hank yells at them.

Jack fits in perfectly with the group. Like all good hockey players, he knows how to bullshit. He talks about game techniques with Bill and shares gossip from his time in the NHL. Having a boyfriend who gets along with your friends is a huge win.

"What are you looking at?" I ask Jack, who keeps glancing at the bar.

"Just remembering sitting over there and seeing the cutest guy once upon a time." He runs his hand through my beard, an obvious favorite thing for him to do. "And now I got him."

"Yes, you do." I break out in a smile that takes over my whole body. I didn't know this kind of happiness was possible. I guess any path is ours for the taking, if we're open to it. "And you're never getting rid of him."

———

ONCE THE CELEBRATION winds up at Stone's Throw, Jack and I make our way to C&J pizza for an early dinner. Jack suggests we get our pizza to go so that we can continue the celebration. I'm embarrassed to say that it took me a moment to realize what kind of celebrating he meant.

The trip back to his place is one long form of edging. Our knees touch in the front. Jack finds my truck to be a major turn on, so this car ride is essentially foreplay for him.

"Just so you know, I'm hard," he strokes himself over his jeans.

"I'm not even touching you!"

"You're that good. Simply looking at you behind the wheel of your big truck in your gray sweatpants."

"Wait, my sweatpants are a turn-on?"

"Yeah. It's a thing. I can't wait for you to fuck me and make me come all over myself."

I grab my stiffening cock in an attempt to calm myself down, but it only does the opposite. I pick up the speed, and my cock throbs in my pants when I pull into the parking lot. No sign of any parental figures waiting for us. When we stumble into Jack's apartment, he closes the blinds immediately. Glad we are on the same page. While I am very much turned on by the idea of doing it in front of a window with Jack, perhaps we could try it in a city where nobody knows us.

"Sit on the couch," Jack says.

"I won the game. Shouldn't I be telling you what to do?"

"No."

"Would it be better if we pulled the couch out first?"

"No." Jack is definitive. He obviously has thoroughly thought-out plans.

He dives into my lap and plants an epic kiss on my mouth, instantly shifting the mood in the room. I moan into his lips, wanting this more and more.

"Are you planning to play next season?" he asks, grinding against my cock.

I nod yes.

"Then we should continue having sex to keep the good juju alive, don't you think?"

"Makes sense to me."

"Good." Jack whips off his shirt, and pulls my hoodie off my head so fast I worry the fabric will tear. Our warm chests rub together, sending a rush of heat to my groin.

Jack repositions himself to straddle my lap, and the friction makes my dick stand at attention.

"We need to have lots of sex to keep the good juju alive over the summer, too." He slips a tongue in my ear, sending me crazy.

I pick him up and toss him onto the couch. Jack lands on his back and throws his legs open, like a gymnast doing a very dirty dismount. I want to hug and cuddle him, but also fuck his lights out. At the same time. The heart wants what the dick wants, apparently.

"Let's get these fucking pants off." I undo his belt and unzip his fly. Jack wants to help push his pants down, but I have a better idea.

I throw his legs up in the air and pull them off that way. He holds onto his big, thick, pale thighs, two lumbering tree trunks in this tiny studio apartment. His hard cock flops against his stomach. I slip my thumb into his mouth to get it nice and slick, then I drag it down his length and his balls. His lips quiver with want when he figures out I'm going farther south. He pulls his thighs closer to his body. My thumb slides down his crack to his hole and slips inside.

He throws his head back and lets out a guttural sigh. It's everything.

I dip my thumb in and out of his hole, savoring its tightness. I kiss along his thigh as I plunge inside his tight hole. I replace my thumb with my index and middle finger. They can get deeper.

"Finger that hole." He gasps against his leg, his face scrunched in exquisite pain.

He pushes my face in between his cheeks. I slide my tongue into his tart opening, letting it stretch.

"Yes. Feels so good." He grips his fingers around what's left of my hair, pushing me deeper against him.

I lap circles around his opening, getting it nice and slick. I slap his ass hard and grab, leaving fingermarks on the pale surface.

"Rub your beard on my hole," he begs.

I comply. My rough facial hair prickles his wet heat, rubbing all over him like a sponge cleaning up a delightful mess. I spread his cheeks and go deeper, feeling his body vibrate under my touch.

"You are so beautiful." I stammer as I speak, nervous to be so genuine. Is that too mushy for us?

"I know I am."

I shove two fingers inside him to pull him back down to earth. "You fucker."

"I'm sorry I have such a high opinion of myself."

I twitch my fingers inside him, eliciting a hungry groan from his lips.

"You are...wonderful." He stares at me with a ferocious intensity that underlines the simple word. I suppose coming up with clever things to say when a guy has two fingers inside you is a challenge. He means every syllable with all his heart.

He pushes his legs down to sit regularly and grabs me by the collar. He pulls me close, that twinkle in his eye. "I love you, Griffin."

It's not the first time he's said it to me, but it's just as powerful. I've never had a man tell me he loved me. As a closeted kid and adult, it seemed like a moment that I didn't deserve to dream about. Guys like me didn't get happy endings, right? My chest clogs with emotion. I want to hug my younger self and tell him it's all going to work out in the end.

"I love you, Jack," I say, a bit speechless that I would ever be so lucky to say this to another man. I thought that coming out so late in life meant the time for love had passed for me.

"But I said it first."

"It's not a contest."

"It's not. But I still win." He shoots me a wink.

"Always a fucker."

"You sure you want to be with someone this insufferable?" Jack asks.

I kiss him, showing him my answer.

"My turn to get a taste of you." Jack puts his legs down. I stand up and pull my sweatpants down to just above my knees. My hard cock flops out in front of me, all for Jack.

"Turn around," he says.

"Turn...around?" A fresh round of heat rushes to my loins. My ass twitches with excitement as he gives it a welcoming spank.

I jut my ass out and push his face against my opening.

"Fuck." New explosions of pleasure open inside me as Jack flicks his tongue on my hole. Heat and lust sweep across my body. His tongue circles my opening. His thumb dips in. Everything I do to him, he's doing back to me, and I am a better man for it.

My cock swells, and the ecstasy of getting rimmed gets me achingly close to the edge.

"Need you," I grunt. I could come like this, but I want to feel Jack's ass clench around my dick as I pump into him.

"Baby, I need to fuck you," I say. A man can only hold out for so long. My dick is about to burn a hole in my hand.

Jack gets on the couch and kneels over the back, his hole mine for the plundering. He reaches for the side table and pulls a bottle of lube from the drawer.

"Leave your sweatpants where they are," he says. The appeal of raggedly old sweatpants mystifies me, but I'm not here to yuck his yum. If anything, I want to encourage it.

I coat my cock with lube, and slip two lubed fingers inside him.

"Give me the real thing," he says to me through the mirror above the couch.

"For a bottom, you can be really bossy." I give his ass a slap as if we're going out on the ice. I press inside. Jack punches the couch arm in delight.

"Fuck yes," he screams. "I can feel my ass stretching for you."

"You're mine," I growl. I sink into his hole all the way until he groans. I hug his torso and pull him close.

"You're so beautiful," I say in his ear, kissing his ear lobe. "You're fucking amazing."

He squeezes my hand. I want to keep telling him this over and over. Jack is fucking amazing, and it's time he believed all the hype, not just on the ice.

"Fuck me, Griffin. Please fuck me."

I kiss along his neck, savoring his salty taste as my dick pumps in and out. I watch my thickness disappear between his red cheeks. I caress along his taut stomach and up his chest, pinching his nipple. There was a contest years ago where people had to keep a hand on a car to win it. If Jack's body were a car, I'd win every time.

I stare at us in the mirror, my hairy chest glistening with sweat. The yearning lust flushes Jack's cheek. The abandon in his eyes as he rams himself backward against my cock. I can barely keep standing as the orgasm thrashes its way through my core and squeezes my balls.

"Coming," I grunt out. Jack goes faster, fucking himself against my cock as I feel him tighten around me. I bury my face in his neck as I shoot my load inside him.

I pull Jack up against my chest, wrapping a hand around his neck as I kiss his ear. He strokes himself frantically, his body coiled and possessed with impending release. His ass clamps around my still-hard cock as I continue to fuck him.

"Yes! Make me come. Make me come," he gasps out, practically speaking in tongues as he comes over his fist. I keep Jack from collapsing, holding him against my chest, rocking with him as we come down from our high.

"I love you," I whisper to him, wanting our connection to be this strong always.

34

JACK

A few weeks later

"And Daddy was so fast on the ice. When he hit the puck and it whooshed all the way down to Mr. Des, it was so cool," June says.

"I think the puck went faster than the speed of sound..." Annabelle squeals.

It's been a few weeks since the Sourwood Cup, and June and Annabelle are still talking about their first hockey game. They each have a million questions about the sport. How long does it take us to put on all of our hockey padding? What if we have to go to the bathroom during a game? Do all players usually kiss at the end of a game like their Dad and me?

Earlier today at their tea party birthday, they bragged to all their friends about watching their dad play hockey. Isabella H. was impressed. Isabella J., not so much.

"Your dad is quite the hockey player," I tell them inside their ice castle tree house.

Because the tea party place had limited capacity, Griffin decided to throw an afterparty in his background that doubles as an official treehouse-warming. Players from the Comebacks mingle around the backyard, some with kids. I can now put names to hockey jerseys.

"Are you and my dad going to get married?" Annabelle asks as she straightens up inside the treehouse.

Shit. Kids have no filter and no segue.

"Yeah." June crosses her arms. "What are your intentions with our father?"

"I, uh...what a question." I break into a nervous laugh. "I mean, we haven't really discussed anything."

Is it hot in this treehouse? Am I allergic to wood? Is that why I'm starting to itch?

"Girls." Griffin calls from the ground. "Stop interrogating Jack."

"We're just having a conversation." June sits on the beanbag chair we moved up there. She crosses her legs like a power lawyer in the middle of a high-stakes negotiation.

"I'm going to check on my friends." I scurry down the ladder and collapse into Griffin's arms with relief.

"You okay there?"

"Your daughters are lovely, but they also scare me," I whisper.

"Well, what *are* your intentions with me?" Griffin arches his right eyebrow as he curls his arms tighter around my waist. If he were a cocoon, I'd never want to become a butterfly.

"I don't want to ruin the surprise." I tilt my head up and give him a kiss.

The truth is, we haven't had any discussions about the state of things. We've been spending time together, having sleepovers, hanging with his daughters. I've been researching careers as well as looking into going to college. It's a bit overwhelming. To pay the bills, Marcy has let me work at Summers Rink, cleaning up and helping her with administrative tasks. Being with Griffin is one area of my life where I'm living in the present. I don't see things ending anytime soon. For now, I'm enjoying the ride. As long as I get to spend time with Griffin, and he lets me see him naked on a regular basis, then all is good. Griffin makes me feel like everything will be okay, and that feeling is more powerful than a label.

Griffin leans in, a hesitant crease in his forehead. "Hey, so I bumped into your dad when I went to Ferguson's the other day. I didn't mention the party, but if you wanted to invite him...there're a lot of people here..."

"So we won't make a scene?" Sadly, Griffin knows us well. "Are you guys friends now?"

"No. But I can make an effort if you're making an effort."

My chest tightens for a moment. Since Dad showed up at the Sourwood Cup, our relationship has been slowly thawing. Very slowly. It's hard to forget the years of him being an asshole. Showing up at one game and telling me I played well doesn't wash the past away. It isn't like Ted Gross magically transformed. We're both taking baby steps toward a normal relationship. It's going to take a while.

"I'll see him another time," I say quietly.

"Yeah. Of course. I'm sorry for bringing it up." Griffin rubs my shoulders, trying to get us back into the party mood.

"Hello!" Derek and his teenage daughter Jolene stroll up to us, a perfect diversion.

"What's going on!" I pull Derek into a bear hug.

Behind them, a man in a bright red button-down shirt furiously texts on his phone with one hand while carrying an iced coffee in the other.

"Hey, buddy!" Griffin gives him a hug.

"I have some time before I head to the firehouse for my shift, so I wanted to stop by." Derek hands over two wrapped gifts. Griffin ferries them to the table with the other presents. The girls have gotten a nice bounty.

"This is my boyfriend Cary." Derek whacks him on the shoulder to get him off his phone.

"Hi! Sorry!" Cary instantly springs to attention. "It's so nice to meet you. Sorry I wasn't at the Sourwood Cup. Sunday is a big open house day, so I was running around like a chicken that had snorted cocaine before having their head cut off."

I try to picture that visual, and the manic energy seems on point for Cary.

Cary turns to Jolene. "That analogy was in no way an endorsement of cocaine. I've never done cocaine, for the record. But from what I hear about cocaine..."

Derek gently tips the iced coffee up to Cary's lips, unfazed by his boyfriend's word vomit. Cary gives him an appreciative look.

"I got the girls a telescope," Jolene says, tucking her bright red hair behind her ears. "The treehouse is a great place for stargazing."

"They'll love it," I say. It's amazing that Annabelle and June will be this big and this mature in only a few years.

Cary's phone buzzes. He tries to ignore it, but the pull is too strong. "Sorry. I'm not a workaholic. I just really, really love my job."

"He's very good at his job," Derek adds.

"Oh my God." Cary throws a hand to his chest with a hearty gay gasp. "I got an offer on this farmhouse I've been trying to sell forever. Freaking finally." He has Derek hold his drink while his thumbs peck away at the screen. His gleeful smile reminds me of charging to the net in games, arcing my stick back with the knowledge that I was totally going to score.

"I'm going to check out the snacks," Jolene says.

"Bye lady." Cary blows her a kiss as she goes. "And remember what I said about not doing cocaine."

She tips her head, as confused as I am about how to respond to that. She lands on a thumbs up and runs off. If Cary can be a parental figure to Jolene, then maybe I have a shot at being a good one to Griffin's girls.

"One second." Cary jumps back on his phone. "I have one other person mildly interested. I'm going to let her know about the offer and see if I can generate a little bidding war. And...there." He cackles a maniacal laugh and tucks his phone in his back pocket. "So when you're not playing hockey, what do you do?"

"I'm figuring that out. I'm looking into college." I shrug.

"To study what?"

"I'm not sure." My plan quickly unravels in my mind upon scrutiny.

"Have you ever thought of being a real estate agent?" Cary slurps some of the final remnants of his coffee from the clutches of the ice cubes.

"You think everyone should be a real estate agent," says Derek.

"Not everyone. But I think Jack could be a good fit."

"You just met him."

"Let the man talk, Derek," I say, suddenly very intrigued by Cary's confidence in his assessment.

"There are a few former athletes in my office, and they love it! It's a good transition for them because they're not chained to a desk, and sales lets you be competitive for a living. You don't need a degree. You have to get licensed, which takes a few months and at a fraction of the cost of a college tuition."

"Huh." I hadn't considered being a real estate agent, but I love competing. Cary seems to be having more fun with his job than anyone else I know. Plus the thought of sitting in a classroom for the next few years doesn't set my world on fire.

"If you do well, you can make really good money. You seem like a schmoozer, too. I get a flirt vibe from you." Cary takes a business card from his wallet and hands it over. "My partner and I have an opening on our team for a trainee agent. Our last one was great, but then her grandmother died and left her *everything*, so she moved to Mykonos to be a lifestyle influencer."

"Nice work if you can get it," I say.

"Tell me about it." Cary slurps the last drops from his coffee, persevering until he sucks down every last drop. "I tried the college thing, and it wasn't a fit for me. I'm so glad I found real estate. Listen, college doesn't start up until the fall. You have a few months. Be my trainee, and if you're not feeling it, then you can go to school."

"I think I'm sold," Derek says.

"Me too." For the first time in my job hunt, I feel excited about something. I picture myself using my charm to sell houses and creating bidding wars. It's worth a shot. Like Cary says, if I don't like it, college will always be there. I stand on my tiptoes, feeling down-right giddy. Cary really is a good salesman.

"Why don't you swing by the office on Tuesday, and we can talk more?"

"Sounds great. I'll stop by Starbucks and pick up coffee for us."

I must have asked if I could murder Derek's daughter by the way Cary reacts. Derek puts a comforting hand on his boyfriend's shoulder.

"He doesn't know," Derek whispers to his boyfriend.

"Starbucks is warmed-over toilet water. I have so much to teach you." Cary shakes his head but eventually breaks into a smile. He's a character, dancing on the edge of crazy. "We're going to mingle. Great meeting you, Jack."

I shake hands with him and Derek.

Cary turns to Derek. "I need to find your teammate with the nice ass who likes martinis. I want to get the inside scoop on his condo complex. I heard a unit is coming on the market."

"Des?" Derek asks as they walk off. "You think Des has a nice ass?"

"You don't?"

They trail off, back to their friends. I amble through the party, saying hi to old friends and new friends. My life in Sourwood was solitary and quiet, but now it's full of people and noise that enriches my soul.

I stroll over to Miller and Fuentes playing bocce ball in a corner of the backyard.

"MOTHER—"

Fuentes clamps a hand over Miller's mouth to keep him from finishing his expletive. Holding it back only makes his face get more tomato-like.

"You knocked my ball away!" Miller seethes.

"That's the point of the game." Fuentes massages his shoulder to calm him down. "Reminder: we are at a *children's* birthday party."

Miller pinches the bridge of his nose and shuts his eyes. "I am in a field of daisies. I am in a field of daisies. I am in a field of daisies."

I look down at our feet. "I think these are dandelions."

Miller sucks in a breath so all-encompassing, his lungs might explode.

I pull Fuentes aside for a moment. "Hey, I want to thank you again for being cool with the rent. I'm going to start paying it this month now that I'm working at Summers Rink."

"It's all good, man. No rush."

"I appreciate it, but I'm paying rent this month. And I'm going to repay you for the months that I missed, and that's that." I don't know what I did to deserve such good friends. I've overdrafted from the favor bank, though. I need to restore the balance.

"Cake time!" Carmen yells.

She and Griffin bring out the cakes. Both cakes have pictures of Elsa on them, presumably to avoid any fighting. I can't get enough of watching Griffin in dad mode. The girls run over. They cram onto his lap.

His love for his daughters makes me love him even more. I used to think it wasn't worth getting close to anyone, but there are a few select people in this world that make it worth the risk.

Everyone gathers around to sing "Happy Birthday."

"Make a wish," Griffin says to his daughters.

The girls close their eyes and blow. I don't need to make a wish. I may not be a professional hockey player living in a mansion, but it seems all of my wishes still came true.

EPILOGUE
GRIFFIN

Five months later

"How do I look?" Jack comes out of the bedroom dressed like I've never seen him. He wears a crisp shirt that's a blinding bright shade of aquamarine tucked into gray slacks and shiny black shoes. This for a man whose normal wardrobe consists of jeans and old hockey T-shirts. He cleans up very nice.

"A-plus," I say. "It can double as your Halloween costume."

"Funny." He pulls me into a kiss.

On top of it being Halloween today, it's also Jack's first day as a licensed real estate agent. When he accepted Cary's trainee agent offer a few months ago, he was excited but unsure. He worried that the high would wear off. Instead, Jack took to the business as quickly as he took to hockey. He loves getting to talk to people all day and the thrill of closing a sale. He diligently studied for his licensing exam for months, with me as tutor. The future is bright for him.

"What time is trick-or-treating?" he asks as he puts bread in the toaster.

"Five, but we want to get to Carmen's by quarter to."

"Not a problem." He checks out his shirt in the mirror. In addition to learning the real estate ropes from Cary, he's also taken sartorial advice from him.

The toast pops up, and Jack smears it with a layer of butter. "The girls are going to look so cute as dual Moanas. Take lots of pictures."

"That reminds me, we need to do some work on the treehouse this weekend to convert to an ocean paradise."

Naturally, as soon as the ice castle tree house was finished, the girls were over *Frozen*. They're currently obsessed with *Moana* and want nothing to do with ice. They're all beach all the time. I told them we'd transform their tree house, which means painting it a turquoise blue like the ocean and putting a fake palm tree inside. I'm sure every parenting guide would tell me not to placate the girls like this, but they're only young once. And slapping a new coat of paint on a treehouse is a minor ask.

We had lots of movie nights in the treehouse this summer and even moved up an old loveseat. Stars twinkled in the sky as Jack and I cuddled, the girls nestled between us. It feels like we're becoming a real family. I want to make an honest man out of Jack, and I'll bet he feels the same.

"The big question is what is your costume going to be?" I put my arms around Jack as he eats his toast. I kiss his neck. "A fireman? A ghost? A vampire?"

"I'm not dressing up."

"You should. This is your first time trick-or-treating."

"I am not trick-or-treating tonight. I am accompanying your two precious daughters, and if I happen to get any candy, it's a happy accident."

"People will love your story. You were so busy playing hockey that you never got a chance to trick-or-treat on Halloween. They'll happily give you candy."

"Silence." He spins around and puts his hand over my mouth.

I plant a kiss on his palm, tasting the toast crumbs and butter.

Jack pushes me against the counter and lunges his tongue deep into my mouth.

"Stop being so sweet to me, Griffin."

"Never."

Jack grinds against me, his hardening dick tenting in his chic pants. "Do you think we have time for a quickie before we go to work?"

Before I can answer that, someone knocks at our door.

"Who's coming here at this hour?" Jack tries to look out the front window.

"It's the police," yells the officer from outside.

Jack's eyes bolt open in panic.

"We should answer it," I say. I hold Jack's hand as we go to the front door.

An officer wears sunglasses to block out the shiny morning sun. He walks inside without being asked. "Jack Gross?"

Jack raises his hand. "Yes, officer?"

"You're under arrest."

"Why? For what?" Jack looks to me, more confused than scared.

"For being a sexy real estate agent!" The officer yells. He presses play on his phone, and a thumping club anthem pounds from the speaker.

I pull up a chair and force Jack to sit down.

"Did you set this up?" he asks me.

I shrug and lovingly plead the fifth. "He's the police. You should listen to him."

The officer gyrates his hips to the music, thrusting his crotch in Jack's face. He turns around and rubs his ass on Jack's groin. No tent appears in the gray pants this time.

Jack mouths *I'm going to kill you.* I blow him a kiss back. Is there a better sign of a strong relationship than that?

The officer moonwalks away from Jack and spins around, giving his ass a shake.

"Good luck on your first day, sexy!" And with that, the officer rips his pants off and throws them in Jack's face.

Thank you for reading!

For access to an exclusive spicy epilogue and NSFW artwork, join me on Patreon.

How did Bill Crandell wind up banging (and falling for) his assistant? Read their love story in the free prequel novella Cherry Picker when you sign up for my newsletter or join the free tier on my Patreon:

It's my last night with my boss. I'm breaking all the rules.

Bill

At the end of a long business conference, I'm eager to get home to my daughter. But a snowstorm strands me in Chicago for the night with my assistant Tate Cherry.

He's very cute and very off-limits, no matter how much he's flirting with me tonight. My willpower is put to the test though, when we're forced to share a hotel room.

Even more so when he makes me an offer I'm unable to refuse.

Tate
After two years of working under Bill Crandell, and fantasizing about being under him in other ways, fate is shining down on me. Tonight will finally be the night we consummate the unnerving tension crackling between us.

It's my last shot with Bill. I can't screw it up and develop real feelings for my boss. Not tonight.

Cherry Picker is a boss/employee, snowed in, forced proximity prequel novella to Gross Misconduct, but can be read as a standalone.

Join my newsletter to start reading Cherry Picker: **www.ajtruman.com/ outsiders.**

Please consider leaving a review on the book's Amazon page or on Goodreads. Reviews are crucial in helping other readers find new books.

Join the party in my Facebook Group and Instagram. Follow me at Bookbub and Amazon to be alerted to new releases.

And then there's email. I love hearing from readers! Send me a note anytime at info@ajtruman.com. I always respond.

ALSO BY A.J. TRUMAN

The Comebacks

Gross Misconduct

South Rock High

Ancient History

Drama!

Romance Languages

Advanced Chemistry

Single Dads Club

The Falcon and the Foe

The Mayor and the Mystery Man

The Barkeep and the Bro

The Fireman and the Flirt

Browerton University Series

Out in the Open

Out on a Limb

Out of My Mind

Out for the Night

Out of This World

Outside Looking In

Out of Bounds

Seasonal Novellas

Fall for You

You Got Scrooged

Hot Mall Santa

Only One Coffin

<u>Big Boys Small Spaces</u>

(co-written with M.A. Wardell)

Marshmallow Mountain

Cut to the Feeling

ABOUT THE AUTHOR

A.J. Truman is a gay man living in Indiana with his husband, kids, and fur-babies. He writes books with **humor, heart, and hot guys.** What else does a story need? He loves spending time with his family and occasionally sneaking off for an afternoon movie.

www.ajtruman.com
info@ajtruman.com
The Outsiders - Facebook Group